THE DOOR

JOHN BOYNTON PRIESTLEY was born in 1894 in Yorkshire, the son of a schoolmaster. After leaving Belle Vue School when he was 16, he worked in a wool office but was already by this time determined to become a writer. He volunteered for the army in 1914 during the First World War and served five years; on his return home, he attended university and wrote articles for the *Yorkshire Observer*. After graduating, he established himself in London, writing essays, reviews, and other nonfiction, and publishing several miscellaneous volumes. In 1927 his first two novels appeared, *Adam in Moonshine* and *Benighted*, which was the basis for James Whale's film *The Old Dark House* (1932). In 1929 Priestley scored his first major critical success as a novelist, winning the James Tait Black Memorial Prize for *The Good Companions*. *Angel Pavement* (1930) followed and was also extremely well received. Throughout the next several decades, Priestley published numerous novels, many of them very popular and successful, including *Bright Day* (1946) and *Lost Empires* (1965), and was also a prolific and highly regarded playwright.

Priestley died in 1984, and though his plays have continued to be published and performed since his death, much of his fiction has unfortunately fallen into obscurity. Valancourt Books is in the process of reprinting many of J. B. Priestley's best works of fiction with the aim of allowing a new generation of readers to discover this unjustly neglected author's books.

JONATHAN BARNES is the author of two novels, *The Somnambulist* (2007) and *The Domino Men* (2008), which, between them, have been translated into eight languages. He writes regularly for the *Times Literary Supplement* and the *Literary Review* and is a Lecturer in Creative Writing at Kingston University. His website is http://www.jonathan-barnes.com.

Adam in Moonshine (1927)

Benighted (1927)★

Farthing Hall (with Hugh Walpole) (1929)

The Good Companions (1929)

Angel Pavement (1930)

Faraway (1932)

Wonder Hero (1933)

I'll Tell You Everything (with Gerald Bullett) (1933)

They Walk in the City (1936)

The Doomsday Men (1938)★

Let the People Sing (1939)

Blackout in Gretley (1942)

Daylight on Saturday (1943)

Three Men in New Suits (1945)

Bright Day (1946)

Jenny Villiers (1947)

Festival at Farbridge (1951)

The Other Place (1953)★

The Magicians (1954)★

Low Notes on a High Level (1954)

Saturn Over the Water (1961)★

The Thirty-First of June (1961)★

The Shapes of Sleep (1962)★

Sir Michael and Sir George (1964)

Lost Empires (1965)

Salt is Leaving (1966)★

It's an Old Country (1967)

The Image Men: Out of Town (vol. 1), *London End* (vol. 2) (1968)

The Carfitt Crisis (1975)

Found Lost Found (1976)

★ Available from Valancourt Books

THE
DOOMSDAY MEN

AN ADVENTURE

by

J. B. PRIESTLEY

With a new introduction by

JONATHAN BARNES

VALANCOURT BOOKS

The Doomsday Men by J. B. Priestley
First published London: Heinemann, 1938
First Valancourt Books edition, 2014

Copyright © 1938 by J. B. Priestley, renewed 1965
Introduction © 2014 by Jonathan Barnes

Published by Valancourt Books, Richmond, Virginia
Publisher & Editor: JAMES D. JENKINS
20th Century Series Editor: SIMON STERN, University of Toronto
http://www.valancourtbooks.com

All rights reserved. The use of any part of this publication
reproduced, transmitted in any form or by any means, electronic,
mechanical, photocopying, recording, or otherwise, or stored
in a retrieval system, without prior written consent of the
publisher, constitutes an infringement of the copyright law.

ISBN 978-1-941147-14-6 *(trade paperback)*
Also available as an electronic book.

All Valancourt Books publications are printed on acid free paper
that meets all ANSI standards for archival quality paper.

Cover by M. S. Corley
Set in Dante MT 11/13.2

INTRODUCTION

It is often the case that the works which reveal most about their authors' preoccupations are not those which have been laboured over for great periods of time, honed and refashioned with punctilious dedication, but rather those which have been produced quickly and even distractedly—art that is hurried, instinctive, improvisatory. Without the gloss that patient redrafting can apply, the author's unconscious fears and concerns seem more apparent than in those instances where the patina of craft has been diligently applied.

J. B. Priestley's *The Doomsday Men* is just such a text. It was typical of Priestley to write swiftly: his most famous play, *An Inspector Calls*, was completed within a week and in the years between 1932 and the start of the war his output included a quartet of novels, thirteen plays, three non-fiction books, several film scripts and numerous lectures and articles. Nonetheless, *The Doomsday Men*, finished in just three weeks, seems especially hectic in its production. Intended as a lucrative diversion (given that big-screen adaptations of Priestley's novel *Benighted* and his stage drama *Laburnum Grove* had recently been hits, one wonders whether the possibility of film rights were in the author's mind), the novel is not amongst the best-known or most beloved of Priestley's oeuvre. His biographer, Vincent Brome, states that, in taking on the project, Priestley was "throwing literature to the winds" and notes also that reviewers "treated it as a *jeu d'esprit*." Priestley himself was to opine that *"The Doomsday Men* was a mistake." Melodramatic in its conception, it is often slapdash in execution. The plot, with its three, initially discrete, strands takes an age to be set in motion, the characterization is flimsy and the ending, rushed and perfunctory, relegates its three heroes—Edlin, Hooker and Darbyshire—to impotent bystanders. Satisfying only in parts, the whole is distinctly ramshackle.

Nonetheless, this rickety entertainment is not without its moments of interest, in part, perhaps, because the speed of its composition. As the narrative progresses into penny dreadful vil-

lainy, fuelled by memories of Sax Rohmer which would a couple
of decades later be popularized all over again by Ian Fleming, the
story takes on the qualities of a fever dream. Episodes which seem
as though they might become crucial end nowhere, characters
appear and disappear almost at random and, once the protagonists
stumble into the Mojave Desert, the lightly-drawn real world
begins to dissolve entirely. This oneiric quality becomes embedded
in the text itself as, over and over again, Priestley associates his
characters' bewilderment at the course of events with the state of
dreaming. "This was a dream," Darbyshire thinks, "in full glaring
sunlight." Later he "dreamily" accepts "every turning and new
bumpy climb, not knowing where they were going" and stares
"in dreamy astonishment." "The dream through which he had
moved all day was taking on something of a nightmare aspect," he
thinks, and, when imprisoned, wakes from "several long confused
dreams." Hooker too has "just had a most peculiar dream." The
eyes of John MacMichael "were not used to observe the world but
only to see with in dreams and visions" and he is later to declare
that all men "live in an uneasy dream of life, pursued by and pursuing shadows." Even in the final paragraph, with peril apparently
averted, Rosalie Atwood stares "dreamily down at the other four
below."

If this line of imagery has a resolution, it is not in the pallid
climax but rather in a more persistent element to the narrative,
an insistence that Priestley's characters—and, by extension, his
readers—wake up. The real world intrudes repeatedly into this land
of colourless derring-do and the shadow of the coming war falls
heavily upon the narrative. Andrea tells her lover that "I haven't
time to waste even reading any more about their armies and navies
and bombing planes and spies and executions; but I know everything's getting worse." Darbyshire remarks that "I ought to be able
to manage it during the next three years, unless we have a war or
something equally damnable." The physicist Paul MacMichael is
said to look "not unlike Stalin," the old journalist Rushy Drew tells
Jimmy Edlin that "Hitler and Mussolini and Stalin weren't exactly
expected either" and John MacMichael, in Hooker's opinion, is
"the Hitler of the Brotherhood of the Judgment." Most suggestive
of all, walking through London, "a mournful Old World monster

of a town," the American scientist George Hooker notes that the whole place is "terrified now that it would have all hell bombed out of it at the drop of a hat." Written in 1937, the novel was not published until the following year by which time such instances of accidental prophecy would have seemed not in the slightest bit fanciful.

Amongst this often confused and even uneasy novel, then, are clearly to be seen the author's overwhelming concerns at the time of its composition. There is also perhaps an implicit warning—to nations asleep whilst all around them grave, palpable threats grow ever stronger. Even when it comes within a hairsbreadth of disaster, the world is only interested temporarily in its "night of terrible dreams," forgetting all too soon and going back to its selfish slumber: "men returned to their ordinary tasks and thoughts, perhaps to destroy the world piece by piece."

Reading *The Doomsday Men* in the twenty-first century it is apparent that whilst the specific geo-political circumstances may have changed, little else has done so. Out of this hasty yet unconsciously revealing attempt to entertain, the voice of Priestley speaks to us again. He would be disappointed, one suspects, to learn that we ignore it still.

JONATHAN BARNES
April 2014

THE DOOMSDAY MEN

To

DOROTHY BROOKE

Dorothy, I must begin
  By warning you: here's fantasie,
  A fairy-tale in Western rig
  (For a wet night in some country inn)
  Which please accept in memory
  Of Jane and me, Grahame and Fig,
  Of desert, mountains and blue air,
  The canyons, camps and buffalo steak,
  The maestro-works you crayoned there,
  The nonsense that we'd find—or make.
  (Sometimes I thought there seemed to be
  Not five but six: as if we'd share
  Our laughter and the heart's quick shake
  Of joy with one we could not see).

  As through the desert hills we'd go
  And bounced inside that dusty car,
  I cast us in this puppet show
  And made each puppet bravely shine;
  Though you, I think, are braver far
  Than these adventurers of mine;
  And being wise as well you'll know
  The idle tale is not quite all,
  As children playing games may throw
  Strange threatening shadows on the wall;
  In such a world could I do less?
  So here, it's yours. Good night, God bless!

CONTENTS

CHAPTER ONE

THE ADVENTURE OF THE TENNIS PARTNERS

It was the last day of the Tennis Tournament at Beaulieu, on the French Riviera. The late winter afternoon was fine, with plenty of brilliant sunshine, but as usual there was an undercurrent of cold, even of impending frost, beneath the surface of sunlight, giving the golden afternoon an unreal, theatrical quality. The little stand on the centre court was crowded with those people—the rich and the entertainers of the rich—who appear to be living a zestful and glittering life of pleasure in their photographs in the illustrated papers, and who so often are as dull, fretful, bored, as the other people who stare with envy at those photographs. They were not bored now, however, for the final of the Mixed Doubles had just begun, and it was a good match. On one side were Grendel, that long-haired, temperamental Czech, who would sometimes double-fault himself out of a game and then at other times hurl thunderbolt services like a maddened Jupiter; and Madame Tissot, a squat and powerful young Frenchwoman, as calculating as if every point cost a hundred francs, an icy terrible female to see across a net. The other pair presented a very different appearance. Malcolm Darbyshire was English, and slim, fair, good-looking, an Englishman of the more expensive films. He was not like most of the finalists, a tennis amateur who spent as much time playing as most professionals; he did not go from tournament to tournament, and his life was not bounded by Wimbledon and Forest Hills; he had no official rating from the Lawn Tennis Association; but instead had a profession—that of architect—and actually worked at it. But he was a good player, no doubt about that, and was playing well now, though he and his partner were in danger of losing this first set. She appeared on the blackboard as Andrea Baker, though nobody there could say whether this was her real name or not, for she was even more of a dark horse than Malcolm Darbyshire. But unlike many of the women players present, she did not look like a horse.

She was a dark, golden-skinned American girl, a beauty, who was playing a quick sure game, darting like a great bird from the base-line to the net; and yet with something puzzling about her, not merely because she was an unknown who ought somehow to be well-known, but also because there was something about her oddly untrue to type. She ought by this time, after a week of play on those courts, to have been alight, all fire and energy and enthu-siasm, with eyes like caverns filled with smoke and flame. It was all wrong. This girl was no blonde champion of the world, and had no excuse for wearing a poker-face. Who was she that she should look so composed, almost sleepily composed, almost listless, except when actually playing the ball? Some of the spectators, who were not all fools, wondered about her. She had been the mystery girl of the Tournament. Throughout she had played her matches, and then promptly disappeared, a large car, driven by a little brown chauffeur, taking her away. She appeared to have no friends; she was obviously rich, and an American, young and a beauty, and a good tennis player, and yet she merely played, made a polite remark or two, nodded, smiled faintly, and then disappeared. No lemon-squash or cocktails in the bar of the Bristol Hotel; no dancing nor dashes at night to the Casino at Monte Carlo; no moonlit kisses, no fun; she hurried into the extravagantly large car every day and vanished. So players and spectators alike had announced, in five different languages, that this was a very odd girl.

Malcolm Darbyshire had been telling himself this all the week. Now, when he ought to have been concentrating entirely on the match they were losing, he was still worrying about her. As her partner from the first day, when they were brought together because neither of them had arranged to have a partner in the Mixed, he ought to have known more about her than anybody there, but he knew no more than the rest did, and had been compelled, rather reluctantly, to say so a good many times. But whereas they were still merely curious, he was worried. This was their last day. In an hour or so she would disappear into that confounded car again, and this time disappear perhaps for ever. And now he did not want her to disappear. He wanted to know all about her, not merely where she came from and where she had played before, but every little thing about her; and in exchange for her confidences he had a great desire to tell her all about himself, how he had decided to drop out of first-class tennis because he was really keen on his profession, how he had just secured a very junior partnership in a good London firm of architects and had been allowed to submit designs in minor competitions, had already had a hand in the building of a Council School, a church, and a small country house, and what he thought about politics, novels, music, food, drink, tobacco, travel, clothes, his two uncles, his sister's husband and a thousand other things. Not for years, perhaps never before, had he felt so strong a desire to impart these confidences to a girl, or to listen at any length to any confessions she might like to make. He was twenty-eight; his tennis and good looks had taken him round a bit; he felt a mature sceptical male; and yet now, instead of enjoying this hideously expensive, tennis-playing holiday, snatched from the winter as a reward for an extra spell of hard work, he was spending most of the day and half the night thinking about this Andrea Baker girl, who might have been the Venus de Milo in shorts for all the response he had from her. True, she now answered his smiles of approval, which he felt were developing in their despair into idiotic broad grins, with tiny reluctant smiles of her own; and she had admitted that it was a nice day again or that they might have a hard match; but he was as far away from any possible exchange of confidences, any rapturous midnight confessions, as he had been a week ago. Now he found himself alternating between being angry with her and with himself, for being such a chump, and behaving like a neglected spaniel, an unpleasant role and one not easy to sustain on a public tennis court. Damn her eyes! And what eyes too!

They lost the first set, by two games to six, and Malcolm felt that it had been his fault. Not enough good tennis, and too many glances across at his partner to see if at this last minute she was coming to life. That is, coming to life as a girl, not as a tennis partner, for she was playing better than he was.

"Sorry, my fault!" he said, during the break and the buzz of talk from the stand.

She nodded, not reproachfully. "We've time. Grendel isn't so tough. He's going to tire soon."

This burst of conversation from her, about the longest she had given him, filled him with delight. "Yes, Grendel soon tires, though he can come up again at times. But that Tissot woman is terrible. She's all steel and rubber. We'll never wear her down. But we'll snatch this set, and then wear Grendel out." He could have gone on in this vein, but she nodded again, as if to dismiss him, and now they had to open the second set. It was Malcolm's service, and he put into it all his feeling of angry frustration. Twice he aced Madame Tissot; Grendel sent one flying out, and his other return, a more cautious drive, was cut short by Andrea with a neat little stop volley, one of her favourite shots. "But the trouble is," Malcolm said to himself, with a certain gloomy satisfaction, "she's stop-volleyed me too."

With the first game against him, Grendel now squared his massive shoulders, swept back his dripping mane of hair, and launched his thunderbolts, making it game all. The next game went to the Anglo-American pair, for Andrea served accurately, if not very fast, and Malcolm was able to kill three returns at the net. Madame Tissot lost her service, chiefly because her opponents directed their returns away from the mighty Grendel at the net, sending them short as well as obliquely, and though the French-woman was like Verdun itself when she was on the base-line, she did not move quickly up to the net. Malcolm served again, with the set three-one in their favour, and again got the game, but only after a long struggle. Grendel now entered one of his berserk spells, went roaring about the court, served and smashed as if the fate of Prague depended upon him, and won his own service and Andrea's as well, making the score only four-three in favour of the Anglo-American partnership. It was now that Malcolm began lobbing against Grendel, to wear out that giant. It was a dangerous policy, for Grendel's smash was terrific and he could hurl his two hundred pound bulk up into the air, to cut short a lob, like an over-size ballet dancer; but it was worth trying, especially as Grendel now began to sweep back his wet mane every minute or so, and his heavy breathing could be heard across the court. That game, with Madame Tissot serving, the lobbing did not work, for Grendel jumped and smashed down the first lob Malcolm sent him, and ran back and returned the second with a piercing forehand drive that almost knocked the racket out of Andrea's hand. Four all. Malcolm's service. But this time, instead of serving hard to Grendel, he gave him two slow soft ones, both of which Grendel bungled; but he served as hard as he could against Madame Tissot, who would have had no mercy upon any soft stuff. Five-four, and now Grendel's service. Grendel made all the usual preparations for going berserk, and it looked as if his flashing racket would be murderous in its service; and so it was for the first two services, which could hardly be seen; but then, tiring rapidly, he double-faulted twice, making the game thirty-all, followed that by wildly driving a return of Andrea's out of court, and finally smashed a lob of Malcolm's into the net. So the second set went to Baker-Darbyshire at six-four, making the match set-all.

Before they began the final set, Miss Andrea Baker, now an entrancing figure of warm gold, nearly came to life. She looked at Malcolm with those astonishing eyes, in which there was now just the faintest trace of warmth—as if at least a match or two had been struck somewhere in those caverns, even if no fires had yet been lighted—and said to him, in what amounted with her to tones of the most delicious intimacy: "Can we do it, Mr. Darbyshire?" His name too, though of course with the chill Mister attached to it! She was almost human.

"Yes, we can do it. Concentrate on Madame Tissot. Either smack 'em hard at her, or drop 'em short—she can't run. And I'm going to keep on lobbing Grendel. I know it's risky, but I'll have him running miles, and he's tiring fast. We'll pull it off all right." He sounded more confident than he felt, but, dash it, when the girl was coming to life, right at the last minute, he couldn't appear dubious. He gave her his broadest, friendliest grin yet.

Then she did a curious thing, which he was never to forget. The little light there was died out of her face, not leaving it composed, reserved, almost frozen, as it had been so often, but giving it an unexpected air of melancholy, almost wistful sadness; and she looked around, taking in all the court, the stand and the thin line of spectators at each side, the other courts, the hotel, the hills and the mountains beyond, the whole landscape, it seemed, the whole fading and chilling gold of the afternoon, just as if she were looking at all these things for the last time; and then she turned to him, as if at last in this moment he was a real person to her, and said quietly, rather sadly: "I'd give anything to win this match. I don't think there'll be another for me."

Now that she had said something personal to him, he could only stare and stutter, for he was completely taken by surprise, by dismay, too, a score of fantastic tragic speculations about her leaping into his mind and conflicting there. What on earth did she mean? And why, after being so frozen, was she suddenly, at this place and time, not only coming to life, but being disturbingly tragic about it? And whatever it was, he was sure, there was no affectation there. She was not talking for effect. On the contrary, she was giving him a glimpse, the merest hint, of her real self, which she had kept so carefully tucked away. And now of course there was no time even to ask a sensible question. The umpire was calling from his high chair; the spectators were settling down, and turning curious glances their way; the final set must be played.

But he had time to look her straight in the eyes—and what eyes!—and mutter with awkward sincerity: "It's all right. We'll do it."

That final set was the best game of tennis Malcolm Darbyshire ever played. He stopped worrying about the girl now, and concentrated entirely upon the game. Grendel and Madame Tissot were no longer two pleasant fellow-creatures, with whom he had exchanged cigarettes and stories and cold drinks in the Bristol; they were menacing monsters, one small, female, cold, infinitely cunning, the other a man-eating giant, roaring destruction and doom. The court was the whole world, and the adventures of the great white balls upon it were his whole destiny. He sent fast top-spinning drives to Madame Tissot's feet, and killed the slow half-volleys she returned. Grendel he lobbed, and went on lobbing, sometimes chasing the giant's tremendous smashes far out of court; and did not even hear the applause that followed him. He served with a fierce despair, as if trying to turn himself into another giant, and he banged away hell-for-leather at Grendel's terrific services, sometimes throwing the point away, but at others scoring glorious winners. But most of the time—and it was not ordinary time but the years of an epic struggle—Grendel seemed to be smashing and he seemed to be lobbing. Andrea was playing well, but she had not the cold, almost venomous concentration of the Frenchwoman; and Malcolm could not pretend to equal Grendel's colossal strength. They arrived at five-all, and it was anybody's match.

The eleventh game of the set brought the service back to Malcolm, and as he went to the service line, he suddenly realised that he was almost done. After all, he had been working hard, mostly indoors at the office, during these last two months, with the fog and sleet of London about him, and not, like most of these people, keeping himself in good trim at other tournaments. And this was the last day of a week's intensive play, in a climate that had been a sharp change, not altogether agreeable in its sudden alternations of warm afternoons and cold nights. Every joint seemed to sag and ache. He tried to deliver two fast services, but he winced as he brought his racket down over the ball, and both went into the net. His partner gave him a sharp glance as she crossed over. Next service—another fault. This wouldn't do. He sent a safe slow second one, and of course it was promptly annihilated. Love-thirty—and this a key-game. He took his time crossing over, then sent across a medium-pace service towards the centre. It was returned quickly as he was running in, and he gave a despairing scoop at it, to find, to his astonishment, that he had achieved a beautiful little half-volley that Tissot could not reach in time. Then the next point was theirs, for Grendel drove hard into the net. Thirty-all. Now Malcolm tried a fairly fast slice service, which went curving away, so that it was hit out. The next return was neatly volleyed by Andrea, far out of the Frenchwoman's reach. The game was theirs, making the set six-five.

It was Grendel's service, and this was clearly to be his last and most terrible effort. Rather painfully, he drew himself up to his full height, sent ball and racket flashing in the sky, and produced an ace. He went across, taking his time and shaking the perspiration off him like a dog just out of the water, and then delighted the stand once more by producing another terrific ace. But now his next service was a fault; the second, much slower, was returned; Tissot drove deeply and Grendel came roaring up to the net; Malcolm lobbed high, but Grendel jumped back and smashed, but Malcolm lobbed again, there was another smash, again Malcolm lobbed, and this time Grendel fumbled and lost the point. Again his first service was a fault, and again the much slower second was returned; and this time Andrea won a short but sharp duel of drives against the Frenchwoman. Grendel tried to make it forty-thirty by another ace, but lost the point with a double-fault. Set point, in favour of the Anglo-American pair. Grendel got his first service in, but it was returned, and now the ball flew across the net from a series of hard drives, which ended with a stupendous forehand drive from Grendel. Malcolm just succeeded in putting his racket to it, and the ball went high above the net. Grendel smashed, and Malcolm ran achingly after it and retrieved it with another lob. This time Grendel could not reach it, but Madame Tissot did, with a fairly slow dropping drive. Malcolm rushed forward, despairingly slammed his racket at the ball, heard in wonder and delight the deep grunt of the strings that told him he had hit the ball fairly and squarely, and then saw it shoot, a perfect drive-volley, between his opponents, to give him game, set, and match.

There was the usual clapping, hand-shaking, towelling and muffling up, congratulations and snapshots, but Malcolm saw and heard it all as if in a dream. After that final stroke of his, when the match was over and won, for one dazzling second the strange Andrea Baker had come to life. With eyes like lamps, she had put out a hand, and said, in her agreeable deep American voice, now a little choky and breathless: "Thanks a whole lot, partner. You were grand." That was all, but it was, as this mysterious girl said, a whole lot.

Now, with the match over, the whole afternoon fading, that horribly cold wind of the Riviera chilling everything, he had only one desire, and that was to prevent this girl from vanishing for ever. He must see her again, and probably there was only this night for it. He carried this determination through the confusion and congratulations that followed the end of the match. He saw her exchange a few remarks, and then go to change. The car, the large fateful mysterious car, was already waiting, with the little brown chauffeur, to take her away for ever. He dare not go and change himself, for fear he might miss her. Shivering a little and horribly anxious, he hung about, dodging acquaintances, and putting off those he could not dodge with the briefest replies. Doubtfully, he rehearsed speeches, and could not help feeling a fool. The girl had had a few good games of tennis with him; they had contrived to win the Mixed Doubles; and that was that. She had shown no real interest in his existence. She liked tennis, not young architects from London who happened to play pretty well. She had her own life—though he could not possibly imagine what it was, probably something distant, immensely rich, very American—and had shown not the least desire to share even half an hour of it with him, off the tennis courts. She was not only self-possessed but also self-sufficient, it seemed. Where did he come in? But then, just when he was deciding he did not come in at all, he remembered the look she had given everything, the way she had turned to him, the odd sudden sadness, her strange tone and equally strange remark. So he gradually edged nearer the car, now parked in front of the hotel.

She seemed faintly surprised, but not displeased, to find him waiting there. But she looked still more remote, out of her tennis clothes, a very haughty dark beauty indeed, and it took him a moment to find a voice. "I was wondering," he stammered, not using any of the rehearsed appeals, "if you were going to the dance to-night."

She shook her head, and surveyed him calmly, making him feel as if there was nothing else he could possibly say to her. "No," she replied, with an awful finality, "I'm through here now."

"I'm not going either," he hastily informed her. Then he stopped, faced that calm dark gaze, summoned up fresh courage, and plunged in with: "Look, Miss Baker, couldn't we—I mean, I think we ought to do something about winning this match—can't we—I wish you'd dine with me to-night!"

She did not reply at once, but merely looked thoughtful. "I'm leaving for Paris early in the morning," she announced, finally.

"Well, there's all to-night. Couldn't you manage dinner?"

She hesitated a moment, looked at him quite solemnly, so that he felt he was going to be denounced for daring to suggest such a thing, then lifted him clean up into the sky by suddenly declaring: "Yes, I'll come. Where?"

Wherever was most convenient for her, he told her, but as she did not seem to care, and he did not even know where she was staying, he ended by naming a very good but shockingly expensive little restaurant overlooking the sea just outside Beaulieu, a famous place. To this she agreed, and fervently he fixed the hour. "I don't suppose you'll want to change, will you?" he concluded.

She gave this some thought too—she was a most deliberate young beauty—and then, just when he was beginning to feel gloomy about her again, she lit up, quite genuinely lit up, actually smiled at him, and said: "I've a dress I'd like to wear, so you change too."

"Right. Eight o'clock then. You know the place?"

"Yes. I think I'll drive myself over."

"Grand!" He could feel himself bubbling.

Before getting into the car, she looked at him calmly but not unkindly, and to his astonishment observed: "You're *very* English, aren't you?" Rather as if being English were some amusing little game he played with himself.

"Well, I suppose I am—just as you're American. I mean, that's all right, isn't it?"

She nodded. Then, with a quick change, asked: "Did you ever play a better game than you did that last set?"

"No, I think that was about the best I ever turned in," he told her, adding, "I'm apt to be a bit lazy, and I don't care enough as a rule about winning."

"Why did you this time?"

Well, she'd asked for it, and she should have it. He looked her in the eye. "Perhaps because I thought you were so keen on our winning."

She stepped into the car, but then leaned forward and looked at him gravely. "That's what I thought. Eight o'clock then." And she had gone.

He limped happily into the hotel, and after a long luxurious bath, he stretched himself out and enjoyed his first smoke of the day. He had that sense of accomplishment and fulfilment which follows hard exercise and a bath, and which accounts for the spurious moral value attached to the playing of games in England. Malcolm, as the girl had said, was very English; but at this moment it was neither conscious virtue nor a feeling of physical well-being that was keeping his mind aglow. It was his success at preventing the girl from disappearing again that made him happy. True, she was leaving for Paris, probably soon afterwards for Cherbourg to embark for America, early in the morning; but then he himself was returning to London within the next two days, his little holiday over; and meanwhile there was to-night, and a table for two, and a good chance that he might know all about her before they parted. Now he was wondering—though he was still happy about it—what there was to know. There might be nothing; he had met people like that before, mysterious tantalising façades covering a blank; a girl might easily achieve such an appearance, especially a girl having nothing else to achieve. Yet even as he told himself this, he did not believe it.

Clearly he was doing a very silly thing; he was falling in love with the girl. He had not the least desire to fall in love with her or with anyone else; he was not looking for romance, but for further commissions to design schools, large or small, churches of any size, villas, bungalows, mansions, castles, and for a few good games of tennis between jobs. To prove that he was really heart-free, instead of dressing he read several chapters of a detective story, one of those bright new tales in which the characters made funny remarks across each fresh mangled corpse; then, in a panic, hurled on his clothes like a quick-change performer, and arrived breathless fully fifteen minutes too early. This gave him plenty of time to ask himself what he was doing, for of course Miss Andrea Baker arrived fifteen minutes late. He had decided to be cool, off-hand, a trifle contemptuous, but the moment she sailed in, looking like a Western princess, he became the young man she had left three hours before.

The head waiter, an artful fat Gascon, treated them as if they were not only a superbly handsome young couple, which indeed they were, but also as if they were fabulously rich and fastidious *gourmets*, to Malcolm's secret dismay. He confided to them, rather than merely handed to them, an immense menu bewilderingly covered with a spidery writing in pale-blue ink. They were led to order the special cocktail of the restaurant, which cost more than any other cocktail in the world simply because it contained a little tangerine orange-juice. It was, Malcolm realised fearfully, that kind of restaurant. Gazing across at the exquisite being who now shared his table, he could not help hoping that she was not the sort of rich American girl who demands a large helping of the very best grey caviare and then drops cigarette ash into it and decides that she prefers cantaloup. He was far from rich himself, and he knew that his bill at the hotel would be stiff, inevitably much stiffer than he could possibly anticipate, and that there would be added to it fantastic, inexplicable taxes *de séjour* and *luxe*, which represented nothing but the disapproval of the frugal French, who saw no sense in the spendthrift antics of visiting foreigners. He noticed there were no French citizens entertaining their families or business associates in this restaurant. They would be all tucking in economically at some sensible place in the town. The bill here would be monstrous. He looked anxiously across at Andrea, and was much relieved when she ignored the vast menu and firmly ordered consommé, chicken and a salad.

Throughout the first part of the dinner they chatted about the tournament, comparing notes as partners; all of which was pleasant enough, but was only a slight extension of the impersonal relationship they had had already. He discovered—though he had guessed most of it before—that she had been coached for some years by one or two good professionals, at first in or near New York and later in California; had played a great deal in private; but for some reason not mentioned had not had much tournament play. She had seen a good many first-class matches, however, and they compared their impressions and opinions of the outstanding players. In the end, Malcolm confessed that though he still enjoyed the game, and hoped to go on playing it until he could no longer totter up to the net, he was now rather bored with tennis society and talk, and had indeed deliberately withdrawn himself from it. This, she said, she could understand, and asked him to tell her about himself.

This was better, much better, and took him happily to the coffee and cigarettes. He told her all about it, his professional ambitions, admitting he was no genius nor even superlatively clever, but assuring her earnestly that he was keen and had no nonsense about him. He told her a little about his home, his parents and sister, his three years at Oxford, and hinted at such plans as he had, which included designing and building a little house for himself, somewhere on the North Downs.

"I ought to be able to manage it during the next three years, unless we have a war or something equally damnable," he babbled on, happily. "I've some ideas for the place now—jolly good ideas, too—saving expense and making it more convenient. Look, what do you think of this?" He began sketching on the table-cloth. "Just imagine that perched up, about five hundred feet, on top of a great green hill, miles from anywhere."

"Miles from anywhere," she repeated, with a not too unpleasant touch of scorn. "In England! You ought to see—no, go on. Sorry!"

It took him a moment or two to recapture his enthusiastic stride. "I know you Americans have all the space in the world. Still, it's relative, you know. Once you're out of London, really in the country, you feel you're miles from anywhere. And anyhow, I can't live there all the time. I have to go to the office, and I'll only get down for week-ends at first, though I hope afterwards they'll let me do some of my work down there. You see, right at the top, I'll have my own work-room—drawing-table, books, everything. A bedroom underneath for myself. Then two guest-rooms there—you see. I'll put a hard court in—you can make one quite cheaply if you know the tricks—and a squash court, if I can run to it. One big sitting- and dining-room combined, of course. You see the idea? Look, here's a rough plan."

"It might be a cunning little place," she admitted, with, he thought, quite unnecessary reluctance.

"You wait!" he cried triumphantly, almost as if he had an invitation to his house-warming party in his pocket for her. "It'll be a grand little job. Something to work for, too. And when they see it, other people will want one——"

"Have you lots of friends?" she asked sharply.

"Well, I don't go in for lots of friends, y'know, but I have some good friends—fellows I was at Oxford with—and—oh!—some of my sister's pals—you know? I suppose you've plenty of friends, haven't you? Must have."

"No, I haven't." She said it without any particular expression, just announced it.

He looked his surprise. She met his glance calmly. He said nothing for a moment, then, with an attempt at a lightness he did not feel, he ventured: "I can't understand that. In fact, I can't understand you at all, if you don't mind my saying so."

She showed none of the usual feminine pleasure at being hard to understand, inscrutable, unfathomable, mysterious, older-than-the-rocks-among-which-she-sits; no Mona Lisa reaction at all. She merely accepted his lack of understanding, then coolly dismissed it with "Go on."

"Go on? With what?"

"About your house and what you're going to do."

"Oh—that! Well, there really isn't a lot more to say, unless you want some technical details—and I don't suppose you do. But, believe me—" and now he lit up again "—I'm going to have some fun with it in a quiet way. Three years and——"

But she cut him short, though not rudely. "You're happy, aren't you?" And she eyed him strangely.

He found this embarrassing. Was he happy? He had never thought much about it. "Well—I think I've been pretty lucky, really. I've a job I like, and I'm not doing too badly at it. I have"— he caricatured it—"me 'ealth an' strength, y'know. I've some good friends——"

"No," she cried sharply, "can't you see it's not really like that at all?"

He stared at the surprising girl. "What do you mean?"

"I mean," she went on, harshly and with a vehemence he had never expected, "it just isn't like that. You've never looked at things properly. You're talking like a child. This job of yours—what does it amount to? How long are you going to keep your health and strength, as you call them? How do you know these people are really good friends? Have you tried them out? Have you tried anything out yet? You know you haven't. You're just talking a lot of pipe-dreams, that's all. You don't know yet—you've never tried even to think—what life's really like——"

"Here, wait a minute," he stammered, beginning to recover from this astonishing outburst and onslaught. "How old are you?"

"Oh—what does that matter?" she returned impatiently. "Don't tell me I'm not as old as you. I know I'm not, though I'll bet I'm only four years younger. But that's nothing to do with it."

"What has, then?"

"Oh!——" then she checked herself, and suddenly pulled her wrap over her golden shoulders. "Let's go."

Reluctantly he stood up. "It's quite early, y'know."

She hesitated a moment. "I know it. But I'd like some air. If you like, I'll drive you to the top where we can see something."

That was very different. Happily he paid the bill, which was unreasonable but not completely monstrous, and then joined her in the car, which she was driving herself to-night. This was certainly a very odd girl. He gave her a glance or two as they moved off, saw she was now sunk inside herself, not wanting to talk, so he did not break the silence. She drove at a frightful speed up the steeply curving road, but there was nothing about her to suggest that she was aware of the fact. As the night swirled about them, and lights flashed and then fled out of sight, and destruction seemed to wait round every corner, he felt very uneasy. This she sensed, without so much as a look at him.

"Don't worry," she said, with a touch of scorn. "I can drive. You won't be killed."

"Thanks very much," he returned tartly.

"Sore?"

"Sore? No, I ache a bit after this afternoon——"

She laughed, it seemed for the first time. "I meant, sore at me. Mad. Angry."

"Oh—no, not at all." But even to himself he sounded rather stiff. And a bit pompous. Very English, no doubt.

She said nothing more until she had brought him, by a series of heart-shaking miracles, to the high top road, along which they roared until at last they arrived at a place that showed them miles of the Riviera coastline glittering below. It was a clear but moon-less night, rather cold, and below the immense darkness in which they now came to a halt the promenades and casinos and hotels far below were picked out in twinkling light. The scene had a certain hard beauty typical of the region, like that of some handsome woman of the world wearing all her diamonds. They got out, and looked down at it all, silently, for some moments.

"Like Southern California," Andrea announced at last, "only not so good."

"I've never been there."

"And don't want to go, eh?"

"Yes, I'd like to. As a matter of fact, there's a chance—just a faint chance—I might. One of our clients—he's one of these film magnates who came to England, and now he's in Hollywood, but he's coming to England again—and wants to build a house near the English studio—and he's very impatient, wants to discuss plans and all that—so one of us might have to go—don't suppose I'll nab it though, no such luck." As she made no reply, he felt compelled to go rambling on. "Don't much care for this part of the world, though. Too faked and dolled up. No real atmosphere. Not real at all. Like most of the people who come here—they're not real either. I only came for the tennis."

"Well," she said, softly, slowly, "you've had that. Even if your partner wasn't so hot."

"My partner," he replied firmly, "was good, very good. Also, my partner, besides being shatteringly handsome, is a very puzzling, mysterious young woman. Nobody seems to know anything about her. Some people say Baker isn't her real name. I have a feeling myself it isn't, though I don't know why." He turned to look at her in the darkness, and could just see her face, mysteriously illuminated by the distant lights, a dim enchantment of a face. She did not return his look.

"If you must know," she replied, "it isn't."

"I hope Andrea's all right. I like Andrea."

"Yes."

"And the other?"

"What does that matter?" She sounded impatient.

He hesitated a moment, then replied quietly: "It matters rather a lot, I think, to me." She did not reply but made an impatient little sound and a restless movement or two. These did not deter him. He moved closer, so that their shoulders were touching. "You see," he began, "I seem to have done a very silly thing this week. I seem to have spent most of the week, when we weren't playing together, thinking about you——"

"Oh, don't start that," she cried, and moved sharply away from him. "Don't think because I haven't been around all the time, I haven't had plenty of that stuff handed to me, specially on dark nights. If you thought I brought you here for that, you've got me all wrong." She stared away from him.

He felt as if she had hit him in the face. "I can't walk back to my hotel in thin dress shoes," he explained carefully, "so would you mind driving me back?"

She turned without a word, and he followed her into the car. Their descent was even more terrifying than the climb had been, and the girl appeared to care little if she should kill the pair of them. But this time he did not show his uneasiness. He sat there rigidly, ready to make a polite reply to any remark she might make. But she made none. It was a most unpleasant half-hour.

Within sight of the hotel, she was compelled to slow down, and finally she stopped altogether, close to the entrance. Then she looked at him, it appeared reproachfully.

"Well?" he enquired.

"Oh—why did you?"

"Did I what?"

"You know—start that stuff. I hoped——" but she did not tell him what she had hoped.

What he said now surprised himself, being entirely unrehearsed. "I think," he began slowly, quietly, "you've got me all wrong too. I'm going to say something important—I mean, important to me —so if you really don't want to listen and are going to lose your temper again, please stop me now." He waited.

But this, after all, was a girl, however strangely she might behave. "Go on then. I'll be quiet."

"I want to say something I've never said to a girl before. I didn't intend to say it, didn't know, in fact, that I could say it, and if you think I'm a bit barmy—all right. But it's this. We've done nothing but play some tennis together—and, after all, I've had plenty of good tennis partners in my time—and I don't know anything about you, and apparently you don't want me to know—and, if you like, it's all crazy—but the fact is, I seem to have fallen in love with you. I know now—it's the real, genuine thing. It's never happened before like this, and I have a feeling it won't happen again. It looks to me as if I'll go on thinking about you for a long, long time. I don't want to, but it looks as if I'll have to. And I don't know why. You're beautiful, I think—really beautiful—but I've met beautiful girls before, and this didn't happen. There's something about you—and I'll be hanged if it's the way you behave—that does something very strange to me. I wish to God it didn't. And now

I've said what I wanted to say—just some more of the old stuff
you've had so much of——"

"No!" She was vehement again, but now with a very different
tone. "I didn't mean—this. This is different."

"I see. Well—you know now how I feel. And, I suppose, that's
that." He made a movement, as if to get out, but she stopped him,
and then remained, leaning towards him a little, looking at him
with great dark eyes. He could see her face now, for the light from
the lamps along the curved roadway to the hotel found its way into
the car. He was not to forget the look on her face for a long time.
But having stopped him, she did not speak.

"It's all—quite hopeless, I gather." He tried to be easy.

She nodded, tragically. "Yes. But not—in the way you think——"

"Why, then?"

"I can't explain."

"I see," he replied shortly, for he felt he deserved a little more
confidence from her than this.

"No, you don't—and it's no use getting mad at me again—
specially now—after what you've said." Her voice trailed off as
she looked, at once searchingly and sadly, at him again. Then she
said, almost to herself, and almost as if about to repeat something
memorised carefully already: "Malcolm Darbyshire."

"That," he observed, rather bitterly, "is the name."

"Don't talk to me that way now," she said hastily. "I've got to go
in a minute—and go for good." She seemed to study him again.
"I like you," she added slowly. "I like you a whole lot, Malcolm
Darbyshire. More than you think."

"And yet—it's hopeless."

"Yes, it's hopeless—because everything's hopeless."

"Now that's just nonsense," he cried angrily. "And you're not
playing fair. You know very well everything isn't hopeless."

"I don't. But it's no use talking."

"Why not? I can't see——"

"I know you can't," she cut in, sharply but miserably, "and I
can't make you see—so what's the use? I must go now."

"No—please—Andrea!"

"Yes. And listen!" She came closer still, and took his hand in
a fierce little grip. "Forget what you've just told me. Forget me.

Don't worry the least little bit again about me. It's all useless. And I do like you a whole lot. You're sweet. So it isn't that. Good-bye!"

There was a glitter of tears in the face so close to his. He stared at her dumbly, then suddenly stirred to action, turned a little and put his free hand on her shoulder.

"Really good-bye?" He was hugely incredulous.

"Yes," she replied, very simply now and solemnly, like a small child. "And—for ever."

And then the astonishing girl kissed him, warmly, passionately, despairingly kissed him, but as his arms tightened round her, she pushed him away, made no reply to his incoherent protestations, sat blindly at the wheel until he had reluctantly climbed out; and then she drove away at full speed, leaving him standing there, bewildered, wildly oscillating between misery and joy, still feeling her lips on his, and yet watching her go rocketing clean out of his life. In this whirlpool he remained, to be twisted and tossed round endlessly, until nearly daybreak, by which time he began to sleep fitfully on his wreck of a bed.

Next morning he knew at once that she had gone and that the Riviera was a mere empty shell, the whole witchery and glamour of life having departed for Paris and further mysterious destinations. He enquired eagerly at the desk for letters, hoping that she might have left one of those little notes of farewell that few women can resist leaving. But there was nothing for him. He did not know where she had been staying. He did not know where she was going, though he imagined that she lived in California and was probably returning there. He did not know her real name. There he was, left hopelessly and idiotically in love with a girl about whom he knew next to nothing, a girl who either was not quite right in her head—and this he did not believe for a moment—or was deeply unhappy and compelled to appear remote and mysterious. He spent the day, his last there, moodily hanging about and doing a little listless packing and occasionally trying to find out if anybody knew anything about Andrea, and not succeeding. She was not in the tennis world nor in smart society, just one of those good-looking American girls who sometimes blow in to compete, and usually have a good forehand wallop. It was like enquiring about a comet among the members of a planetary system. He knew no more about her by five o'clock than when he had wakened that morning.

Just after five, however, a telegram arrived for him, with all the dramatic unexpectedness of telegrams. It had been sent from Lyons, and ran: *No dont forget all about me but goodbye Malcolm—Andrea.* Forget her? He was in for a hell of a time trying to keep her out of his mind for five minutes together. He read this telegram at least eighteen times before dinner, looking at it again and again as if there might, idiotically, be some word he had missed, or that she herself might somehow miraculously peep out at him between the now familiar words. A new feeling of tenderness for her now overcame him, because of this deeply feminine last message, which brought her back to him as a real breathing girl and not as a mysterious departed figure. Yet there was precious little consolation in it; all the glamour of the world had gone; and he was left—though making ready to depart himself—in a Riviera that was a weary emptiness. Thank God he too had to go!

It came, that precious little piece of information, that blessed light in darkness, as such things so often do, when he was least expecting it. In the dining-car of the Paris express he found himself sharing a table with old Bellowby-Sayers, a wheezy fat old snob and gossip, who had come over from Cannes several days to watch the tennis, not because he really cared about the game but because he liked to be in at everything when the spotlight was on it. As the spotlight had been on Malcolm too for at least one afternoon, old Bellowby-Sayers was glad to notice his existence, though Malcolm would have preferred being left alone. Afterwards he thanked his stars for that seat, none too comfortable, next to the snobbish old gasbag.

"Had a good tournament, didn't you, my boy?" said Bellowby-Sayers, after pulling a face at the fish set before him. "Let's see—semi-final in the Singles, wasn't it? Ah—yes—that Austrian lad was a bit too quick for you. Don't get the practice most of these regular fellas do, I suppose? Good show, though. And, of course, the Mixed Couples. Played a great game that last set, I thought. How did you like your partner? Fine gal, eh?"

Malcolm admitted she was, and said to himself, "Yes, the finest gal you've ever seen, you old chump."

Then it came, a gift from the gods. Old Bellowby-Sayers chuckled. "Bet you don't know who she is!"

This time Malcolm did not talk to himself. "No," he replied eagerly. "Nobody seemed to know. I was wondering if you did. You meet a lot of people."

"Yes, I get about a bit. Matter of fact, I recognised her at Cannes. She was staying there. She's the only daughter of a fella who played merry hell in Wall Street a few years ago, and then cleared out, with a colossal pile. One of these American metal men—copper, silver, all that. The real thing—multi-millionaire—but a queer, miserable sort of fella, I thought—probably no digestion left, like most of these fellas. Met him several times, and the gal with him once. Yes, she's his only daughter—and coming in for a packet, believe me. Fancy he's made one of his quick trips over here—though he's out of the market now—and she came with him and rushed down for a bit of tennis. Heard she played a good game. Fine-looking gal, but not very lively—not like some of these American gals you see about—gay little devils!"

While he was rambling on, Malcolm was telling himself that he was in love with the daughter, the only daughter, of some fantastic American multimillionaire, probably a dyspeptic old tyrant. But did that explain the girl's queer moods, the inexplicable things she said, that strange last minute with her? Just too much money? Dollar princess nonsense? No, it didn't. She wasn't that kind of a girl. There was something more, he felt sure, something that no Bellowby-Sayers would be able to account for, something that was going to haunt and tantalise him endlessly until he saw her again. And for all her good-byes-for-ever, her millions and Californias, he was going to see her again, somehow or other. Now he heard himself, above the beating of his heart, asking her name.

"Probably means nothing to you, my boy," replied Bellowby-Sayers, "and it's dropped out a bit over there. But one time in Wall Street it frightened the lives out of some of 'em. Henry MacMichael. He's retired to California now, I believe; probably one of these ranch places up in the hills back of Los Angeles."

So there she was then, living in the hills somewhere in Southern California when she was at home, his girl if he was ever to have a girl: Andrea, daughter of Henry MacMichael.

CHAPTER TWO

THE ADVENTURE OF THE MISSING PROFESSOR

In an unfashionable and not very comfortable hotel within sight of the British Museum a tall young American sat in a little chair, now perilously tilted back, with his stockinged feet on the bed, eating an apple and staring gloomily at the steamy window. It was the middle of summer, but here in London the summer did not seem to know when to begin. This morning it had rained again; though the sun was somewhere about, so that the streets appeared to be smoking and the window was steamy. The young American was deciding that a good baking hot day would do him good. His name was George Glenway Hooker; he had long large bones with very little flesh on them, deep-set eyes and delicate finger-tips, untidy dark hair, an awkward manner, and clothes that appeared to have been made for somebody else; he had three different scientific degrees and a gold medal; already he had been a demonstrator, a research student, an assistant professor, a full professor, and now he had a research fellowship from the Weinberger Institute of Technology; but what he really was—although he would have been the first to deny it—was a magician. It is doubtful if anybody in Bloomsbury would have given the tall young man more than one quick glance, for within the shadow of the great Museum there are always dozens of young men who look very untidy, rather learned, dullish; yet the fact remains that this George Glenway Hooker was the only genuine magician in the neighbourhood. And he was not only a magician; he was also an explorer, moving slowly forward in regions where he left the rest of mankind, with its pitiful fusses and squabbles, far behind. Most of them neither knew nor cared what he and his handful of colleagues, scattered over the world, were doing. Now and again when he made an attempt to tell a few of them, they almost yawned in his face. They did not realise—and he never told them, because he did not realise it himself—that they were staring, with a glazed bored eye, at a magician, a fantastic explorer, one of the greatest of the American pioneers, working along the very frontier of life itself.

What George Glenway Hooker could do, and had done several times already, was to transform what we call matter, but which he knew as the tiniest charges of positive electricity, into light, and also to conjure light itself, in the form of photons, back again into the bases of matter. He spent his working hours in a magical world of infinitely minute solar systems, where the very elements themselves can be instantly transmuted. He and his friends had forced their way into the secret laboratory of Nature herself. It was quite possible, that is, if the next barbaric outburst did not blow them and their workshops to smithereens, that one of them might emerge, with a handful of mathematical and chemical symbols, to announce that the universe that houses us is quite different from what we have so far imagined, and might prove what many have guessed at, namely, that Newton, with his solid engine of a cosmos, was wrong, and that Shakespeare, with his dissolving towers and palaces and universal stuff of dream, was strangely right. There was, indeed, nothing too fantastic that they might not announce at any moment, they were so far removed, in their adventure of research, from the common run of men. Yet all this did not prevent George Glenway Hooker from being an awkward young man with a shy manner, disgraceful trousers, and an ability, almost amounting to genius, for landing himself in uncomfortable hotels.

He had come to England this summer not simply because he was temporarily free to travel, for he did not enjoy travelling, being a poor hand at it, and regarding it as a waste of precious time. He had two reasons for crossing the Atlantic, and the second of them he hardly acknowledged even to himself. The first was far more sensible: he wanted to visit that Mecca of good physicists, the Cavendish Laboratory at Cambridge, and indeed had just returned from a happy visit there. It had been during the vacation, what these cool drawling Cambridge men, with their elaborately off-hand manner, called "the Long," but several good fellows had been still at work, at some very pretty little experiments too, and once he had accepted their odd manner, which had seemed conceited at first until he had realised that it was their English equivalent of his own gruff shyness, he had had a fine time with them. Now that was over, and he ought to be thinking about getting back to New York. This brought him, reluctantly, face-to-face with his second reason for coming over here.

It sounded foolish, just to say it, but there it was: a distinguished American physicist had disappeared, vanished as completely as if every electron in his being had suddenly been charged with positive instead of negative electricity. He had not disappeared dramatically, with the police and the newspapers looking for him: that would have been much easier. No, Professor Paul Engelfield had coolly and quietly resigned from his last chair, at Chicago, had given out that he preferred independent research, which was not surprising for he was known to have plenty of money at his disposal; and then he had completely vanished. Nobody Hooker had talked to, and he had made a special journey to Chicago, only this Spring, to enquire, knew where Professor Engelfield had gone. For nearly two years now, Hooker had been waiting for some dramatic announcement—for the missing scientist was not without a touch of the histrionic—from Professor Engelfield about his favourite heavy *nuclei*, which he had been persistently bombarding with both electrons and photons, in his own type of cyclotron. But not a word. This might mean that he had failed and was sulking in some obscure laboratory of his own. (And Hooker could imagine him sulking.) It might mean that he was on the edge of something tremendous, and refused to say anything, even to admit he was experimenting, until he was certain of success. It was just possible that he was ill somewhere, but it was not likely, for Hooker, who had met him once or twice at conferences, remembered him as a strong-looking man only in his early fifties, filled with energy, not at all the kind of man to be feebly decaying in some unknown nursing-home. And if anything had happened to him, there would have been something in the Press, for Engelfield was a very distinguished scientist indeed, a man who might have walked off with a Nobel Prize at any moment. Other physicists were puzzled by his disappearance, but not one of them had been fool enough to go looking for him. And now Hooker was compelled to admit to himself that *he* had been fool enough, had not only enquired extensively throughout the States but had also come over here to England in the hope that he might discover that Engelfield, now free to roam and with ample means from some private source, had decided to continue his experiments in Europe, probably in Cambridge. But he had not come upon a single trace of him. At the Cavendish, of course, they had heard of Engelfield, but, ironically enough, had asked Hooker what Engelfield was doing now. And that was precisely what was worrying George Glenway Hooker. What *was* Engelfield doing now?

For they had both been working in the same remote field, with Engelfield, older by twenty years at least and with far more resources of every kind at his command, some way ahead. Hooker was anxious to get to work again, but first he badly needed some news of what Engelfield was doing. His interest was purely scientific and professional. Remembering Engelfield again now, as he stared at his steamy bedroom window and finished the apple, Hooker decided that he had disliked rather than liked the man, even though he had been such a swell. He called to mind again Engelfield's thick-set figure, heavy dark face, with its bristling brows and big moustache (he had looked not unlike Stalin), and fiercely arrogant manner, which had kept him changing, to the bewilderment of his colleagues, from one university or technological institute to another. There was nothing of the teacher about Engelfield; he had been the pure research student, looking always for a good laboratory and a university president who would leave him alone with his apparatus and not be always summoning him to clap-trap conferences. That was all right. George Hooker could understand and sympathise with that. But there had always been a bit too much of the lone wolf about Engelfield, who would arrogantly demand information when he badly needed it, but hated to give any; and he had been very contemptuous, very much the sneering senior, that time they had had a sharp clash at the Cleveland Conference. "Our promising young colleague, in his praiseworthy enthusiasm, but rash endeavour to obtain results . . ." that was the line of talk he had handed out, and Hooker still smarted a little at the remembrance of it. But he was not a young man who bore malice, and after all, they were both scientists, weren't they, both working in the same remote field? "Aw, shucks!" cried Dr. George Glenway Hooker, neatly pitching the remains of the apple into the wastepaper basket, and uncoiling his lean length. Where in hell was Engelfield?

The Cavendish crowd at Cambridge didn't know where he was. Bergler had replied from Berlin that he was sure Engelfield had not been in Germany recently. Stuvert from Brussels hadn't heard anything about him. The Radium Institute in Paris had not seen him, for Hooker had gone there himself when he first landed. There was Russia, but Hooker didn't believe Engelfield had tried Russia: he looked too much like Stalin himself, Engelfield did, to try Russia. So Hooker told himself now that he might as well pack up and get a little real sunshine before settling down to work in the fall. Engelfield, the selfish devil, had meant to walk right out and leave the rest of them guessing, and he had done it only too well. How he had done it, Hooker could not imagine. All that he could imagine, unfortunately, was that just when he was in distant sight of a result, Engelfield would suddenly bob up from nowhere to announce the success of some tremendous experiment of his own.

So George Hooker walked from his hotel down Charing Cross Road and then along Shaftesbury Avenue to Piccadilly Circus, to tell the American Express that he had decided to sail as soon as possible. He did not enjoy the walk; in fact, he did not enjoy London at all; it seemed to him an unnecessarily squat, cheerless, dingy sort of city, with a lot of old buildings in it that were not worth preserving, and a good many new buildings that were only a poor and miniature imitation of New York and Chicago. The museums were good, but the best place in it was the National Gallery, which he had visited several times, for he had an eye for pictures, and there, he had to confess, was a dandy collection. Take the National Gallery out of the city, adding to it the Science and British Museums, and you could have the rest—too damp, too cold, too dark, too gloomy, a mournful Old World monster of a town, terrified now that it would have all hell bombed out of it at the drop of a hat.

The American Express was busy, as usual, and there was the customary chattering swarm of American women with bright orange lips and hard eyes, the sort of women Hooker never noticed at all when he was back home. But there was one he knew, the wife of a chemistry man now at the Rockefeller Institute, and this little woman, who had been quiet and sensible enough at home, now behaved like a mad magpie and screamed all kinds of nonsense at him. London seemed to do something to these women. The thought of royalty and Life Guards and glass coaches and ostrich feathers just round the corner appeared to be too much for them. Usually he was a tolerant young man, so long as he was allowed to work in peace and wear comfortable old clothes, but now he meditated sourly on these phenomena. But after waiting half the morning, he was lucky enough to obtain a berth in the *Queen Mary*, sailing from Southampton in two days' time, on Wednesday afternoon.

After a watery and absent-minded sort of lunch at his Bloomsbury hotel, he did a little packing, so that he could send his trunk on in advance, then decided to pay a final call on the Camford Instrument Company, from whom he had bought a few things and whose calm clean showroom seemed to him a haven of peace and good sense. He had still to finish his talk with Morrison there about evacuated tubes. The Cavendish crowd had shown him a thing or two that Morrison ought to have known, for he sometimes did jobs for the Cavendish, and Hooker thought he could cheer himself up and pass the remainder of the afternoon nicely by having a good companionable jeer at Morrison. So, a little after three, he arrived at the entrance to the Camford Instrument Company's premises, which hid themselves away, like so many concerns in this strange dark island, up a mouldy little side-street, just as if they made burglars' tools. Just inside the door he waited a moment, to see if Morrison were visible. He was not. But there was a thick-set fellow giving instructions to one of the assistants, and there was something about the cut of this fellow, even from the back, that seemed vaguely familiar to Hooker. So he waited a little longer.

The thick-set man had now finished with the assistant, who brought him a step or two nearer the door. But the thick-set man now waved him away, as if he did not need any further attendance.

"Now don't forget," Hooker heard the man say, sharply, "Suite Seven A—the Savoy. Everything else delivered to Barstow, California. Got that? Right."

Now he was rapidly approaching Hooker, who still stood just in front of the door. The man was wearing spectacles and a short but thick beard; the face was thinner, browner, than the one Hooker remembered; but nevertheless, if this was not Professor Paul Engelfield, late of the University of Chicago and other American institutions of learning, then George Glenway Hooker was no longer quite right in his head. And what luck! At the last minute! Quite excited now, Hooker took a step or two forward, held out his hand, smiled broadly.

"Professor Engelfield," he cried rapturously, "I've been looking everywhere for you. Gosh!—this is great!"

The bearded man stopped dead, stared at him, then said coldly: "There's some mistake, my dear sir. I don't know you."

"But you're Professor Engelfield, who used to be at Chicago, aren't you?" said poor Hooker. The light was not good where they had stopped, and he might have made a mistake. But the voice, he could have sworn, was the same.

It had been the same, but now it suddenly changed, was harsher, more guttural, almost a foreign voice: "No. My name's not Engelfield. Some mistake. Good day to you." And the man brushed past him and marched straight out.

Hooker remained rooted, staring. Something was wrong. On a sudden impulse he hurried outside, but the man had disappeared, possibly into the taxi that was just pulling out of the street. He returned slowly, trying to puzzle it out, then went across to the assistant, one of those superior dim young Englishmen who never seemed pleased to see a chap.

"I'm Dr. Hooker of the Weinberger Institute of Technology," he began, giving the assistant the works in a vain hope of impressing him. "I've been here before." He paused, to let this sink in.

If the assistant was impressed, he gave no sign of it. He merely made a polite sound towards the back of his throat.

"Now wasn't that Professor Engelfield who just went out?"

"No, sir."

Hooker stared at him. The stare was returned, and there was the faint dawn of an outraged look on the assistant's pale fair face. This kind of thing, it was beginning to say, simply was Not Done.

"You sure?" Hooker sounded incredulous.

The assistant raised his pale fine eyebrows. Bad Form, they proclaimed, Very Bad Form. "That is not the name, sir. Evidently you've made a mistake."

"Well, what *is* his name then?" Hooker demanded.

The assistant did not say "Mind your own business!" He merely looked it. The effect was the same.

"Look here," said Hooker desperately. "Didn't I overhear him tell you to deliver some stuff to Barstow, California?"

"We are delivering an order there," replied the assistant distantly.

"Then he must be an American. And he *looked* like Engelfield, except for the beard and the spectacles, and talked like him too—at first. I don't understand this. And I might as well tell you, I've been looking for Engelfield all over the place. Now—come on—I'm a customer here just as much as that chap is. Tell me the truth."

"I can only assure you, sir," said the assistant, wincing a little at all this crude Americanism, but quite firmly, "that the gentleman who just left, so far as I know, is not your Professor Engelfield. I am sorry I can't give you his name, but as I saw you address him yourself and he did not choose to give it, I really don't feel at liberty to do so myself. That would amount to a breach of confidence."

"I see. And I suppose it would be another breach of confidence if you told me what it is he wants over there at Barstow?"

"Naturally, sir. This company regards all its commissions as being strictly confidential. You would expect that yourself, I imagine, sir."

"I might—at that," said Hooker gloomily. He hesitated a moment, then added: "Tell Mr. Morrison I called but couldn't stop. And tell him the Cavendish crowd agrees with me about the evacuated tubes." And out he marched, feeling defeated.

What next? Had he made an ass of himself, or was that really Engelfield, plus a beard and spectacles? If Engelfield, for some reason best known to himself, wanted to disappear, perhaps so that he could experiment in secret, he might easily have grown a beard—the spectacles were probably necessary to him now—and have changed his name. It was not, Hooker reminded himself as he walked moodily away, as if he had seen the man anywhere, in an hotel, at a theatre, having a drink; then he might have understood that he could have been mistaken. But this fellow not only looked and talked like Engelfield, but he had actually been giving an order—and Hooker had a notion that it was no small order—at one of the most famous firms of laboratory instrument makers in the world. As a coincidence, that was a bit thick. Then again, his manner, if that of a total stranger, was all a mistake. Why be so gruff, peremptory, and hurry out like that? To be mistaken for Professor Engelfield was no insult to a man who could give an order to the Camford Instrument Company. Whichever way Hooker looked at it, something was wrong. Well, what next? Did he give in and tamely take the next boat home? If he did, he concluded, he would be spending the next six months calling himself names instead of getting on with his work.

So the tall young man who strolled into the Savoy Hotel, an hour later, did not announce himself at the desk. He looked about him in the big busy entrance hall, where so many of his fellow-countrymen and women were asking questions about boats and baggage, buying theatre tickets and copies of the *New Yorker*, or waiting for Father, Mother, Sis or Junior; and then he went upstairs to find suite Seven A. After several walks along warm corridors, he found the door he wanted and knocked sharply on it. Actually it was not properly closed, and he heard a voice inside roaring "Come in." Once inside, he felt the fool he had anticipated feeling, for the man sitting in there was not the man he had spoken to earlier that afternoon.

No, this was a heavily-built, clean-shaven man, about sixty or so, with a square jaw and a permanent slight scowl; and he had that indefinable look of wealth and power and successful bullying which suggests big and not too scrupulous business. Yet—and Hooker saw it in a flash before they had exchanged a single word— he too reminded him of Engelfield, a rather older, richer, big business Engelfield.

"Well?" asked this big man sharply. "What do *you* want?" His tone suggested that people were always wanting things from him—and generally not getting them.

And what *did* he want? Hooker asked himself this, desperately, and decided that what he chiefly wanted was to be safely outside.

"I seem to have made a mistake," he stammered. "I used to know a Professor Engelfield, and I've been looking for him———"

"Why?" This was as sharp as it was unexpected.

"Well—we happen to be doing—roughly—the same sort of research. I'm a physicist, you see—and—well—I had an idea Professor Engelfield was staying here——"

"Where did you get that idea from?"

"I thought I saw him—and overheard him giving this address——"

The other grunted, and stared hard at Hooker, as if to discover what his little game was. "You didn't send your name up, did you?" he said, finally, with an unpleasant intonation. "Just came charging in, eh?"

"Yes. But I only wanted to make sure——"

"Well, now you have—because I can tell you right now I'm not Professor Engelfield or whatever his name is—you'd better charge out again, eh?"

"All right. Sorry I made a mistake."

And Hooker turned and opened the door, only to find himself face-to-face again with the bearded man who had been at the Instrument Company. And the bearded man, startled, muttered something very rude. But that was not all. This time Hooker noticed a little old scar above the left eyebrow of this bearded man, and the last time he had noticed that scar was at the Cleveland Conference. Yes, this was Engelfield all right, whatever he might say. Triumphantly, Hooker stepped back and let him enter the room.

"How did you get in here?"

"I wanted a word with you, Professor Engelfield."

"I told you before——"

"Yes, and you needn't tell me again," cried Hooker in triumph, "because now I *know*. That little scar. I remember it. You're Professor Engelfield all right—and it's useless denying it."

"And what if I am?"

This was not easy to answer politely. Hooker longed to say, "Well, what in the name of science and decency is the idea of pretending you're not, growing that beard, changing your name, trying to disappear? What are you *after*, man?" But all he did was to mutter: "I wanted to find you, that's all."

The other two exchanged a quick glance, neither of them

looking very pleased. Then Engelfield hung up his hat, and sat down. Hooker remained standing, near the door.

"Who *is* this?" the older man asked irritably.

"He's what he looks like, Henry," replied Engelfield with a grin. "A young American scientist—and not a bad one as they go—called—let's see—Bunker——?"

"Hooker," said that young man sharply. Engelfield was as arrogant as ever, it seemed. This other fellow, Henry, might possibly be his brother. A nice family.

Then he made up his mind to say what he had to say and then clear out. "Listen, Professor Engelfield," he began earnestly, "I'm sorry if I'm butting in where I'm not wanted, but I've been trying to find you for a long time. After all, we were working in the same field, and I felt you might be able to tell me something——"

"I might—at that," said Engelfield, sardonically.

"Well, nobody knew anything about you—and I tried to find out where you were—knew you must be working somewhere— then this afternoon when I heard you asking for those instruments to be sent out to Barstow——"

"How's that?" This came like a pistol shot from the older man, who glanced angrily at Engelfield. The latter gave a shrug, exchanged a further glance with the other, then suddenly, as if he had now made up his mind, turned and smiled.

"Your guess was right, of course, Hooker," he said, quite pleasantly. "I haven't been wasting my time. But—well, this is difficult. I'll have to have a word with my brother here—he's been paying the piper lately—before I can decide if I can tell you anything. Now if you'll excuse us a minute—just sit right here—have a cigarette?—fine!"

In a glow of triumph, for here at the last minute he seemed to have pulled it off, not only having found Engelfield but now standing a fair chance, it seemed, of being admitted to his confidence, George Glenway Hooker smoked his cigarette, and had come to the end of it before the brothers returned from the neighbouring room in the suite. They returned smiling, confident, and for some obscure reason Hooker did not like the look of them. Yet they were now quite friendly.

"Well, that's all settled," said Engelfield smoothly. "I don't say I can tell you everything—but I might be able to tell you one or two things you don't know."

"Fine!" cried Hooker, so delighted that he began to babble a little. "And I don't mind telling you, Professor Engelfield, I'm so dead keen I'd have followed you right out to Barstow or wherever you are in California—just to see what you're doing."

"You would, eh? What did I tell you, Henry? These boys mean business. And when were you thinking of sailing, Hooker?"

"This week."

"Well, we've time. Now what I suggest is this—and of course it's up to you—I've nothing here, and for the next twenty-four hours I have to stay here, to clear things up—but I've been staying at a little place in the country that Henry rented—and all my notes are down there. Now if you could get down there to-morrow night, when we could be quietly by ourselves, I could give you some idea of what I've been doing—and, believe me, it's worth a little trouble."

Hooker was all enthusiasm. His ship did not sail until the day following; he could just manage it. What a break! "There's nothing I'd like better," he cried. "Where is it?"

"The house is called *The Old Farm*, and it's just outside a village called Ewsbury, about twenty miles this side of Oxford. If you're going down by train—you'd have to, eh?—all right, then—it's what they call a Halt on a side-line of the Great Western Railway. You get down there about nine to-morrow night. I'll be there then or as soon afterwards as I can make it. Now, there'll be nobody in, because we've just dismissed the servants—we're giving the place up—but if I'm there, the front door will be open. If I'm not, don't wait outside, go round to the back—you can easily get in through a window if the door happens to be locked—and go right upstairs, turn to the right at the top and it's the far room, and wait in my study. I left a sheaf of notes on the table there, and if you have to wait, you can amuse yourself trying to decipher 'em. How's that?"

It sounded a bit complicated, but Hooker enthusiastically agreed, and made a careful note of the place and all the other directions.

"You're a fortunate young man," said the heavy brother Henry, rather grimly.

"I'll say I am," cried Hooker, who felt he was. "There's something pretty big coming, I guess. You're sure to be there to-morrow night, aren't you, Professor Engelfield, because my boat sails pretty soon?"

"Don't worry about that." He waited a moment. "There's something you could do for me. That bag, Henry." The latter nodded, and went into the adjoining room. Engelfield smiled at Hooker, and continued: "If you want to be sure I'll be there, and do something for me at the same time, I wish you'd take this bag down there for me—I'm going to be pretty loaded up and I'm mighty forgetful these days. All you have to do is to take it down with you and, if I'm not there first, see that you take it upstairs with you into the study. All right? Fine! By the way, you needn't bring a bag of your own down there because I can easily fix you up with everything you want, if you stay the night. Now here's the bag I want you to take down for me."

Henry had returned and solemnly handed over to Hooker a small but heavy leather suitcase. "It's locked, young man," he said. "So you don't need to worry about that. And now—if my brother doesn't mind parting from you so soon——" It was a dismissal.

Hooker accepted it cheerfully. Once this ponderous brother was out of the way, and he and Engelfield were together, with a sheaf of notes and the quiet night in front of them, they could really talk.

"To-morrow night then—at the Old Farm, eh?" said Engelfield, steering him and the bag towards the door. "Sorry we can't start right now, but Henry here has too many irons in the fire and we're trying to clear things up—you know how it is?"

"Yes. And thanks. This is a great chance for me," said Hooker earnestly, looking his gratitude. There was a kind of flicker went across the dark bearded face, as if a tiny shadow passed over it, but at that moment Hooker was too intent upon showing his gratitude even to wonder what it meant. He strode out of the Savoy Hotel, heavy little bag in hand, like a conqueror. At one tremendous stroke he had not only found Professor Engelfield but had miraculously contrived to win his confidence. Hooker did not doubt for a moment that there was something sensational coming: Engelfield had the look of a man whose research had been wildly successful. And during the next twenty-four hours, when he was outwardly busy packing and sending his baggage off to the ship, paying his bills, and clearing up generally, George Glenway Hooker was also too happily busy in his mind wondering what form Engelfield's new discovery would take, whether there had been at last some startling results from the heavier *nuclei*, to give more than a passing thought or two to Engelfield's sudden change of attitude, and indeed of character. So far as he came to any conclusion at all about that, he concluded with some self-reproaches that what he and some others had thought was arrogance was really a form of shyness, the equivalent in the older man of his own awkward manner. In his gratitude, in his sense of lively expectation, he felt now that Professor Engelfield was at heart as good a fellow as he was a scientist.

So it was a very happy tall young American who went down, the next evening, on the leisurely little Great Western train to Ewsbury. He dined off a meat pie and bread and cheese and beer in a tiny inn not far from the railway, and began to feel a new affection for this damp green island. The countryside down there was one of rounded hills and sudden hollows, like fragrant cups of greenness and blue dusk, and everything seemed to be touched with mouldering antiquity. Ewsbury itself, however, which straggled along the road for half a mile or so, was not lost in the deep silence of the neighbouring hills and hollows. It was enjoying a fair, a noisy whirl of gilt and coloured lights, which Hooker passed on his way to the Old Farm. It seemed quite a large fair for so small a place, and Hooker, who had a nice taste in roundabouts and sideshows, was sorry he had no time to explore it. The Old Farm, an ancient gnome informed him in a sing-song hard to understand, was about a mile farther on; so the young man, still carrying the bag he had been entrusted with, kept his long legs in motion, waving a farewell to both the fairground and the ancient gnome who stood shakily looking at it. If the miserable parody that the English called a summer had been doing its worst to-night, Hooker would still have marched happily through it, but actually the night was fine, very rich in fragrance, and with a damp green magic of its own. His thoughts hazily expanded with the wide misty-blue night itself; anything, he felt, might happen; miracles were possible in this antique enchanted kingdom, whose influence might explain the sudden change in Engelfield, himself transformed—perhaps like his heavier *nuclei*—under these mild stars. Many a time afterwards, sometimes with regret, sometimes with derision, Hooker remembered that walk.

Not a light showed at the Old Farm, which revealed itself reluctantly and uncertainly in that queer dusk as an irregular low house, at the end of a wandering drive about three hundred yards from the road. Hooker tried the front door, but it was locked. He had arrived first, as Engelfield had said he might. So he groped his way, past beds of sweet-smelling flowers and tall damp weeds, round to the back, where the door was hard to find. It too was locked. The nearest window, however, was open a little, and Hooker was able to open it still more, to let himself in that way, landing awkwardly on a kitchen table. After that it was easy to find the study upstairs that Engelfield had described, a long low room, all beams and nooks and uneven surfaces. Putting down the bag on the table, a big table with several piles of books on it, some small files, and a great many odd sheets of paper, probably notes, Hooker looked about him comfortably, and decided that though the place was too low and beamy and nooky, had too much furniture in it, too many fusty old things, and the electric light was poor, it would be a good place in which to work, once a fellow had completed all his experiments and had his notes in front of him. For a few minutes he pottered about, opening and looking out of the broad low window in front of the table, and examining some of the bookshelves, which did not look as if they belonged to Engelfield. The scattered sheaves of notes on the table obviously did, however, for familiar symbols and equations caught his eye. Engelfield had distinctly said he could amuse himself, if he had to wait, by trying to decipher these notes. So he wasted no more time, but sat down to them.

They were very tough going, these notes of Engelfield's. To begin with, Engelfield appeared to have one or two special symbols of his own, and it took the young man about ten minutes to discover what they stood for. The *delta* symbol could not mean, as it usually did, merely augmentation, for if so the notes did not make sense at all. Then the usual symbol for kinetic energy was missing. Again, some of the notes were meaningless because the formulæ in them clearly referred to elements that were represented here by mysterious squiggles that meant nothing to Hooker. It was all very puzzling, but very fascinating too, and soon, here in this rum study in an empty house, far away from anything he had ever known, in mysterious rural England, Hooker was fathoms deep in bewildered speculation, chasing uncertain deuterons and electrons from formula to formula, now as far away from the surface of things outside that Oxfordshire village as if he had been sitting at the bottom of the ocean. There were occasional sounds from outside, sudden voices or passing automobiles, but they meant nothing to him. The point was, what did Engelfield mean? He had to set foot on this new track before the owner of the notes returned, to make him look an ignorant fool. So there he was, completely lost to the world around him, when the door suddenly opened and the place seemed to be full of people.

Actually, there were three: the large grim brother Henry, wearing a light overcoat, and two hefty middle-aged men in blue uniform, obviously policemen. The one in front with Henry looked a sort of inspector, and the one at the back, standing just inside the door, an ordinary constable.

"Now then!" said the inspector, sharply.

Hooker looked up, grinned vaguely, then stood up. "Hello!" he cried cheerfully, mostly to Henry.

But Henry did not respond. "You see," he said to the inspector. Then he turned again. "And look—there's the very bag." And he stepped forward, held up the bag, suddenly and unaccountably opened it, and with a dramatic gesture spilt some of its contents on the table. Valuable metal shone there: little gold cases, silver-backed hairbrushes, and the like. No wonder, Hooker thought, the bag had seemed so heavy. But what was all this about?

The inspector, who had a very long and reddish nose, looked pleased. "Caught him right on the job, sir," he observed, mysteriously.

"What's the idea?" asked Hooker pleasantly.

This appeared to amuse the policeman. The one at the back suddenly guffawed. The inspector's nose came down to split a wide grin.

"They're all the same," he said, still grinning, to the grim Henry. "Catch 'em right on the job, with the stuff in their 'ands, and they

ask you what the idear is. English, American—all alike—it seems.
Can you beat it? Now," he said, turning sternly on the bewildered
young man, "I'll tell you what the idear is, my lad. You're caught,
fairly caught, not only 'ouse-breaking, but with stolen goods *in*
your possession—*if* I might call your attention to them things on
the table."

"Here, wait a minute," Hooker shouted, suddenly finding himself in a lunatic world, "I was invited here, and that bag was given
to me to bring down here."

"Oh? And who gave it to you?"

"He did." And Hooker pointed to Engelfield's brother, coolly
standing there.

"I did?" The unspeakable Henry coolly laughed.

"We don't want any lip," said the inspector sternly to the amazed
young man. "Must think we're fools. Invited here!"

"And so I was. By *his* brother."

"And that's why you climbed into an empty house by the
kitchen window, eh? Come off it, lad. You're doing yourself no
good, trying to brazen it out this fashion."

"But I tell you," Hooker shouted, "I was with them yesterday, at
the Savoy Hotel——"

"You were at the Savoy Hotel all right," said the inspector, with
satisfaction. "We know all about that. And a nice bagful you got
too."

"And they asked me to come here to-night——"

"Just a minute, inspector," said Henry, as the policeman was
about to interrupt. "We can soon settle this. I don't know you—
but you say you know me, eh?"

"Of course I do."

"Well, what's my name then?"

"Henry——"

"Yes—but what?"

"Well——" said Hooker desperately, "Engelfield, I guess."

"You see," the other said calmly to the inspector. "Claims he
knows me and doesn't even know my name."

"Oh—you needn't tell me, sir," replied the inspector. "It's as
clear a case as ever I saw."

This was the moment when Hooker came to life again. So

far he had been like a man struggling to overcome some night-mare growth in the world about him. If he looked at these crazy events hard enough, he had felt that they would turn ordinary and sensible again. As if he had invented this new Henry and the policemen. But now it was as if he suddenly realised that they were outside himself, actual, and menacing. He must do some-thing, and immediately. In another minute these two beefy cops would be marching him off somewhere. They had no real case; the frame-up was monstrous enough to be almost childish; but he could not help feeling that once he was marched off, it might take him weeks, possibly months, to clear himself; and even at that there would be some people at the Institute telling each other that Hooker must have been behaving queerly, that there's no smoke without fire, and all the rest of it. He had no idea what happened to you here in England when the police laid hands on you—some-thing very leisurely, he imagined—but whatever it was, it must not happen to him. Something had to be done—quick.

He was standing close to the table, the narrow side, not far from the open window. The inspector and Engelfield's damnable brother were standing together, about three yards away, with most of the table between them and him and the window. The ordi-nary policeman was still just inside the doorway. Hooker was long and lean, but no weed; in fact, very active and quite strong; and it was only a few years since he had been one of the star men in his college basket-ball team. And when it was required of him, he could both think and act very quickly.

He appeared to droop miserably and at the same time contrived to edge a little farther round, nearer the window, and let his hands fall until they were underneath the edge of the table, which was long and fairly wide but not a very massive piece of furniture. "I suppose you know," he muttered mournfully to the inspector, still drooping, "I've been framed." His hands were gripping the under edge of the table now, and his knees were bent, to give him a good purchase. He talked slowly, miserably, feeling sure that the sound of his voice would have a lulling effect. "I'd met his brother before. He was a professor. He asked me to come down here, and to climb in at the back if he wasn't here first. So I did, and I was just looking at some notes——"

As his voice trailed along to the end, he summoned all his strength, then heaved the table over, with a crash of books and bag and files and a scattering of papers, so that it fell towards the other two, who instinctively jumped back. Before they could recover and run round, while they were still shouting, he had swung himself out of the window and taken a wild leap into the dark. He went sprawling in the soft earth below, but was soon up and racing down the drive. As he went he could hear shouts behind him. At the entrance a large roadster had been parked. He hesitated a moment, then saw a bicycle leaning against the gatepost. He had not ridden a bicycle for years, but he had had one when he was a boy, and now he wheeled this out, jumped on, not noticing which way he was taking it, and after a few wobbles went sailing down the road at a fair speed. Fortunately, it was big enough for him, and he guessed it to be the property of the police constable. He was adding to his crimes every minute, it appeared, but didn't give a hoot. What did give a hoot, however, in fact several menacing hoots, was that big roadster, which was now undoubtedly coming after him.

He heard again the cheerful noises of the fair and saw its lights glittering before him. Another turn of the road, and there it was, a few hundred yards in front, just to the left of the road, with most of the village beyond. He decided not to take the chance of riding the full length of the village street on that bicycle; even now one of them might be telephoning from the house to have him stopped; so just before the entrance to the fair, where the crowd began and the hawkers were plying their trade, he dismounted, hastily leaned the bicycle against the low stone wall, looked back down the road and saw powerful headlights coming round the corner, so walked briskly into the fair.

Passing a row of coconut shies and hoop-la and other stalls, he came to a small side-show, labelled *Nirobi the Mystic Girl*, paid his threepence and quickly dived into the tent, where about twenty people were staring without noticeable enthusiasm at a beery man in a turban that didn't belong to him and at Nirobi herself, a very thin, dirty-looking, bored girl, who was dancing, in a very perfunctory fashion, with the equally bored and perfunctory assistance of a large snake. Hooker was in no mood, however, to criticise the performance. The point was, it was dark in there; and perhaps by this time the roadster and its policeman were a mile or two farther down the road. Nirobi came to the end of her dance; the snake retired into its basket; and the beery man in the turban announced that for an additional threepence any member of the audience could purchase the wonderful Indian girl's mystic prophecies. As he held up some smudgy little pamphlets, the mechanical organ outside exploded into song, and a voice was heard saying that another performance by Nirobi was about to commence. This had not lasted long enough. As they went out, Hooker made himself as small as possible, and felt very sorry that he had left his hat behind at the Old Farm. It seemed unpleasantly bright outside, too many lights altogether. And one of the first things these lights showed him, above the crowd only about twenty yards away, between him and the entrance, was a policeman's helmet.

Hooker edged himself away in the opposite direction, and was lucky enough to run into a fellow who was selling black-and-white paper caps that had large bright yellow cardboard peaks. With one of these monstrosities on his head, and the peak pulled well down, Dr. George Glenway Hooker of the Weinberger Institute of Technology felt a little better. Fortunately, a good many youths were wearing them. Some of the youngsters, who walked round arm-in-arm, screaming, were also wearing false noses and imitation spectacles, and for the first time for twenty years Hooker felt a keen desire to possess a false nose, with or without imitation spectacles. On the other hand, he was convinced that it would not do at all if a man his size and age solemnly enquired, in an American accent too: "Say, where can I buy a false nose?" He moved slowly round with the crowd, a nice silly innocent lot, mostly very young, and began to wonder if after all he had much to worry about. That policeman, whose helmet he had seen, might be on duty here, and not know anything about him. On the other hand, trailing round like this, not knowing who might be ahead of him, at any moment he might come face-to-face with one of his pursuers. And his knees were aching now: it was hard work trying to be several inches shorter than Nature had made you. But then he had another stroke of luck. There, not two yards away, was a basket filled with false noses, imitation spectacles, and sets of celluloid teeth. He treated himself hastily to a very bulbous nose, which had imitation tortoise-shell spectacle frames attached to it; and now behind these he felt there was very little of his former appearance left. His best plan was to have a good look round the fair.

In the centre of the fairground, its masterpiece, was a blaring, shining switchback, in which cars shaped like gilded dragons and vast staring cockerels went whirling round and round and up and down. It stopped for more passengers just as he was making up his mind. Hastily he climbed into the interior of some glittering farmyard monster, and noticed with satisfaction that it would be easier to look out of this curved car than to see, from any distance, who was in it. They began to move, slowly at first, up and down; and there, below, looking about him sharply, was the inspector. No mistake about that: it was the inspector all right. They had guessed he had come in here. Just as the switchback was gathering speed, and before the whole fairground had turned into a whizzing puddle of light, Hooker had time to notice that the inspector was glancing up at the whirling cars. After that he could not tell where the inspector was looking, was not even sure he was still there. Up and down, round and round, they went, with the organ bleating and blaring, the girls screaming, the whole fair a changing scribble of colour and light. And here he was, Dr. George Glenway Hooker, holder of a research fellowship in physics, and just at the very time he had seen himself following Engelfield's trail into the most distant exploration of deuterons, electrons, neutrons, photons and *nuclei*, here he was, wearing a black-and-white check paper cap with a bright yellow peak, imitation spectacles and a false nose, careering round and round, like an electron himself, in the middle of a country fair. And, police or no police—by heck!— enjoying it too.

But he had to make sure about that inspector, so every time the switchback stopped, he slumped back into his seat, which was at the back of the car, where the monster's tail curved round and threw a dark shadow; and he stayed slumped until they were moving fast again. This he did five times altogether, and during the last three rides he was trying to decide what to do. Either he must sneak away across the fields at the back of the fair and risk having to wander about out there for several hours more, or he must try and hide himself in the crowd returning to the main road, in the hope of getting away sooner. And whatever he did, he had made up his mind that he would not return to London but would try and make for Southampton and his ship. That too was a risk, but Engelfield and his brother did not know exactly when he was sailing; and he had too an obscure conviction that they would not try to prevent his sailing, even if they could, and that the fantastic trap they had set for him, which still seemed to him childish and almost idiotic, was simply to pay him out for what they considered his impudent curiosity. But he could think about all that later, he decided; what was worrying him now was how to escape from this neighbourhood. Then he saw, in a flash, that his very best plan was to attach himself to some other person or people, for it would be a solitary young man that the police would be looking for, and probably they would not pay much attention to a noisy group.

There were plenty of noisy groups, but now the problem was—and Dr. Hooker considered it carefully—how to attach himself to one of them. He was well acquainted with several delicate techniques, but the technique by means of which one young American scientist, hiding from the police, became an accepted member of a gang of Oxfordshire lads and lasses playing the fool at a fair was quite unknown to him. He cautiously descended from the switchback, but could not see the inspector. There was no blue helmet in sight anywhere. So far, so good. And now what? He stood hesitating at the entrance to another side-show (*Demo—the Electric Wonder Man*), among a little crowd who were being roared at by Demo's showman, when he discovered that somebody was talking to him. It was a young man with a round red face, tousled fair hair, and a canary-coloured pull-over. He was arm-in-arm with two giggling young women, and he was genially but definitely drunk.

"Ol' boy," he was saying solemnly, "tha's a hell of a nose you got there, ol' boy. For moment, put wind up me that nose did, ol' boy. Thought it was—real. Didn'd I, girls? Ab-so-lulely true, ol' boy." And he wagged his blond tousled head with great solemnity.

This was Hooker's chance, and, feeling less shy than usual behind this nose, he snapped at it. He invited the trio to see *Demo the Electric Wonder Man* with him, hinting that he knew all about electricity and could see through fifty Wonder men. So in they went, with a warm, moist, giggly girl hanging on to Hooker's arm. Demo's tricks were stale stuff to the American, who explained them to his party. Unfortunately the blond young man insisted on repeating these explanations at the top of his voice, with the result that they were asked to leave, and the blond young man nearly had a fight, and both girls clung hotly and moistly to Hooker, and it looked like being unpleasant. But Hooker got the three of them safely out, brought them to a comparatively quiet dark place behind the show tent, and there they held a meeting. The girls, who had been scared, were rather indignant now with their friend, the blond young man, whose name was Ronnie. They now declared he had had too much.

"Properly over-stepped the mark, that's what you've done, Ronnie," cried one of them angrily. "And how you're going to drive us home, I don't know—what you say, kid?"

The other agreed, and would not accept Ronnie's assurance that he was quite all right. "Quite all nothing!" she said emphatically.

Again, this was Hooker's chance, and he took it. "Let me drive you all home," he said. The girls instantly agreed, for now they had great confidence in the tall stranger with the false nose.

"But it's Newbury," they told him, doubtfully. "How'll you get home?"

He waved this aside, made them all link arms again, and steered the party towards the entrance. They were a noisy little group all right, and looked no different from dozens of others. And they passed within two yards of a policeman at the entrance. Hooker never looked at the face under the helmet; he was taking no chances; so he never knew if it was the same policeman who had seen him at the Old Farm. Whether it was or not, the group system worked; and five minutes later they were rattling down the road in Ronnie's little old open car, with Hooker at the wheel reminding himself to keep to the left; and during the next dozen miles they successfully passed several policemen. All the way to Newbury, Ronnie and the girl at the back with him flirted and quarrelled, slapped and kissed, while the girl at Hooker's side talked without ceasing, telling him about her two sisters, her brother, her brother's wife, her uncle in Australia, and all the people she worked with in the shop. At Newbury, which appeared to have gone to bed, Hooker removed his comic nose and hat, was suddenly and very tenderly embraced by the young woman who had sat by him, and was then shown where to wait for a late cross-country bus that would take him nearer to the coast. He sat there in the little waiting-room, wearing an old cloth cap that Ronnie had found at the back of the car and had insisted upon his taking. The only other people, a sleepy elderly country couple, sitting among a host of paper packages, did not seem to notice anything surprising about his appearance. No policeman came to disturb them. When the almost empty bus arrived, and he was able to stretch himself out on the back seat, with the cap almost covering his face, no questions were asked and there were no sudden halts. The bus rumbled steadily through the night towards the sea.

And Hooker, going again over the events of the evening, remembered now a last shout he had heard from the inspector, addressed to Engelfield's brother Henry. The name he had heard then was one vaguely familiar to him at home, and he dozed off muttering it to himself: MacMichael.

CHAPTER THREE

THE ADVENTURE OF THE MURDERED MAN'S BROTHER

Jimmy Edlin, who had been in many of the strange cities of this world, had now returned to the newest and strangest of them all, that vast conglomeration and gaily-coloured higgledy-piggledy of unending boulevards, vacant lots, oil derricks, cardboard bungalows, retired farmers, fortune-tellers, real estate dealers, film stars, false prophets, affluent pimps, women in pyjamas turning on victrolas, radio men lunching on aspirin and Alka-Seltzer, Middle-Western grandmothers, Chinese grandfathers, Mexican uncles, and Philippino cousins, known as Los Angeles. It was not Jimmy's native city: he had no native city; he was the son of a wandering Irish-American father and an English mother; and since his late teens, thirty years ago, he had roamed the world trying this and that, and had prospected for gold, dredged for platinum, sold advertising space, imported watches and cheap bracelets and fountain-pens, exported rubber and ivory and Chinese pigtails, been a ship's purser, newspaper proprietor (in Alaska), publicity man, general merchant, owner of a restaurant (Shanghai), made tidy fortunes and lost them, and had a roaring good time. For the last few years he had been in China, chiefly in Shanghai, but had cleared out when the Japanese came, after converting a great many Mexican dollars and similar currency into two respectable banking accounts, one in London, the other here in Los Angeles. He had not returned at once to California, however, but had gone down to Honolulu, to taste the first fruits of his temporary retirement, and would still have been there if he had not received startling and very bad news. His only brother, Phil, who for years had been on the staff of the Los Angeles *Herald-Telegram*, had been discovered in the back room of a small down-town café—murdered. Jimmy had caught the first boat—there was only the boat, for the *Clip-per* was not available—but had landed days after the funeral, and now the story of the Phil Edlin murder had vanished from the front pages, there having been two more murders, a prominent suicide, one large and two small political scandals, a juicy film star divorce with "love-nest revelations," since then to blacken those pages. Phil Edlin, in that back room with a great hole in his chest, was now old news, and was being rapidly forgotten. Yet there were some, of course, who remembered.

His wife, Florence, had taken it pretty hard. Jimmy had met her only once before, some years ago, and had not liked her much. One of these peevish thin blondes, slopping about the apartment all morning, eating candy and turning on the radio, then spend-ing hours titivating herself up to go shopping or to the movies, never settling down properly to the job of being a wife, a steno-grapher without an office to go to, who thought the twin-bed just pensioned her off for life, and was always grumbling because the pension was not bigger every three months: that is how Jimmy had seen her then. But now, still in deep black, with the tears welling into her eyes as she told the damnable story all over again, her looks gone to hell, she seemed to him—as he was easy and rather senti-mental in his judgment of women, like most men of his kind—a truer figure of a woman than he had thought she was. Indeed, he felt conscience-stricken, for not only had he probably misjudged

Flo, but he felt too that he ought to have taken more time off to see poor old Phil. Too late now, but he was still angry about the murder; and, so far as he could judge, about the only person in Los Angeles who was still angry, for the enquiry appeared to have led to nothing, and even Flo here, who ought to have been an avenging fury, seemed to accept it woefully and to want to forget about it. But as Jimmy sat there, listening to her, his broad good-humoured face, with its impudent nose and Irish actor's gash of a mouth, was sullen with resentment, and though his big shoulders were deep in the chair—he was a heavily-built man of no great height but square and thick—his fists were clenched and one bright brown shoe beat a tattoo on the carpet.

"But Godalmighty!—Flo——" he protested at last, "aren't they going to do anything? Here's poor old Phil—who never did anybody any harm—a good newspaper man—and they send him round the town, on their business, mind you—and then when this—this—happens to him—they don't do a damn thing—why—hell's bells——"

He pulled himself out of the big chair and walked over to the window, and there scowled accusingly at the mellow and faintly unreal sunlight that was illuminating the Boulevard. He did this to relieve his feelings, but also because Flo, perhaps moved by his vehemence as well as her own recital, was now crying hard. He waited until her sobbing had turned to sniffling, before turning round again.

"You don't understand, Jimmy," she wailed, finally. "They had a long enquiry, and the police asked a lot of questions—they talked to me for hours and it was awful—and what could I tell them, anyhow?—and then said it must have been somebody in that Murro gang—oh!—what does it matter now? He's gone, hasn't he?"

"I know. But why? If he'd been one of these tough lads, who go round asking for it—I could understand it. But Phil! He wasn't that kind of a fellow at all——"

"He couldn't have hurt anybody," she cried, tearful again.

"That's what I'm saying. What's this Murro gang?"

She dabbed at her eyes, and swallowed hard. "They said they'd come here from New York—you know, a lot of them did after they started cleaning up the rackets there—and Phil's paper, the *Herald-Telegram*, had had a lot of stuff about them—Phil had written some of it—and so they think one of them must have done it—and now they say this Murro gang all left town—I don't know"—she ended weakly.

He moved about restlessly for a moment, brought out his pipe then put it back again, and gave his sister-in-law several glances, half sympathetic, half impatient. Here was no resolute ally. They could murder all the Edlins in the world, and she would just give in. But when she looked at him, he contrived a sort of sympathetic grin, and she replied with a wan little smile.

"I'm sorry, Jimmy," she said, "but I just want to forget about it. You can't blame me, can you? And I never want to see this place again. I'm going back East. My mother wants me to stay with her, and that's what I'm going to do."

He admitted it was a good idea. "But what about money, Flo?" he enquired gruffly. And then, remembering what he had first thought of her, he could not help wondering what this might let him in for. If there had been any kids, that would have been different; he would have seen that poor Phil's kids were all right, would have enjoyed it too, for he liked kids and had none of his own that he knew anything about, not having acquired a genuine legitimate wife on his travels, in spite of many strange adventures with the sex; but he was not too keen on handing out Flo another pension. Once more, however, she surprised him.

"Thanks, Jimmy, but I don't need any. There was some insurance and the *Herald-Telegram* gave me something, though it wouldn't have killed them to have given me a bit more—seeing that Phil——" But she left this alone, and went on: "It isn't as if we'd any children, you see."

"No, that makes it better."

"It doesn't," she cried, almost fiercely. "God!—I'll say it doesn't. And we could have had. It was my fault. Phil wanted them. And I always said: 'Oh, let's leave it.' Why don't we know? Oh!—my God——" And now she suddenly dissolved into a really passionate storm of weeping, leaving Jimmy to stare at her awkwardly and sadly, and then to make a few comforting noises and to pat her thin heaving shoulders. It was some time before she was calm again.

"Yes, I'm going back East, perhaps to-morrow," she said, at last. "There's nothing to stay for now. I've done all I can do. I'm sorry you've had to come all this way, Jimmy. What are you going to do?"

"Well, I'm a gentleman o' leisure just now," he told her, grinning a little. "I got out of China in time, made my little bit, and now I'm just looking round and enjoying myself—at least, I'd just *started* looking round and enjoying myself, when I got this packet of trouble. Now that I'm here, I might as well stay here for some time. And I've got my old top floor at the Clay-Adams."

"Are you still trying to paint pictures, Jimmy?" she asked, coming for the first time clean out of her misery.

"Yes," with a grin, "when I can get at it." He was glad to see her looking more normal now. "You needn't tell me you don't admire my pictures—I know you don't—you told me last time, though mebbe I'm improving. When I meet a nice little woman who *does* like my pictures—*really* likes 'em—if she can cook a bit too, I'll marry her—I will, by jiminy! And don't tell me that's why I'm single, because I've heard that crack too many times. My pictures are all right—once you get round to understanding 'em—and I've painted 'em in places where some people wouldn't like to stop long enough to blow their noses." Having coaxed a smile out of her, he waited a moment, then went on earnestly: "Now listen, Flo. You're clearing out, and I'm not blaming you. But I'm staying, because this isn't good enough, and I want to know more about it. If it's a gunman who's left town, then I'd like to know more about him and where he's blown to. Now somebody knows more than's come out. This wouldn't be Los Angeles if they didn't. Now then, Flo, where do I start? That's all I want from you."

He had time to fill and light his pipe before she replied. "Phil had a pal on the paper," she began, hesitantly. "I didn't like him much so Phil didn't bring him here, but they used to go round together—sometimes on stories—sometimes on their own. His name's Drew—Rushy Drew they all call him—and I gave him Phil's notebook, because he asked for it."

"And what does he think about this business?"

"Rushy Drew? I've only talked to him once—it was just after they'd finished the inquest—but—well, he was like you, Jimmy—he wasn't satisfied. He said Phil was on another kind of story altogether round that time. That's why he asked me if he could have the notebook."

"Where do I find this Rushy Drew, Flo? Down at the *Herald-Telegram* office?"

"Well, you know what those reporters are, and Drew's an old-timer—always half-drunk if you ask me. No, the best place to find him is in the far room at *Dan's Place*. It's just across the square from the *Herald-Telegram*. I fancy Rushy's there half the day and most of the night."

"All right, Flo, and thanks. Now is there anything I can do?"

There was not—and, indeed, he could not help feeling that she would be glad to see the last of him, not because of any dislike but because his constant references to the murder made her unhappy all over again. Having no particular liking for her himself, he was glad to escape from her tearful presence and the half-shuttered miserable apartment into the bustle and colour of the city. But he took with him a steadily smouldering resentment. This was not to him the old Los Angeles, where he had had many a spree, sometimes with Phil, possibly with this Rushy Drew if he could only recall him; this was the city in which his brother had been murdered, without so much as an arrest following it. And you couldn't coolly bump off an Edlin like that—no, sir! The whole damned place, which had always been pretty tough, now began to look sinister.

It was not until late that evening that he found Rushy Drew in the far room at *Dan's Place*, a rambling darkish room filled with stained tables, giant spittoons, cigar smoke, signed photographs of second-rate heavy-weights, and a thick reek of rye whisky. He remembered Rushy Drew vaguely when the barman pointed him out: one of those oldish reporters who never get any older, with a decayed hat at the back of his grizzled head, a long fruity nose, ash all over his coat, and the wreck of a five-cent cigar stinking and dying at the corner of his wrinkled dried lips, which no amount of rye could keep moist.

"I'm Jimmy Edlin—Phil's brother—you remember?"

"Sure! Sit down. Glad to see you. Rye or Scotch? Hey, Walter, another rye and a Scotch. Had to come up from Honolulu, hadn't you? Too bad! And too damned bad about Phil!"

Over the drinks Mr. Drew listened while Jimmy explained his doubts and his determination to know more. Mr. Drew himself had that look which Jimmy had often seen before on the faces of newspaper men of his type, that weary, sceptical, infinitely knowing look of the man who feels that he is perpetually behind the scenes, and nearly always the grubbier parts behind the scenes. And if that look did not produce something valuable, Jimmy made up his mind not to tolerate it very long. He had exchanged drinks and doubts with many Rushy Drews before.

"Well," Rushy drawled, finally, "I'll tell you. In the first place, the thing is fairly on the level. They didn't know who did it, and I don't believe there's been any covering up—and, believe me, this is one town where Judas Iscariot could get covered up if he knew the right people—and he would. But Headquarters didn't know, don't know now, who did it. They're supposed to be still working on it, but they've too many things to work on—and *not* work on—right here. The *Herald-Telegram* played up the gunman-gangster angle for all it was worth, because we've been running one of these clean-the-city-of-the-bad-men-from-Brooklyn campaigns, which look so good and don't spoil anybody's friendships. On the evidence—you've seen the clippings, eh?—it could just as easily have been one of these out-of-town boys as anybody else; so that was the angle they gave it. Our valued representative died at his post, helping to clean up your city—and send the rats back to Brooklyn and New Jersey, see?"

"I see. And you don't believe it, eh?"

"You bet I don't. I know it's all apple-sauce." Rushy was emphatic, but stopped long enough to order more drinks. "Those boys don't turn the heat on to a reporter, unless—like that feller in Chicago— he's been playing round with 'em and then tried to walk out. And they didn't come here from New York looking for trouble—they just wanted to keep quiet and see what was doing. And Phil had been off that story for weeks, and had never set eyes on any of these gunmen from the East, and didn't believe there were four of 'em in town. No, sir. All hokum, and of course they know it at Headquar- ters—but—what the hell!—they've too much to do already—and they don't know where to look—you saw the evidence, and it was all they'd got, believe me—not a thing to go on—so where are you?"

Knowing his man, Jimmy confessed that he wasn't anywhere, but said he felt sure Rushy Drew, who knew the town and was, into the bargain, Phil's best pal, would know something.

"You're damn' right I do, though it's not much." Rushy paused for effect, and was not disappointed. "First, *I* know—though nobody else—that Phil was on another kind of story. They don't even know that at the desk, because he used to go round when he'd done his routine stuff and then turn in something juicy of his own. And he didn't like to talk too much before he'd got something. But he'd tell me now and again, because he knew that I'd been around here even before he had and knew the town backwards and sideways. They've built the rotten thing round me while I've been sitting here, ordering ryes that taste more and more like rainwater."

"What was he after, then?" asked Jimmy. "And has it anything to do with the murder?"

"If it hadn't, then I don't know what had. You know this town. They talk about the lunatic fringe in these states. Well, here it isn't a fringe, it's a solid seam of God-awful lunacy six foot thick and thirty miles long. We've more nutty people to the square mile here than anywhere on God's green earth. Every kind, from Hindu prophets with hair down to their knees to fat women who shave their heads and think they're Joan of Arc and Mary Queen of Scots. They're all here. Take any boulevard and in the fourth bungalow on the right they'll be busy raising the dead or talking things over with Dante and Shakespeare. Two doors farther down, they're waiting for the new Messiah. Across the boulevard, they're sitting about in pink robes or starry pants, burning incense until the Grand Panjandrum tells them it's the Judgment Day. We've so many nuts here, they fall so thick and fast, honest to God I haven't been able to get a good laugh out of 'em for twenty years. It's just one big loony-bin."

"And so what?" asked Jimmy, who knew his Los Angeles and could not imagine what was coming.

"I keep clear of 'em," Rushy continued, in his odd bitter drawl. "I'll see things soon enough. But Phil had heard one or two rumours, and so he'd started looking into some of these queer new sects we have here, and he was right in the middle of it, up to the very eyes in it, when somebody put him out."

"Didn't you tell them that?"

"I told them at the desk, but—what the hell—nobody would believe any harm of these religious birds—and anyway it's a lousy angle. We don't want bad boys from Brooklyn here, but we extend the heartiest welcome to all new citizens with a tile loose. L.A. is their New Jerusalem. Come right in, folks, and worship how you please! They pay their taxes and don't ask too many questions—they're too busy with the next world to see what's happening in this one—so walk right in and stay!"

"Yes," said Jimmy dubiously, "I can see all that, and I know the kind of folks you mean. But I don't think there's anything along that line, Rushy. I think you're clean out there." And his tone expressed his disappointment.

"Yeah? Well, that's what I'd have said. But for two things." Here Rushy paused, deliberately, maddeningly, and coolly relit his cigar and swallowed some rye. "Not two days before he was put out, Phil let something drop to me. He told me he thought he was on to something a whole lot bigger than the usual nutty stuff, and asked me if I'd ever heard of a crowd calling themselves the Brotherhood of the Judgment. I hadn't, as a matter of fact; they were new to me, but as I said, I've given it up. But he said he'd just caught the tail end of a story that would make every front page from here to Cape Cod. He wouldn't tell me any more. Probably didn't like the way I laughed and told him I'd heard all that before. That's one thing."

"This might be something. What's the other thing? Come on, Rushy. You're talking to his brother now. Wasn't there something about his notebook?"

"His wife told you, did she? He hadn't it with him that night they let him have the works. Left it at home, which was a bit of luck. I knew he put down things in it. And I was right. There isn't much—just a few remarks about this Brotherhood of the Judgment—but unless I'm going nuts too—they look like dynamite to me."

"Rushy," said Jimmy solemnly, "I have to see that notebook. I'm not playing about. Nobody's going to get away with murdering my brother without something happening. I don't know what all this means to you, but it means a hell of a lot to me."

"Jimmy," replied the other, in almost the same tone, "I'll not only let you see the notebook but you can have it. But whatever you're going to do—and I can't see you can do much—don't count me in. No, I'm not afraid—don't think that—I'd have just as soon gone out when Phil did instead of still sitting here bellyaching. But I'm getting on—I'm tired—and I've seen too many queer things happen that nobody could get to the bottom of—they're always happening in this man's town—and though I'll tell you anything I know, or try and find out if I don't know, I'm not turning detective, not even for Phil's sake."

"All right, please yourself about that, Rushy, but I must have that notebook as soon as possible. Where is it?"

"Up at my place—one room above a mad Mexican widow just out of South Olive—I just sleep there, that's all, and don't always manage that. But you don't want that notebook now, this minute, surely to God, Jimmy?"

But Jimmy did, and after some further persuasion, and two more quick drinks, he almost dragged the unwilling Rushy out of his haunt, which was more his home than the one room above the mad Mexican widow, and moved him firmly towards South Olive Street.

"Come to think of it," muttered Rushy, as they went, "it isn't a room. It's just a damned upstairs piggery. Ten to one you won't even be able to sit down."

"I don't want to sit down," said Jimmy, humorous but firm. "I've been sitting down too long, and I'm getting too wide behind. But I want that notebook."

"Christmas bells!" Rushy shouted, as he let them in, "but it can't be as bad as this. Either I've never had a good look at it for months or there's been a convention in here."

Jimmy had seen many untidy rooms in his time, had lived in them himself without much protest, but this room of Rushy's beat everything. There was a bed and a chest of drawers; so much could be clearly seen; but the rest of the place was a crazy litter of shabby books, empty cigar boxes, bulging or overflowing old files, piles of newspapers, odd shoes, fishing tackle, and miscellaneous rubbish and muck.

"I know I haven't had as many as usual," the owner muttered, looking bewildered, "but I'll swear it wasn't as bad as this last time I noticed it. Sit down on the bed, Jimmy. I know where I put that notebook, though you mightn't think so."

He went to the chest of drawers, looked at the first small drawer, exclaimed in surprise, tried the next, gave another exclamation, and then, cursing himself, went rapidly through all the drawers. Blasting his eyesight, he then tried again, going through them all more carefully this time. Not finding what he wanted, he looked slowly about the room. Jimmy waited, smoking his pipe and saying nothing.

At last, Rushy turned, and Jimmy saw that he was wearing a queer look, half-bewildered, half-frightened, and was suddenly cold sober. "Jimmy Edlin," he began, in an odd quiet voice, "you've got to believe me. Yesterday, I *know*, that notebook of Phil's was in that top drawer. I thought I might have shifted it somewhere else last night, so I've looked through all the drawers. It's gone, Jimmy. Somebody's taken it."

"Here, wait a minute. Let's have a proper look."

"I tell you, somebody's been here and taken it. I knew somebody had been in here the minute I came in. God knows it's always a mess, but not just this kind of a mess. I tell you, Jimmy," he asserted passionately now, "somebody's been all through this room, looking for something. And the notebook's gone."

There was panic in his voice. He looked at Jimmy hopelessly. And in the silence that followed, Jimmy heard the screeching of motor-car brakes outside, and an odd sinister sound it seemed at that moment.

"Now wait, before we start getting all excited," said Jimmy, with deliberate calm. "Are you going to tell me that a bunch of religious loonies sent somebody here to go through your room and take that notebook? It isn't sense, Rushy."

"No? And it wasn't sense that your brother Phil——"

"That's different."

"Well—is it? And if you can blow a hole in a feller, I suppose you can go through another feller's room, can't you? I tell you, Jimmy, they've been here—and it's gone—and I don't like the look of things at all."

"You're getting the jitters, Rushy. Now why——"

"Listen!" And Rushy held up his hand. Up the uncarpeted stairs, heavy footfalls were approaching. Even Jimmy did not feel quite calm, and Rushy was obviously perturbed. "Coming here," he whispered, and held himself rigid. There was a sharp knock.

They looked at one another, and Rushy shook his head. There was a second and a louder knock.

"Go on," said Jimmy. "Hell—there are two of us." But Rushy did not move, so Jimmy went himself and threw the door open wide.

A tall young man in a bright brown suit entered. "Good evening," he began, in a smooth plausible tone. "Now I'd like to interest you gentlemen in our new day-by-day clothes pressing service, collecting coats, pants, tuxedos, or what-have-you, every morning, and returning everything the same afternoon. We guarantee good service——" But anything else he said was drowned by Jimmy's sudden shout of laughter.

"Well, that's how it is, Rushy," Jimmy roared, after they had got rid of the young man. "The big menace turns into a pants-pressing service. And now let's find that notebook. It must be somewhere in this museum of yours."

But it wasn't, and Rushy, who proved that he knew his way among this litter, was able at last to convince Jimmy that the notebook really had been taken, by somebody who had gone through the room very thoroughly.

"But if they did," said Jimmy, making his final protest, "how did they know it was here?"

"How did they know poor Phil was on to them?"

"Perhaps they didn't," Jimmy retorted. "I can think of a dozen more likely ways of being killed, down-town here. Phil goes into that back room because he's made a date there with some fellow——"

"No doubt about that, except I'll bet the feller had suggested that place. It wouldn't be a woman, because that wasn't Phil's line. Something to do with a story, you bet your life!"

"Right! But while he's waiting there—and it's late and a tough neighbourhood—anything might have happened. A couple of Mexican stick-up men might have charged in——"

"And not gone through his pockets? Guess again, Jimmy. That

wasn't any stick-up job. I knew that from the first, just as I knew it wasn't any of these Brooklyn gorillas they talked so much about. No, sir." He turned and looked about him, muttering, "Got a bottle of Seagram's somewhere, and ought to be able to raise another glass besides that one with the tooth-brush in. Here we are. Help yourself, Jimmy, and hurry up, for God's sake. I've got a mouth like Death Valley." But that made him think of something else.

"What's got you?" asked Jimmy.

"Death Valley reminded me. Jimmy, I think I can remember nearly everything he had in that notebook—I mean, about this Brotherhood of the Judgment—you remember, those were the birds he mentioned to me. There wasn't much, all told. Now wait." And he stood there, still holding the bottle of rye and a glass, with his eyes tightly shut, while Jimmy sat on the edge of the bed, staring at the astonishing muddle of the room, and hearing, from somewhere outside, a dance band lolloping away on the radio. "I'll have to think this over when I'm alone," Jimmy was telling himself. "Nothing makes any sense while this wet old file of head-lines is around. He's just as nutty as the people he talks about."

Then Rushy opened his eyes and grinned faintly. But before he spoke, he took a sharp pull at the rye. "Now then, if there's anything I can't remember, it's something that wouldn't mean a dam' thing to you or me or anybody else. He'd written at the top of the page *Brotherhood of the Judgment.* Then something about there being four temples or arks——"

"Arks!" Jimmy snorted. "And we're sitting here, at our time of life, worrying about people who want to have arks."

"Jimmy," the other warned him solemnly, "the folks who are nutty enough to want to have arks might be dangerously nutty. Anyhow, there was an ark, he thought, in London, one in New York, one in Chicago—and, believe me, that'll be some ark, that one in Chicago—and one, the chief one, here in L.A."

"Where?" asked Jimmy, now with an old envelope and a pencil ready.

"Wait! I'll get it. He'd scribbled down—now what was it?— Redondo Boulevard and Centinela—you know, the avenue, out towards Culver City. All right then—that's how he'd started. Then he'd written something about this lot looking different from the other nutty religionists. More dangerous. Something really going on there, behind the ordinary crazy front they were putting up. Not just singing hymns and praying and telling each other how good they are. He was sure about that. And Phil was no fool, y'know, Jimmy."

Jimmy agreed, and waited. So far he had put down nothing but the two streets. "Go on. That's not all, is it?"

"No. I read this page a good many times. Hell!—it was the least I could do, wasn't it? Then there were some queries—you know, the way a feller does when he's trying to puzzle something out. One or two I couldn't read. But I remember what I could read—that is, if I read 'em right. *Tall man—Abram Lincoln with a squint—real leader?—don't think so. Who is Father John? Why Barstow—Granite Mountains—Death Valley? What are the—*now, wait a minute, what was the word?—I was never sure about that—but might have been *initiates—*y'know, the inner circle—anyhow, we'll say it was—*What are the initiates really expecting? What duties are they taking turns at?* Are you putting these down?"

"No. I can remember 'em, and anyhow they don't seem to amount to much," said Jimmy, rather sulkily. "I don't see why Phil was bothering about 'em. Duties! They could be taking turns with the collection bag, couldn't they?"

"Sure! But they might also be taking turns at putting nosey reporters out of the way. Use your imagination, Jimmy, for Pete's sake."

"Trouble is, you've got too much, Rushy. Is that all?"

"No, at the bottom of the page was something about a clock."

"Oh!—clocks are coming into it now, are they? If you ask me, we might as well be doing a cross-word puzzle."

"This is it. Question and answer. *When does the clock strike?* Then below, the answer: *You won't hear it.* Better put that down, Jimmy."

"I've got it down, though God knows why." Jimmy looked at his scribbles in disgust. "*When does the clock strike? You won't hear it.* Well, Rushy, I think we might just as well go out now and play Red Indians. We're on the wrong track. I've thought so all along. Some dirty little down-town rat killed Phil and daren't stay long enough afterwards even to snatch his wallet. You lost his notebook. And nobody's been in this room except you—and I'm not sure even about you." He was very contemptuous.

Rushy was annoyed. "Okay, Mr. Wise Guy, you know it all. But I'll tell you again what I think—just because you are Phil Edlin's brother—and then that lets me out. He was killed because he was getting to know too much, and I know for a fact that the only thing he was deep in was this Brotherhood of the Judgment story, because he told me so himself. He wasn't a fool; he'd plenty of sense and he was a dead keen newspaperman; and he wasn't playing at Red Indians when he went round with that notebook. I may be a fool, but I'm not such a goddamned fool that I don't know where I left something important, like that notebook, or that I don't know when somebody's been and turned over every single thing I possess. Forget it—if you like. I'm not going to do anything, and I've told you why. But don't come round again to me, Jimmy, to tell me you're going to find out who killed Phil, because I'll know you're just talking big. And now that I am here, I might as well stay here. Want another drink?"

"No, thanks, Rushy." Jimmy was a bit stiff but also vaguely apologetic. "I'll get along. Sorry if I sounded too sharp and sure, but all that stuff just didn't seem to fit in, that's all."

"We'd know better what fitted in and what didn't, if we knew more about the whole cockeyed business here in this world than we do. I'm an old-timer, and I've seen plenty, and, believe me, Jimmy, most of it's taken me by surprise. If somebody had told me ten years ago that Franklin D. Roosevelt would be the Czar of these states, I'd have had a good big laugh. And Hitler and Mussolini and Stalin weren't exactly expected either. You don't know what's coming next. Well—I may be seeing you, Jimmy."

Oddly enough, Jimmy, thinking it all over in his hotel that night, staring now and again at the envelope on which he had scribbled his notes, and remembering not only everything Rushy had told him but also the character of his brother Phil, was far less confident than he had been up in Rushy's room. There might be nothing in it; but now he felt that at least it was his duty to make sure. If Phil had thought this Brotherhood of the Judgment was worth his time and attention—and Phil was not the fellow to chase wild geese, unless under orders—then he, Jimmy, with time on his hands and a brother's death on his mind, could not afford to ignore completely this trail, broken, dim, fantastic though it might appear to be. No, the least he could do was to have a look at the Brotherhood, even though he still could not come near convincing himself that its members—probably a lot of idle women and retired Bible-reading farmers—were capable of house-breaking, robbery and murder.

He did not start at once, however, in the morning. He felt dubious, troubled, with an uneasy night behind him, and so, wearing nothing but shirt, pants and slippers, and puffing away at his pipe, he spent the morning painting from memory a scene he thought he remembered from the voyage, completely ignoring the golden, early October morning outside, which was flooding the whole wide city with its own heavy and hazy sunlight. Even among the world's most mistakenly enthusiastic, untrained daubers, Jimmy could be considered unique. He was so bad that he was almost great. He neither knew nor cared much about drawing; what he liked to do was to lay on plenty of colour; but it was the quality of his colour that gave Jimmy's efforts their astounding character. His blues and greens, pinks and purples, all seemed to have come out of some horrible chemical works; they looked like poisonous acids; they had a metallic sheen that set the teeth on edge; they suggested neuralgia in pigment; and when Jimmy had worked away with these nightmare hues, composing them into what looked like lumps of coloured cotton wool until at a closer inspection they revealed their full metallic hideousness, the result was downright terrifying. Canvases presented solemnly by him to wincing friends were to be found, after a hard search at the back of lumber-rooms, all over the world; for though Jimmy liked nothing better than to paint and then to look with pleasure at his creation, he was no hoarder of his pictures; he gave them away freely; and it is a tribute to his friendly soul that so many people had accepted them and even forced up a smile of welcome for the framed horrors. All this morning, then, he spent happily conjuring the Pacific into what appeared to be a dreadful vat of copper sulphate solution, and creating above it an electric-blue sky that instantly suggested a blinding headache. And he was able to finish this monstrous libel in time to give his widowed sister-in-law a farewell lunch.

Afterwards, strolling idly down Figeroa, deciding again to try and see what Phil had been after among the Brotherhood of the Judgment, he found himself regretting that he was alone; not just alone at that moment, but with no companion on this adventure— if it was to be an adventure, which he still doubted. Rushy Drew was clearly no use; even if he had not made it plain himself, Jimmy would have rejected him. Jimmy reflected that he knew at least a dozen fellows round the town, but not one of them could be considered a friend. He had made a great many friends, the real thing, on his various travels, for he was a companionable soul, as gregarious as a starling, but they were all thousands of miles away. A shame too, for some of them would have been useful at this sort of investigation, though Jimmy, who had never suffered from any sense of inferiority, considered that he was pretty good at it himself. It would not take him long to find out if there was anything in this Brotherhood nonsense. And he went over Phil's queries again.

But it was not until the middle of the evening that he actually found his way to the local Ark of the Brotherhood. Phil's directions, just the mention of Redondo and Centinela, had not been too clear, for the building was certainly not at the corner where the two roads met. It was somewhere between them, and it took some finding, for it turned out to be at the end of a narrow side-turning. It looked like any other chapel, and might have once belonged, Jimmy thought, to some other sect. There was nothing suspicious and secret about the outside of the building. Apparently he was just in time for some sort of service, for a few people were going in. An illuminated sign told him that everybody was welcome. He went in, but told himself he was a fool to let himself in for some dreary hymn-singing service.

A rusty little man, with thick spectacles, stopped him just inside the entrance. "Good evening, brother," he said, in a melancholy voice. "Are you a member of our Brotherhood?"

"No," said Jimmy cheerfully. "Just looked in. All right, isn't it?"

"Most certainly," said the little man. "All are welcome to our public services. But kindly seat yourself at the side there—anywhere at that side—because the other seats are reserved for our members."

So Jimmy went down an aisle, between rows of yellow little

wooden chairs, and as he had come to see as much as he could, he went as far down as possible. It was a longish narrow building, with a great deal of yellow wood about it, not too brightly lit. Here at this end was a carpeted platform, with a small organ behind it, and in the middle of the platform there was a reading-stand covered with black velvet. The only decoration was an immense dark banner, hanging down above the organ, and on it had been painted, very vividly and imposingly, an immense single eye, which appeared to look down on the scattered congregation with no enthusiasm. Jimmy was not intimidated by that eye. "You're phoney, my lad," he told it. At his side of the platform, just behind the three or four steps that led down from it, there was a door in the back wall, before which two middle-aged and rather large brethren were standing, as if on sentry duty.

He now looked across at the members, of whom there might have been about a hundred. There were both men and women, but not far more women than men, as he had expected to find; and he soon noticed that there were hardly any young people there. They were nearly all middle-aged or elderly, and a hard-faced lot, many of them with a strong weather-beaten look, not like city folks. But it was not easy to see most of their faces in that light. The ones he could see he did not much care for, for they had a beaky, bony, tight-mouthed look about them. The dozen or so people who were sharing the seats at the side with him were a nondescript collection, except the one person who was sitting on the same short row that he was in, actually only two chairs away. She looked all wrong in there, and, after a few glances, he had an idea that she felt all wrong too. She had a nice impudent little hat on, and was herself a nice but not impudent little woman, perhaps about forty, with a rather flushed soft face, very bright eyes, and, he thought, pretty greyish curls; altogether as nice, bright, perky, chirpy a little woman as he had seen for months. "You're all right, you are," he told her silently, after the third or fourth glance, "and I'll bet any money this is both your first and last time here. Like me. Good luck to you!"

She had been looking about her dubiously and had stolen one or two quick glances at Jimmy, who at last, after they had waited there for about ten minutes, ventured to give her a friendly grin.

She did not look offended, so he leaned her way and whispered: "When do they start?"

"I don't know." She had a nice clear little voice too, and the merriest inch of nose you could wish to see. A merry little tinker of a woman, no doubt about that, and worth a thousand of these long-faced psalm-singers in here. "I've never been before."

"Nor me either."

She seemed glad to be able to talk to somebody, and went on: "I overheard two women talking about it—so I thought I'd see what it was like."

"Doesn't look much to me, so far," said Jimmy, as if he was a great taster of sects and services.

"No." She drew that out as if she were dubious. "But——"

"But what?"

"Haven't you noticed some of these folks, especially the ones in front?" Here she lowered her voice. "I may be fancying things— I don't like it in here, anyhow—but they all look crazy to me, I mean, really crazy, mad people. Honestly, I mean it. You notice their faces. They have just that look. I wouldn't be left alone with some of 'em, not for anything. Batty! Honestly! And not just nicely batty, like some people, but miserable, cruel batty. Oh!—they must be starting." And she leaned back, and looked straight in front of her, like a good little girl.

At first, only the organ growled and rumbled at them, as if it had had quite enough of this sort of thing. Then an elderly man with a long upper-lip and a grey chin-beard mounted the platform, and asked them to sing with him. Jimmy had the pleasure of sharing a book with the little woman, who sang a bit in a shy soprano; but Jimmy only grunted vaguely, and did not care for the hymn, which was all about blood, as if it had been composed in a slaughter-house. Then the elderly man, in an angry nasal voice, read a long piece from the Bible, all about angels standing at the four corners of the earth, and another angel telling them not to hurt the servants of God, who were sealed on their foreheads, and then a lot of stuff about tribes, of no great interest unless you were in the know, and then some pretty grim talk about washing people white in the blood of the Lamb.

"'They shall hunger no more, neither thirst any more,'" the

elderly man concluded, not sounding angry now but very loud and shrill, "'neither shall the sun light on them, nor any heat . . .'"

And now from the rows of people in front there came surprising cries and groans and triumphant shouts, in fact all kinds of quite savage noises; and some of them raised their hands and shook them hard; and one woman made a gurgling sound and fell back, as if in a faint; and one man, a big chap with the voice of a bull, yelled *Halleluyah!*

"You see!" Jimmy heard the little woman whisper urgently and with a slight quaver. "I don't like this at all."

"Anybody can have it for me," said Jimmy.

Now they were all praying, led by a passionate skeleton of a man in a black coat much too large for him. He was, however, a most fluent and powerful leader of prayer. He asked Jehovah to look down on them, sealed in his service, and to abate his wrath a little while, until all who could be sealed were safe in the fold, and then to let go his wrath for all it was worth, fulfilling the most terrible prophecies, it seemed, with hail and fire and blood and darkness and wormwood for everybody except the faithful few. Punctuated as it was by groans and loud *Amens*, his long prayer, delivered with a terrible sincerity, with an outward force expressing an inward fury of impassioned conviction, began to have its effect even on Jimmy's sceptical mind. Something stirred uneasily in the depths of his being. And he knew that the little woman, now rather closer than she had been, distinctly trembled once or twice.

"It's all right, y'know," he told her, when it was all over, and they were about to sing again.

"I know it is. I know it can't happen," she whispered confidingly. "But I just hate the way he wants it to happen. It's the people that frighten me, not what they say. And I'll be glad when it's over, won't you?"

At the end of this hymn, the elderly man with the chin-beard announced that their local leader, Brother Kaydick, would talk to them. Brother Kaydick, a tall, rather imposing figure, came out through the door at the back. At first, Jimmy thought he must have seen him before somewhere, and it was not until Brother Kaydick had begun talking, in a deep resonant voice, that he remembered. This was undoubtedly the man that Phil had described as

Lincoln with a squint. It was a very good description. This man had Lincoln's lean height and long dark face, but the face lacked the statesman's noble breadth and the eyes were wrong. He looked like a squashed-in, not quite sane Lincoln. And suddenly, for no reason that he was immediately aware of, Jimmy's scepticism left him. It was not simply because Phil had described a man who now appeared: that proved nothing, except that Phil had probably attended one or two of these meetings. No, it was not that; yet now he suddenly felt certain that he had been wrong and Rushy had been right, that Phil had guessed there was something really queer, menacing, about these people, who had somehow discovered that he knew too much. He did not reason about it at all. The conviction came in a flash. Meanwhile, Brother Kaydick was talking to them, and being listened to with profound respect.

He began by making various announcements, mostly relating to special services, and also by giving some brief news of the Brotherhood's activities in the three other centres. Then, after quoting by heart a text or two from the *Book of Revelation*, with growing fervour he addressed them, asking them to remember what the greatest and wisest of the Old Testament prophets had said, what was to be found in the *Book of Revelation*, which must be regarded as the keystone of the Bible, and to look about them, to reflect upon the present condition of the world, and to ask themselves if all things were not working together for the end so long and gloriously prophesied. What was the whole world now, into which children were still being born, but the spectacle of that woman arrayed in purple and scarlet, seated upon the seven-headed beast with its names of blasphemy, carrying her gold cup filled with abominations and filthiness of her fornications? The beast had seven heads—yes, and what were now the great powers of the world? They too were seven—the United States, Britain, Russia, France, Germany, Italy, and Japan. Where were the blasphemies? They were everywhere. The whole earth was now Babylon, drenched in the blood of saints and martyrs. Did not every power in the world make war with the Lamb, as the Bible said they would; and shall not the Lamb overcome them, as also it was said? Had not all nations drunk of the wine of the wrath of the fornications of Babylon? Were they not more besodden with them every day? Were the most terrible words of the ancient prophets thus to be mocked? Had not a voice from Heaven, as it was prophesied it would, already spoken to them, and was not that why they were gathered together, the brothers and sisters of the Judgment? The Judgment was certain, nor could it come too early, but they who were already sealed in the service of Heaven must be prepared not only to welcome but also to serve the Judgment, for Heaven worked in mysterious ways and its servants were abroad on the earth even now, a faithful few, as they were in the olden time. And there was much more in this vein, delivered with great fervour and with something like real oratory.

Jimmy listened with growing uneasiness. There was something here, behind the words, though they were strong enough, that he did not understand. The man was a crazy fanatic, like many of them there, but there was about him a sense of certainty that could not easily be laughed away. He *knew* something, and though that something might be explained here in terms of Bible prophecies and the like, Jimmy could not help feeling that there was more to it than that. Somehow, listening to him and looking at him, you could not dismiss his talk to some vague crazy vision of Babylon and old Jewish prophets.

Finally, Brother Kaydick announced triumphantly, while his listeners made enthusiastic sounds: "I have a message for you from our beloved leader, Father John. It arrived this very evening. Father John commands me to tell you, brothers and sisters of the Judgment, that out there, in his lodge in the wilderness, he is praying, and there are signs of an answer to his prayers, that he is seeing visions, and that soon, very soon, what he sees in these visions will come to pass, so that the Word may be fulfilled. He asks for the even deeper devotion and service of those who are sealed, and for the thankful prayers of all members. To-night's public service is ended, except for the singing of the usual hymn. Will Servers Eight, Eleven, Fifteen and Twenty-three, join me in the small room?"

It was then, while Brother Kaydick was making for the door at the back and the elderly man was reading the first lines of the hymn, that Jimmy came to a decision. As the organ began, he found himself sharing the book again with the little woman.

> *Jehovah said "Vengeance is mine"*
> *The sinful could not flee,*

they sang lustily.

"Listen," whispered Jimmy urgently. "You don't know me and you mustn't think I'm crazy. This is serious. I'm going round to the back in a minute."

"Oh!" cried the little woman, in dismay. "You're not going to join them, are you?"

"Not me. But I have to know more about 'em, and I'm going to try something on."

> *When Pharaoh and his hosts were drowned*
> *In the Red devouring sea*

the others roared happily.

She looked up at him, her delightful little round face puckered with bewilderment and doubt. Certainly her curls were grey—or greyish—but they were very charming, only making her eyes seem brighter. Even at that moment he could not help wondering—and it came in a flash—if by any possible miraculous chance she would like his pictures. "I thought you were the one person who was all right," she said, dubiously, rather reproachfully. "And now you're talking queer."

"No, I'm not. Can't explain now. But my name's Jimmy Edlin, and I'm staying at the Clay-Adams. Are you on the end of a telephone?"

"Well—yes," she replied, still doubtful. "I'm at my cousin's— only for a day or two—down here at Inglewood—"

> *It rained for forty days and nights*
> *After that Ark was sealed*

they chanted triumphantly.

Jimmy lowered his head a little, to speak close to her ear. "I asked because I want to give you a message later on to-night or early in the morning, to say I'm still all right. If a message doesn't come through from me—and, don't forget, Jimmy Edlin's the name—say, by to-morrow morning at ten, send the police along here. Yes, I mean it."

"Gracious me! But couldn't you——"

"I want to get on with it now," he continued, "and I believe I'm taking a chance. So you've got to help me. Don't worry. It'll probably be all right, but I'd like to be prepared. Do you mind giving me your name and telephone number, please?"

Still bewildered, she gave them. Her name was Mrs. Atwood, and at once he hoped she was a widow. "I'll ring up your husband if you'd prefer it," he told her quickly.

"I haven't a husband any more. Haven't had for five years. Now do you really mean this? It's not some silly game, is it?"

The walls of Jericho were strong
But then the trumpet blew

they proclaimed joyfully.

"Do I look like a man who'd play a silly game with you?" he demanded.

"Yes, you do," she told him, coolly. "But I can see you're serious now. Now, if you don't ring up to say you're all right by ten in the morning, you really want me to tell the police?"

"That's it."

"I never heard of such a thing! But I don't think I'd mind seeing some of these folks get a crack over the head—with their blood and Babylon and miseries! Do some of 'em good! But what are you going to do, Mr. Edlin? And why do you think something might happen to you?"

"Can't tell you now."

"Then you'll have to tell me when you telephone. Making me so curious! Else I'll think you're just a show-off. You're not, are you?"

"Sometimes." He grinned. "But not this time, I give you my word."

The earth shall be our Promised Land
And Satan reign no more

they concluded confidently, and the organ rumbled on alone. Jimmy gave a final look of understanding at the nice little widow's bright eyes; she nodded and smiled at him as she passed; he watched her trip down the aisle a moment; then he turned and went towards the door through which Brother Kaydick had disappeared. He had no proper plan, but he had often been content before to let instinct guide him, and now was willing to risk it again. The two large brethren, a tough pair at close quarters, were still doing duty, and now they promptly stopped him.

"I want to see Brother Kaydick in there," he explained. "It's important."

"But you are not a member of our Brotherhood."

Now for it! "Yes, I am. Tell him I've just arrived from the centre —the Ark—in London."

"From London?"

"Yes, and not only a member, my friend," he continued, with an easy air of confidence he did not feel, "but also a Server. Number Nineteen—London. And, I tell you, it's very important."

"I'll tell Brother Kaydick," said the older of the two, and left Jimmy with his colleague, a gloomy raw-boned chap who looked as if he had spent the first thirty-five years of his life behind a plough somewhere and had not enjoyed it. He continued to eye Jimmy, who knew only too well that his appearance was not in his favour. With his heart thumping a little, Jimmy could only hope that they would decide that a brother from London might be excused so worldly an appearance. Then the other returned and took him down a short corridor and into a small room, which might have served once as a vestry. On one wall was a large map, and on a desk in the far corner were files and piles of booklets and what looked uncomfortably like a couple of boxes of revolver ammunition. There were five men in there: the imposing Brother Kaydick, with his dark height and menacing squint; and the four Servers whose numbers had been called out, four hefty, big-boned, hairy-wristed fanatics, who looked a very tough proposition. This was no joke at all. He was in for it now. And under Brother Kaydick's doubtful, searching look he felt more wildly unlike any possible Brother of the Judgment, from London or anywhere else, than he had done before. Unless he bluffed like blazes, he decided, this was not going to be a very healthy adventure.

"Well, friends," he said ingratiatingly, as they continued to examine him as if he were a talking alligator, "I am very glad to be able to report to you—at last."

"You say you are from our ark at London?"

"Yes," replied Jimmy, hoping he did not sound too unsure of himself. It was not easy to meet Brother Kaydick's pronounced squint. "I'm—er—Number Nineteen."

There was a look of surprise, still mixed darkly with doubt, on their five long faces. Perhaps the brethren in London didn't have numbers. Perhaps, even if they did have numbers, there never had been a Nineteen. Perhaps——

"Number Nineteen—from London," Brother Kaydick was repeating slowly, and to Jimmy's ear as if he did not like the sound of it at all. Then, very quietly and casually, he enquired: "When does the clock strike?"

So that was it. Thank God he remembered!

"You won't hear it," Jimmy told them all. And gave them a smile too.

This certainly made a difference. Their faces were not the kind that clears easily, but undoubtedly they now cleared a little.

"You are welcome, brother," said Kaydick with grave politeness. "We were surprised because we had not been warned of your coming."

"No. I—I——" and now what? Why was he there? What was the line now? Out it came: "You see, I've a very important message for Father John."

"You can give it to me, brother. I will see that Father John receives it."

That would get him nowhere, and, besides, what on earth was the message? "Sorry, Brother Kaydick. I know what a big—that is, I know what your position is here—we all know that, of course— but I was told to give this message to Father John himself. So I want to know where he is."

Brother Kaydick did not look pleased. The other four merely stared. "It would be better," said Kaydick slowly, "to let me have the message so that I can send it to our leader."

"I dare say, brother. But—well, those were my orders."

"I shall be communicating with Father John to-night," Kaydick continued. "And I will tell him you are here. No doubt one of our Servers will be instructed to meet you at Barstow, and then will either take you to Father John or will accept the message. You will probably have to leave the message there with him."

"At Barstow?"

"Yes. On the Mohave Desert. There!" And Brother Kaydick pointed to it on the large map. "Be there to-morrow evening—you may go either by road or on the railway—and wait at the Harvey House there. You will know the Server who is sent, of course, by asking or answering the question about the clock striking."

"There's just another thing," said Jimmy, rather desperately. "In London—I wasn't given Father John's name among—er—unbelievers—his ordinary—I mean, his—er—worldly name. And I was told that you would give it to me here—y'know, in case I might need it up there on the desert."

To Jimmy's instant relief, this did not surprise Brother Kaydick, who nodded gravely, then scribbled something and handed the folded slip of paper over to Jimmy, who felt it would be better to read it outside. So now, after repeating that he would be at the Harvey House, Barstow, the following evening, to meet the messenger, he withdrew at once, telling them that he was tired and must rest before his trip. Then, conscious of the pleasant task before him of telephoning Mrs. Atwood that he was all right so far, in the light of a lamp outside he read the name of the mysterious Father John, leader of these grim fanatics.

It was John MacMichael.

CHAPTER FOUR

THEY MEET AT BARSTOW

The little town of Barstow does not cut much of a figure on the map—there it is, a dot on the Mohave Desert—but once there, or even if you are only on the way there, you realise it has its own importance. It may now have several hotels, gasoline stations, drug stores, bars, pool rooms, and a motion picture theatre, all bravely picked out in neon lights, but it remains what it has always been—an oasis in a desert. And its situation is important. Two main roads enter it from the West: one coming down from Bakersfield and Central California; one coming up from San Bernardino and Los Angeles. Two equally good roads leave it eastwards: one wandering over the barren hills until it reaches Needles and enters Northern Arizona; the other going forward into Nevada and taking the tourist to the new magnificence of Boulder Dam. Moreover, the little town is on the main line of the Santa Fe railroad, and now it sees the silver-gleaming, stream-lined coaches of the *Chief* and *Super-Chief*, caravans to and from the Arabian Nights of Hollywood. There is a new hotel now, facing the main street, but the older hotel, operated by the Fred Harvey Company, a building in the Harvey tradition of compromise between Spanish-Indian and Chicago styles, still does a brisk trade down by the railroad tracks.

On this October evening, however, there was only one guest in the dining-room of the Harvey House. Over in the lunch room, where you eat at the circular counter, there were plenty of customers, chiefly railroad workers, washing down slabs of pie with hot coffee. But the bright lights in the astonishing floral candelabra of the dining-room shone extravagantly in this desert only to illuminate one guest and a solitary waitress. The guest was dubiously examining one of those hard lumps of lettuce decorated with bits of pineapple and grapefruit and cheese and smeared all over with a thick pink paste, which are considered by all American caterers to be salads. The waitress, a severely virtuous young woman in spite of her musical comedy uniform and musical comedy make-up, was examining the guest. He was a very handsome young man and was wearing a brown tweed coat, a pretty blue shirt and tie, and neat grey flannel trousers. His hair was fair and rather wavy; he was nicely tanned; he had a charming shy smile and an English accent; and the waitress, who noticed all these things and fifty more, hoped that he was one of those young Englishmen who were now finding their way to Hollywood. Here she was both right and wrong, for the young man, Malcolm Darbyshire, had just come from Hollywood, but he was no film actor but an architect, who had been fortunate enough to wangle the job of conferring with an impatient client of his firm who wanted to build a house near the English studios. And Malcolm, pulling every possible string, had not wangled the job simply because he liked the idea of a nice long trip from London to Los Angeles (though he did not despise it), but because for the last six months he had found himself a dreamy, a haunted, a lunatic young architect, desperately in love with a mysterious girl, a sad sleeping beauty of a girl, a bewitched princess of a girl, with whom he had played tennis and exchanged a kiss. And he was here, poking at a fantastic salad, in Barstow, when he ought to have been returning home, because he had been told that Andrea MacMichael might possibly be found somewhere in this desolate region.

The waitress did not know all this, of course, but perhaps some mysterious intuition of the handsome young man's state of mind, at once idiotic and wonderful, reached her, so that there was a certain sympathetic tenderness in the way in which she now placed before him two dishes of vegetables and a plate of lamb chops. She was rewarded with another charming smile, though it seemed a trifle absent-minded. And well it might be, for Malcolm found himself now, after six months' haunted lunacy, living in a fantastic dream. He could not come to any sort of sensible terms with this vast continent, with its dusty plains and great mountains and hundreds of enormous rivers, its immense darknesses and sudden glare and glitter, its railway trains like small towns on the move, its incomprehensible mixture of cruelty and kindness, cleverness and stupidity, daring and cowardice, its equally mysterious politics, jokes, drinks, salads: and the whole monstrous thing had been crammed down his throat with one colossal shove. And now here he was, at the end of a dusty day, miles from anywhere that made any sense at all, in the middle of a desert that looked like a scrubby Sahara, looking for a girl who probably never wanted to set eyes on him again. He was, he knew, behaving like a complete and hopeless chump, unfit to be a member—and only a recent young member too—of the Royal Institute of British Architects. Yet he could not help feeling that he was also a glorious chump. He could not be certain if Andrea was really in this part of the world at all, yet already these barren hills, the roads he had seen running out to nowhere, this little town, were invested with glamour, as if they existed in a fairy-tale world. Before coming in to dinner, he had stood on the bridge, stretching its white length over a river that wasn't there, and had stared at a sunset, immense, fiery, startling, that had ended the day as if it had been an epic; and though it was all so remote and strange, and at last the mountains had turned black and were like a savage silhouette against the pale-green receding sky, and the very first stars seemed to tell him he was in another world, he had been oddly comforted in his folly. Anything, it seemed, might happen here, even the reappearance of Andrea, and possibly an Andrea he could understand.

Malcolm looked up from his lamb chops, which were not so tender as the waitress had been, to observe that that young woman was now pouring ice-water into the glass of another guest, who was accepting that solemn ritual, which almost appeared to be the new American substitute for grace, with the grave calm of a fellow-citizen. He had seen this chap once or twice before: a tall untidy chap with shocking clothes flapping about him, but a pleasant, thoughtful-looking fellow, perhaps a year or two older than himself. They had, in fact, exchanged a nod and a word. Malcolm wished now he had suggested that they shared a table, for this American, though he was not dressed in the semi-cowboy rig of these parts, might know the district and the people in it. So far Malcolm had not asked anybody about the MacMichaels. He had only arrived from the Coast that afternoon, and he shrank from enquiring about his beloved at the hotel desk. Obviously Andrea and her millionaire father didn't live here in this little town, and now Malcolm could not imagine where on earth they could live. The large map hanging in the little entrance hall had been anything but a comfort, for it simply showed him hundreds of miles of desert, sprinkled with grim names like *Granite Wells, Dry Silver Lake, Devil's Playground, Death Valley*. Talk about a needle in a haystack! This was like looking for one wisp of hay in twenty thousand mountainous acres of needles.

As Malcolm lit a cigarette and wondered how to open a conversation with the tall young man in the other corner, another man arrived. But this newcomer waved away the waitress, and stood in the middle of the room, looking at the two who were seated there. Then Malcolm saw him go to the other corner, say something to the tall young man, who looked up, frowning his surprise. In half a minute the interview was over. Now the newcomer came to Malcolm. He was a broad, plump, middle-aged fellow with a wide mouth and a snub nose and a general air of cheerful impudence, though at the moment he was looking rather solemn and mysterious.

"Say," he began, in a rich conspiratorial whisper, coming so close that Malcolm could see a bright green stripe in his rich brown suit, "when does the clock strike?"

"What clock?" asked Malcolm. "I'm afraid I haven't noticed a clock. But if you want to know the time——"

"No, no, that's all right," replied the broad, green-striped man apologetically. "Just forget I spoke. It's a gag—just a gag." And out he went.

Malcolm took his cigarette over to the other table. "Hope you don't mind my coming over——?"

"Surely not! Sit down."

"Thanks! Have a cigarette? I was wondering if that fellow who's just gone out asked you about a clock too."

"He did," replied the tall young man, grinning. "Then said it was a gag."

"Yes. What did he mean—a gag? A joke?"

"That's it. He looked the type too." And the tall young man finished his coffee.

"There doesn't seem anywhere to sit in this hotel—no bar or anything."

"No. Some bars up town, if you want a drink."

"I don't particularly," replied Malcolm, "at least, just now. I suppose you wouldn't care for a stroll?"

"Certainly." He stood up, then looked solemnly at Malcolm, who knew at once that he was now about to introduce himself. "My name's Hooker."

"Mine's Darbyshire."

"English?" asked Hooker.

"Yes."

"Thought you were," continued Hooker, as they went out. "I was over in England this summer. Had a nice time—mostly."

After leaving the hotel, they turned away from the town, and strolled towards the bridge where Malcolm had watched the sunset. The night was cool, almost cold after the heat of the day, and very clear, with a fine show of stars, among which Malcolm noticed several familiar constellations at odd angles in unusual parts of the sky. That made him feel a long way from home. He could feel too a sense of immense distance, remoteness, in the velvety blackness of the country all round him. Meanwhile, he and Hooker had exchanged a few confidences about their respective jobs.

"But you're taking a holiday out here, I suppose," said Malcolm.

"I've just been back to the Institute, since I was in Europe," replied Hooker. "Research is my job, not teaching, so I can come and go more than most of others. But I wouldn't quite call it a holiday—I had my holiday this summer—in fact, I don't know what I'd call this particular trip—a piece of foolishness, I guess."

Malcolm's heart suddenly warmed to the chap. Could there be two of them here behaving like chumps?

Hooker changed the subject. "I suppose you're on your way to have a look at Death Valley or Boulder Dam, aren't you?"

"No," replied Malcolm. "I'd like to have a look at them, of course —though I haven't a car and I imagine it's a bit difficult without one—but actually I've come out here—I mean here, to Barstow— to make some enquiries about some people—anyhow, one person—I know, who are supposed to live somewhere round here. Haven't asked anybody yet about them. I was wondering if you knew—though of course you're a stranger too, so I don't suppose you would. Their name's MacMichael."

Hooker stopped. They were now at the near end of the long bridge. "Did you say MacMichael?"

"Yes, MacMichael."

"Boy—oh boy—oh boy!" chanted the young scientist, to Malcolm's astonishment. "Now can you beat that?"

"What's the matter? Do you know them?"

"Never mind for a minute," cried Hooker excitedly. "Just tell me some more." He leaned against the parapet, looking down at the river that wasn't there, and Malcolm followed his example. "I'll tell you this much—I'm looking for MacMichaels too—and if you like you can come along—and I *have* a car, not much to look at but it can travel. But tell me some more."

They were interrupted for a moment by the passing of a large car, travelling slowly away from the town, over the bridge. Malcolm was glad of it. He did not know how to begin, yet he felt that here was a possible ally of great value.

"Well," he began hesitantly, "I met a girl—playing tennis on the French Riviera, last February—and—well—I've come to find her—and that's about all. Sounds silly, I know, but I simply have to find that girl."

"Want to marry her, I suppose?" said Hooker, with a calm detachment from all this fuss of mating.

"I would marry her—yes, like a shot," Malcolm admitted, "though the chances are pretty thin. But there's more than that in it. You see——"

"Just a minute. Who is this girl?"

"She was competing under a false name—a lot of tennis players do, for various reasons—but I was told afterwards that her name was really Andrea MacMichael, and that she's the daughter of a copper millionaire called Henry MacMichael, who has a place—though that seems unlikely to me—somewhere round here."

"Fine! Go on."

"Well, there isn't a lot more to say. But—there was something funny about this girl—she was very unhappy, I think—strange—repressed—secretive—and—well, I want to see her again to find out what's wrong. I know there's something wrong."

"What's the matter with those people, anyway?" cried Hooker. "I didn't know anything about a girl—didn't know there was one—but I ran into the father——"

"What's he like?" enquired Malcolm anxiously.

"A pain in the neck, and a good big pain too. Now what's the matter with 'em? I don't care what Engelfield may be doing, it doesn't explain the way they go on."

"Who's Engelfield?"

"He's a physicist, like me, only older and better known, and he disappeared and I went looking for him, and now he turns out to be Henry MacMichael's brother—as a matter of fact, I checked up on that—and, like your tennis girl, he changed his name—well, he left out the MacMichael—his real name's Paul Engelfield Mac-Michael——"

"I'm sorry," said Malcolm, "but I'm not following all this."

Hooker laughed. "My fault. I'll have to tell you the whole story —hey, what's that?"

It was the sound of a shot, very sharp in the immense night, and it seemed to come from the road just beyond the bridge. They could see the lights of a car along there. Then there was a second shot. Then the sound of somebody running, over the bridge, towards them. A figure appeared, pounding along their way. The next moment, a heavy man came up, gasping. It was the man who had asked them the question about the clock in the dining-room. He had another question this time.

"Got a gun, you fellows?" he gasped, and when he found they hadn't, he continued, fighting for breath: "All right. I'll take a chance. Can't run much farther—thought I might—hide under the bridge. Any water down there?"

The headlights were turned in their direction now, and moved slowly forward.

"Cover me up, boys. Say you saw me go down the road. I'm clean out o' breath." And the man crouched down behind them, wheezing and groaning a little, as the headlights came nearer. The two young men stood close together, not feeling too comfortable about this hide-and-seek game that included revolver shots. The car came up slowly, invisible behind its big lights, but then, when it was very close, suddenly gathered speed and swept past them and was soon out of sight.

"That's better," said the stranger, getting up again, "and thanks a lot, you two. I know I might have got you both tangled up in a very nasty piece of business, and I apologise for it, but I was in a tough spot. Not a mile outside the town too. And I'll tell you this—if I hadn't run for it then, within these next two or three hours I'd have been laid out stiff somewhere among those hills, with a couple o' vultures pecking my guts out of me to-morrow morning. What an escape! And I'm no coward, boys, believe me— but that's just a bit too thick. Ugh!"

"And what time," asked Hooker calmly, "*does* the clock strike?"

"Yes, of course," said the other, "you're the two I asked first— in the dining-room. You must think I'm clean off my nut—don't blame you if you do—but I'm not. I'm just crazy enough to go and let myself in for something when I might be having a nice quiet life—but that's all. I think I'd better tell you something about it—I've got to tell somebody—can't go on like this—and I owe you two something. Here, are you staying at the Harvey House? So am I. Well, let's get back there—can't talk here—and I'm cold. I was nearly cold for ever that time."

On the way back they gave him their names and he told them his—Jimmy Edlin, late of Shanghai and Honolulu, more recently still of the Clay-Adams Hotel, Los Angeles. He seemed an amusing and adventurous sort of chap, and Malcolm was curious to know what had been happening to him and why he should go about asking a question about a clock striking, yet he could not help regretting this interruption in the talk between him and Hooker about the mysterious MacMichael family. Also, he was anxious to hear Hooker's story, which might closely concern Andrea. Nevertheless, he asked both his companions to join him in his room at the hotel, for it turned out that he was one floor lower down than Hooker and nearer the stairs than Edlin, whose room, Number Twenty-two, was round the corner of the long corridor.

Once inside Malcolm's room, Jimmy Edlin lit a pipe and the other two lit cigarettes, and they settled down cosily. Before he began talking, Edlin had a good look at both of them, though he had already done this once before, in the dining-room. "Don't mind me, boys," he said. "Yes, I'm looking you over again. You see, if I'm to talk, I've to trust you. I'm up against something, believe me. And there's more to it than I thought there was, and that's saying a lot. But I know you two are all right, and you've done me a good turn. Does either of you know anything about a sort of religious society called the Brotherhood of the Judgment?"

Neither Malcolm nor Hooker had ever heard of it, and said so.

"I'll try again," said Edlin, puffing away at his pipe. "The head of it—and I've not seen him so I can't tell you what he's like—is living somewhere up this way. They call him Father John—which doesn't get you very far—but I happen to know his name is MacMichael— hey, steady, boys!" He added this because, to his great astonishment, both his listeners had given a shout.

Malcolm began to wonder if the whole thing was simply getting out of control. This was too fantastic. It really would not do. And he told them so. "I've been doing a lot of travelling," he told them. "All very rum—to me. I've just had five days in Hollywood with a client of ours, who seemed to be living in a sort of film nightmare, and as I stayed with him I was in the nightmare too, with one girl coming to dinner bringing a leopard with her, and another girl who said my aura was bright blue with yellow stars in it, and a chap so tight he said he could only go round on all fours, and an awful quarrel between my host and two other fellows about whether they should use real elephants or have them made of rubber; and not much sleep lately; and then I come here, feeling a fool and not quite real, and it's all desert and I haven't the least idea where I'll find this MacMichael girl I'm looking for; and then you, Mr. Hooker, begin talking to me about MacMichaels and professors with wrong names who are missing; and now you, Mr. Edlin, after coming running up with people firing at you, begin talking about clocks striking and some brotherhood or whatever it is and a Father John and he turns out to be a MacMichael too—well, what I mean *is*, it's all right, isn't it?—nobody's simply being funny, are they?—just taking advantage of the general dither I'm in—now, tell me, honestly, you fellows."

Jimmy Edlin, taking his pipe out of his mouth, stared in astonishment at the end of this outburst; but Hooker, after grinning sympathetically, said slowly: "I know just what you feel, Mr. Darbyshire. I feel a bit that way too. But it seems all right."

"I thought you boys were stone-cold sober," said Edlin reproachfully. "I know I am. If you've started on a blind, I'll either retire or catch up, just as you say, but I think in that case we'd better postpone the talk."

They assured him they were completely sober. Neither of them had had a single drink that night.

"Then let's get this straight," said Edlin earnestly. "Do I understand that you're both looking for this MacMichael lot? And separately? And here we are, the three of us. Now this is what they call coincidence, isn't it? Well, coincidence my foot! I tell you, boys—and I'm older than you and I've seen a lot in my time—these things don't work by chance. We were brought together for a purpose, believe me."

"What purpose?" asked Hooker, who was obviously sceptical.

"I don't exactly know yet. But I'll tell you this much. And if I didn't believe it, I wouldn't be here—running down desert roads with fellows taking potshots at me. There's something going on—back there—" he waved a hand, presumably to indicate the distant mountains "—that's all wrong."

Malcolm stared, bewildered, but Hooker merely shook his head and muttered something about a possible scientific experiment.

"No, sir," said Jimmy Edlin emphatically. "I'm not talking about scientific experiments—in fact, I don't see where they come in—though you may. I'm talking about something that these religious fanatics are working for—I don't say they all know about it, but some of 'em do—and whatever it is they're at, it's important enough to them so that they don't stop short at murder." And he shot the startling ugly word at them.

There was a moment's silence, during which Edlin looked hard from one to the other of them, while they exchanged puzzled glances. Then a queer hateful thought, the ghost of which had haunted him several times when he had been awake late thinking about Andrea, came to Malcolm, to explain the girl's reserve and secrecy and melancholy. He dismissed it hastily, though he knew it would return, probably later that night, to haunt him more fearfully than ever.

"You see," said Jimmy Edlin gravely, "I got into this because my brother Phil, who was a reporter in Los Angeles, was murdered." He went on to tell the story of his evening with Rushy Drew and of what happened the following night at the meeting of the Brotherhood of the Judgment, and how he had arranged to meet one of the brethren here at the hotel at Barstow. "I was a fool, of course," he continued, "to think I'd get away with it. I was too pleased with myself, and didn't stop to think, that was my trouble. I hired a car and came along here—I'd only just arrived when I asked you two fellows the clock question. Then I went out and met a fellow down there in the lobby—weather-beaten ordinary sort o' fellow in the usual Western rig-out—and he stared at me hard, so I took him on one side and we exchanged the password all right, and he said he had a car there, waiting to take me up among the hills to meet Father John. There was another of 'em in the car. No sooner had we started off than I felt it was all wrong. I could feel it in my bones. And something about the look of those two fellows too. They didn't like me, and I knew it. When we got just beyond the bridge, I shouted to 'em I'd forgotten something and asked 'em to slow up. They slowed up all right, probably without thinking, and then I made a dash for it. You heard 'em taking a pot at me. It was only being so close to the town that saved me. Of course what had happened was that after that meeting, perhaps after Kaydick had got in touch with Father John, they'd made some enquiries—perhaps sent a cable or something—and tumbled to the fact that I was an outsider. So they sent for me all right, but only to take me into that desert and leave me there—cold."

"But you don't really know that," Malcolm protested. "They may have been genuinely taking you to see Father John."

"And then tried to kill me because I decided to refuse the invitation," Edlin retorted grimly. "No, sir. You try riding behind two fellows who know they're going to do you in, it's quite a different sensation from the usual pleasure trip. Even their backs look different. And just notice this. Even if they only suspected I wasn't a real member of the Judgment troupe, they'd only to refuse to send anybody, and I'd have been stranded here, because it's new country to me and how the hell would I know where Father John is. That's what ordinary people, who had somebody butting into their affairs like that, would have done. Just ignored me."

"I don't see why these people didn't, if you think they really had found you out," said Hooker.

"Because I knew too much. I didn't know a lot, but it was too much."

"But anybody could walk into their meetings," Malcolm pointed out. "You said that yourself."

"Certainly. And we could all join the Brotherhood to-morrow, I reckon, and sing hymns and listen to prayers and be told that God loves us so much he might burn us up at any moment. But there's obviously an inner circle—Brother Kaydick and his tough boys—and to be one of them you've probably to take an oath and all the rest of it, swear to obey orders—and you're given a sort of password. How my brother Phil discovered it, I don't know, probably heard two fellows in this inner circle—they're the Servers and they have numbers, all the old bag of tricks—doing their clock-won't-

strike act together. But he did know—that, and a few other things—
and they found out he knew—and went for him. And if I hadn't
had a quick hunch to-night—and broken the two hundred yards
record—that would have been the last of me. And from now on, of
course, that clock question is out—they'll have changed that now."

"What was it again?" asked Hooker, thoughtfully. And when
the question and answer were repeated to him, he went over them
slowly. "You know, that's a very odd thing to say. I don't suppose it
means anything, but still—it's very odd."

"It ties up with all that gloomy *Revelations* stuff they handed out
at the meeting," Edlin remarked. "I told you. They were a gloomy
lot. I took a great dislike to 'em myself. So would you have done.
There was a very nice little widow there, sitting near me, and she
hated 'em on sight—like a sensible woman."

Forgetting for the moment that there might possibly be some
connection between his mysterious Andrea and these ferocious
fanatics, Malcolm remarked: "But I don't really see why you don't
report the whole thing to the police, and have done with it."

Edlin chuckled. "That's the English touch all right. Send for the
police."

Hooker smiled at this, though he might have been remembering his own encounter with the English police.

"Well, why not?" Malcolm persisted.

"It wouldn't work. If I knew somebody in the police here, and
could get a good man put quietly on the job, really collecting
evidence against them, then it might work. But I don't, and what
would happen if I complained would be that this Brotherhood of
the Judgment would prove it was a nice respectable organisation,
with all its members paying taxes and living with their own wives,
and Father John would turn out to be a nice old gentleman with a
long beard and sandals, first cousin to a senator or a federal judge,
and Mr. Jimmy Edlin would be given a sour look and would be
asked to go away and not make a nuisance of himself, and I'd be
farther away from knowing anything worth knowing than I was
before."

Hooker considered this carefully. "You're right, I guess, Mr.
Edlin. You'd have to know a lot more before you could bring the
police in. But I still don't begin to understand why these people,

however silly they may be about their beliefs, should be ready to risk murder."

"And I don't. That's just the point. But there must *be* something they're up to, and, if you ask me, it's not there in Los Angeles. This is the real end, though where, what or how—I don't know. But then I don't even know yet how you boys come to be in it."

Malcolm did not reply because he happened to glance across at Hooker, who was looking very thoughtful and clearly was about to speak. So Malcolm waited; and Edlin looked across at Hooker too. The latter stretched his long legs out at full length, appeared to examine his socks, which were wrinkled round the tops of his dusty shoes, and then observed slowly: "The queer thing is—that if the MacMichaels are really in this—they worked, or tried to work, the very same trick on me. I've thought it over a good deal, and I've come to the conclusion that the only possible reason why they should have tried that ridiculous frame-up was to keep me out of the way and keep me busy defending myself because they thought I was too curious." And having made this maddening statement, which tantalised both his hearers because they did not understand what he meant by his "frame-up," Hooker sighed hard and stared again at his wrinkled socks.

"Now, Mr. Hooker," Jimmy Edlin began.

"It's Dr. Hooker really, if you must talk like that——"

"I didn't know you were a medical man."

"I'm not—thank God—just a doctor of science—mainly physics—but just call me Hooker——"

"Fine! It looks as if we're all in this thing together, though I don't understand why yet—but then that's what you're going to tell me, both of you. But before you start, I must have a drink. I don't know how you boys feel, but I need a drink badly, and as it happens I put a bottle of Scotch in my bag."

"But isn't your bag in that car?" said Hooker.

"No, I got in just as I was. Lucky too! Anyhow, I'll get that Scotch and bring a couple of glasses from my room. It's just round the corner. Back in half a minute."

But he was not back in half a minute. Malcolm and Hooker waited in silence for several minutes, as people so often do when one party in an important conversation has just left them but has promised to return very soon. Each went over in his mind what had recently been said, and they had plenty to think about.

Malcolm finally broke the silence. "Taking his time, isn't he? He seems all right—rather a likeable chap, I think—but I don't know what to make of this yarn of his."

"No," said Hooker slowly, "but he didn't invent those shots we heard. If it wasn't for them, I'd think he was imagining things, just because his brother had been killed and nobody knew who'd done it. But what happened to him to-night—and we were witnesses— proves that he isn't imagining things. There is a John MacMichael too. I found that out when I came home and began making enquiries about the MacMichaels."

"Tell me about them," said Malcolm eagerly. "I couldn't find out much."

"Old Thomas MacMichael, that's their father, was one of the old Western copper men, and he made a pile. Henry, who was the eldest son, went into Wall Street and made a whole lot more—still has most of it, I guess. The next son, Paul, became a scientist, and didn't use his last name, perhaps because he didn't want people to think he was getting by because of the old man's money. John's the other, and I couldn't find out anything about him. Perhaps he's off his head. They're a queer lot. I never liked Paul—the one I knew— though he's a swell physicist."

There was a long pause. Finally, Malcolm said: "Look here, I think you'd better tell me now, while we're waiting, what happened to you. I'm dying to know—and Edlin seems to be enjoying most of that whisky by himself."

So Hooker described his search for the missing Engelfield, the discovery of him in London, and then his adventures at the Old Farm and the fair at Ewsbury. It was a long recital.

"It didn't make a lot of sense," Hooker concluded, "but all I can think is this. Paul found himself on the track of something really big in his own field, which is roughly the same as mine, research in atomic structure, and especially experiments in the transmutation of elements—I don't know if you understand what that's all about," he added, hopefully.

"No, I don't," said Malcolm hastily, "and if you don't mind, just now I'd rather not try. Some other time."

Hooker grinned. "Whenever you say. But, as I said, I think he saw something big ahead of him, so cleared out and dropped his old name. He's money of his own and, besides, probably he has his brother Henry backing him. And whatever he's doing, he wants to keep it to himself, which doesn't surprise me, knowing him."

"You mean, you think his discovery may be valuable from a commercial point of view?" Malcolm was not clear as to the drift of Hooker's remarks. "So it has to be a secret."

"No. I'll bet, after I said 'transmutation,' you began thinking about alchemy, gold from lead and all the rest of it, didn't you? Thought so." Hooker's grin was sardonic, but friendly. "No, that's not it. In fact, I don't believe there's a commercial angle to this thing, though it's always just possible that a man experimenting in that field might discover a new cheap form of energy. You've heard the line of talk? The *Queen Mary* driven across the Atlantic with the energy from a bit of coal about as big as a walnut. Sounds fine. Only they don't tell you how much it would cost, even if you could do it, to get the energy out of that bit of coal. No, what he's probably working on is something simply of value to science, but he's an arrogant and solitary and anti-social devil—all wrong for a scientist, of course—and he doesn't want to share anything or be criticised or risk being laughed at, so he's keeping under cover until it's all perfect and he can come out and say, 'Now look what I've done, you boobs!' That's Paul Engelfield MacMichael. I could see by the look in his eye, when he said a few things to me that time in the Savoy Hotel, that he was tackling something very big and was pleased with himself. Now if it had been you, say, who walked in on him, he wouldn't have minded. The trouble was that it was *me*, George Hooker. I don't want to boost myself, but after all it is a fact that I'm one of the few fellows who've been working in the same field, and of course he knew it because we'd had arguments before. So, not like a decent scientist, which he ought to be, but—" and here Hooker suddenly lost his deliberate calm and raised his voice excitedly "—just like a copper king's son and a Wall Street shyster's brother, he plays a God-damned dirty trick on me. And he hasn't heard the last of it either."

"I don't blame you," said Malcolm. "But where does this other brother, John—Father John or whatever he is—come in?"

"He doesn't, so far as I know. I don't care about him. Probably he's crazy. These families nearly always produce at least one crazy one, and I doubt if the other two are strictly sane."

"That might possibly explain Andrea—the girl, y'know."

Hooker struggled with a yawn. "Don't ask me. Nothing explains girls to me. I gave that up years ago, when I stopped dating 'em. What time is it? Must be late."

Malcolm looked at his watch. "Nearly eleven. Look here, this is absurd. Do you realise, Hooker, how long that chap's been gone for his whisky? Why, it couldn't have been much after nine when he went, and he said he'd be back in half a minute."

The other did not reflect the alarm in Malcolm's tone. "Decided to finish the Scotch himself, I guess. I'll bet he's snoring now."

But Malcolm was still uneasy. "He seemed to me too keen on this mad business—with his talk about murder and God knows what— just to do that. We'd better go and see if he's all right, Hooker. Number Twenty-two, he said. It's on this floor somewhere. Come on."

Hooker yawned again, pointing out afterwards that he had been driving since early morning, but agreed to go along. They went down the corridor, and, turning a corner, came to Twenty-two. The door was open, and the lights were on inside the room. An elderly chambermaid was in there, tidying up. A half-empty bottle of Scotch stood on the table, and by its side was a pipe, the one that Edlin had been smoking when he left them. There was also a decided reek of whisky. But there was no sign of Edlin, no sign even of his baggage. After peering in for a moment or two, Malcolm and Hooker stared at one another. The chambermaid went on grumpily with her work, taking no notice of them.

"Could you please tell us where the gentleman is who had this room?" asked Malcolm.

"No, I couldn't." The chambermaid sounded as cross as she looked. "He's gone, that's all I know."

"Gone where?"

"I wasn't told that. All I was told was to come up and do the room out. You'd better ask at the desk."

"Mr. Edlin *was* in this room, wasn't he?"

"Don't know the name," she snapped, as if she strongly disapproved of everything connected with this business. "You'll have to ask at the desk. Whoever he was, he seems to have been powerful fond of liquor. Place stinks of liquor."

They withdrew slowly, feeling somewhat defeated as well as mystified. On their way downstairs, Hooker gave it as his opinion that Edlin, a little shaky after his escape, must have taken a few enormous swigs of whisky, and then, suddenly drunk, must have forgotten all about returning to their room and have gone reeling out of the hotel. Malcolm felt that there was more in it than that, though he was not prepared even to guess at what had happened.

The reception clerk was more communicative than the chambermaid, though he spoke with a certain reserve. Yes, Mr. Edlin of Twenty-two had left about an hour ago.

"But did he say why he was going?" asked Malcolm.

No, he hadn't said anything.

Malcolm looked questioningly at Hooker, who was frowning now. Then they both looked again at the young clerk, who showed some faint signs of embarrassment.

"We can't make this out," Hooker told him. "Mr. Edlin was talking to us, about two hours ago, went to his room, saying he'd be back in a minute, and we haven't seen him since."

The clerk leaned forward a little and became confidential. "He oughtn't to have been out, you see. And the doctor and an attendant came for him. Good job they did too, because he'd got himself pretty bad even in that short time. Practically passed out. But they got him away all right."

It was left to Hooker to ask the questions. Malcolm felt that everything had now escaped any kind of control. His own lunacy had brought him here, and he had wandered into an ever-enlarging and more spectacular lunacy.

"One of these sanatoriums for fellows who can't quit the liquor," the clerk explained. "The doctor didn't say much, but I knew that was it. They came for him from Riverside or somewhere down there. Pretty bad case, I reckon. He'd only just checked in, but when they carried him out, I could smell the whisky from here. He'd had plenty, believe me. And I don't mind telling you gentlemen I wasn't sorry to see him go."

After a struggle, Malcolm now found his voice. "Did you know this doctor?"

"No, sir. Stranger to me. From Riverside—or Pasadena, I forget which. Johnson, the name was. A tall dark man with a terrible squint."

Malcolm seemed to have heard just recently of a tall dark man with a terrible squint, but could not remember in what connection it was. At the moment he felt all at sea. No sense in any of this.

"Thanks," said Hooker, rather dryly.

"You bet!" replied the clerk, beaming, and turned away.

Without a word, Malcolm and Hooker moved across the little lobby and went outside, where a locomotive, which looked to Malcolm of an incredible size, was ringing its warning bell. Another train, away in the distance, was giving that long mournful hoot that seems to make the night spaces of America even vaster than they actually are. Away across the gleaming railroad tracks the coloured lights of Barstow's main street shone bravely, very small in the immensity of the night. Malcolm felt a long way from home; not only bewildered but lost.

"Well," he asked, at length, "what do you make of it?"

"You've got to take one line or the other," replied Hooker, slowly. "Either he's one of these crazy drunks, and he never had a brother who was murdered and there isn't a Brotherhood of the Judgment and a Father John and all the rest of it—or——"

"He was telling the truth, and those fellows came back and somehow took him out of the hotel, eh?"

"That's it. Either one or the other. Take your choice."

Malcolm thought a moment. "He seemed all right to me."

"They often do, those drunks, when they've just had enough and not too much," said Hooker, almost as if he enjoyed making it all more difficult. "But I'll tell you what I'm going to do."

"What?" Malcolm had nothing to suggest himself.

"I'm going," said Hooker firmly, "to bed."

CHAPTER FIVE

BEING THE FURTHER ADVENTURES OF MR. EDLIN

"Back in half a minute," said Jimmy Edlin, over his shoulder, as he opened the door. When he came out into the corridor, he had a feeling that somebody had just gone round the corner, towards the stairs, but he did not attach any importance to this fact. After all, they hadn't the whole hotel to themselves. He went along to his room in a pleasantly excited state of mind. The last thing he had expected was to find here a couple of fine young fellows who seemed to be as curious about this MacMichael business as he was, and who appeared to have seen it so far from an entirely different point of view. In a minute or two he would know what that point of view was, and might learn something valuable, over a drink or two of that excellent Scotch he had had the sense to put in his bag. This was going to be great. Nice fellows, and the three of them all after the same queer crowd. Jimmy liked company, and so far he had not been a big success working by himself on this job, which he was convinced now was a very rum job indeed. The little widow, Mrs. Atwood—and there was an attractive little piece of woman-hood for a lonely man—had been very much interested, very sympathetic, almost excited it seemed when he told her over the telephone where he was going—but you couldn't land a woman into this nasty mess, as he had been careful to tell her. (She hadn't liked that either, he remembered, and had even been a bit short and sharp with him, saying Good-bye abruptly and cutting him off. A pity! Though he was no hand at saying things that might please a woman over the telephone; something too inhuman about that lump of vulcanite.) But now it looked as if he had two very useful allies in these fine alert young chaps. Yes, he'd been lucky.

In this pleasantly excited state of mind, then, Jimmy hurried along to his room, and, not bothering to close the door behind him, he rummaged in his bag, which he had not unpacked yet, for the Scotch. He took the lead foil wrapping off the top of the bottle, to make sure that he would not need a corkscrew. Then he looked up, remembering the two glasses he had promised to take along, to discover that he was facing the barrel of a large revolver. The man who held it, now standing with his back to the door, was the very man, a youngish fellow with queer light eyes and almost bleached hair, who had answered the Brotherhood password and taken him out to the car.

"Get back and raise your hands, mister," came the command.

Jimmy did as he was told, breaking out into a sweat. This was going to be tough.

"I can tell you exactly what our orders are, mister," continued the unpleasant bleached young man. "We're to take you along. But if you won't come along, if you give any trouble, then we're to make good an' sure you don't do any more interferin'."

Jimmy knew only too well that this was the truth. These people were capable of killing him there and then, and to hell with the consequences. Whatever it was they were planning, it obviously made them both relentless and reckless.

"All right," he muttered, with a mouth that was drier than ever. "I haven't got a gun. Better put that one down."

"No, *sir*. We let you off too easy last time," said the other, now coming forward. He moved until he was near the telephone, but kept Jimmy steadily covered.

"I don't know what you think you can do," said Jimmy uneasily. "But this happens to be an hotel, don't forget."

"Sure! I hadn't forgotten." And the young man, without taking his eyes or his large revolver off Jimmy, reached down with his left hand and took up the receiver. Jimmy stared in amazement. What did the fellow think he could do? But the fellow seemed to know. "I want to speak to Doctor Johnson," he remarked, coolly, down the telephone. "That's right. Oh—doc—I've got him. Yes—twenty-two. Sure I can hold him. Okay."

The young man put down the telephone, still watching Jimmy, then slowly backed towards the door.

"You might give me some idea what you're doing," said Jimmy. "Where does the doctor come in? Are you sick—or am I?"

"I reckon you are, mister," was the reply, delivered without the ghost of a smile.

Jimmy felt more puzzled than alarmed. So long as he kept quiet and gave them no trouble, as the young man admitted, they had no intention of using that gun on him, which, anyhow, would be a very desperate move on their part, here in the hotel. On the other hand, how could they "take him along"? Was there some back way out that they knew about? And what was this doctor business? While Jimmy asked himself these questions, the young man kept silent, but very watchful, obviously not intending that Jimmy should escape a second time that night.

A knock and a voice outside. The young man had the door open and shut again before Jimmy could even think of making a move. But now Dr. Johnson, complete with a black bag, was in the room. And there could be no possible doubt as to who it was. Brother Kaydick had now taken charge.

Brother Kaydick muttered something Jimmy could not catch to his assistant, then stood looking hard at Jimmy and rubbing his long chin. At least, Jimmy felt that Brother Kaydick was looking hard in his direction, but, so powerful was that squint of Brother Kaydick's that he might have also been looking at the bottle of whisky on the table. This silence seemed to Jimmy unmannerly.

"Good evening, Brother Kaydick," he remarked. "When did you turn into Dr. Johnson? And what have you got in that bag?"

"Quiet!" commanded Brother Kaydick harshly. He muttered again to the bleached young man, then, to Jimmy's surprise, stalked into the bathroom, taking the bag with him.

"Keep your hands up," said the owner of the revolver, sharply.

"You don't mind me being in this room, do you?" Jimmy enquired. He was tired of this, and so were his arms, which now ached to be anywhere but up in the air. "I couldn't rent you fellows another room here, could I? I'd like the use of this myself. I don't want to be unreasonable——"

But Brother Kaydick had reappeared. "Turn round."

"Why should I?" But he did. He also heard Brother Kaydick and his assistant coming closer, and smelt something sickly, something that might easily have a place in Dr. Johnson's black bag. Then he found his arms seized and pulled down behind him; a sickly-smelling cloth enveloped his nose and mouth; he was suffocating, and he struggled hard to free himself; they were choking him, the devils; but now, though he was still struggling, he was half-floating about too, and there seemed to be rockets whizzing and exploding all over the room. And, oddly enough, the last thing he remembered was the appearance from nowhere of a sudden fountain of Scotch whisky. . . .

He was back in China, in the native quarter of Shanghai perhaps, and they were celebrating some festival, and never had he heard so much beating of gongs, so many fire-crackers; and though he kept telling them to stop, they only grinned at him, and brought out bigger gongs and more strings of firecrackers; and then there was a procession, with everybody making the most devilish racket, and at the end of the procession was an enormous gilded car, with dragons carved all over it, and seated high in this car, dressed like a mandarin in full regalia, was Brother Kaydick; and though Jimmy tried to hide himself in the crowd, it was no use, because always the Chinese in front of him mysteriously melted away, leaving him open to the view of the figure in the car; and though he ran and ran, that was no use either, because the car was always just coming round the corner; and at last Brother Kaydick saw him and cried in a terrible voice, "There's the man," pointing a long talon of a finger, and a big Chink soldier, with a club, rushed at him and hit him—bang!—on the head. . . .

He could still feel the bang on the head. His head seemed to be enormous and every bit of it ached like the devil. He was cold too, stiff and cold. Slowly he opened his eyes, but made no sense out of what they saw, so closed them again. This happened several times. Then he really began to take notice. It was hard work at first, with such a head on him, but he persevered. He was lying among some packing cases in the corner of a small dim room that had unpainted deal plank walls. He was cold because he had had no covering over him, and was not even wearing his coat. Bright sunlight was coming in, through a few cracks in the walls and between the edge of a small window and the rough curtaining tacked over it. He thought about all this for a long time. Cold and stiff though he was, somehow he did not want to move yet. There were sounds outside, but he did not feel like bothering about them. The thing to do was to keep quiet, just to think a little, not too much, and try to forget that his head was far too big and apparently split open in several places. He felt as if he was just recovering from a three days' crazy binge-and-blind, yet he knew that he had been up to nothing like that. This would have to be carefully worked out before he began to move. What exactly had he been doing? He began to work it out, very cautiously. He wasn't still in China; that had been a dream. Honolulu? No, he left Honolulu for Los Angeles.

His half-opened eyes were pained to behold an ever-widening bar of brilliant light, so they closed again. Might that be a door opening? He lay quite still. Then a voice remarked: "No, he's still out." It was a voice he had heard before and had disliked. There came the sound of the door closing, then being locked.

Within five minutes, Jimmy was thoroughly awake, though feeling groggy. He remembered all the events of the previous night, up to his having a struggle with Kaydick and the other fellow in the hotel room. They had doped him somehow—he could still smell chloroform or whatever it was they had on the cloth—and there was also a puzzling smell of whisky, though he could not remember having had any the night before. Very carefully and quietly, he moved and then rubbed his stiff and cold arms and legs. Evidently they had dumped him in here, last night, after taking away his coat. But where was he? And how had they smuggled him out of the hotel at Barstow? And what in the name of thunder was he going to do now? Beneath his surface bewilderment, however, there was a growing anger. Doping him, then dumping him in here like a parcel!

Now that he could feel his arms and legs again, he began to take careful stock of the place he was in, which seemed to be the back store room of a not very large, rough wooden structure. There were a good many packing cases of all sizes about, along with various wooden boxes and tins. The floor, which like the walls was made of rough deal planking, was littered with packing straw, paper, bits of rope and twine. The window was high up and very small. Very cautiously, for it would be easy to make a noise that would give him away, he rose and tip-toed to the nearest point of light, where a knot in the wood had fallen out. He put an eye to this hole, but all he could see through it was a yellow bit of desert, brilliant in the sunlight. There were, however, some narrow lighted streaks in the wall where the door was, and through which he could just hear voices, so now, moving more cautiously than ever, he went on tip-toe across, and tried two of these. They were better for hearing than seeing, but he was able to catch a glimpse of Kaydick and the bleached young man, and he came to the conclusion that the third fellow there was the other man, who had driven the car from which he had escaped near Barstow the night before. He saw too, on the table, a package about three foot long and one foot high, very securely tied and sealed, and looking as if it had come a long way, for there were various labels and stamps on it. This was all he could see. What he heard was more important.

It was not easy to put together their short and disjointed remarks, obviously those of men who understood one another and had plenty of time on their hands. You had to do, at some speed, a jigsaw puzzle with plenty of pieces missing. But Jimmy was no fool, and he knew he had to think quickly. What he gathered was that they were waiting for the arrival of a truck that had been delayed, and that this truck would take Kaydick and the bleached young man, whose name was Joseph, up to a place called Lost Lake, where, Jimmy shrewdly surmised, Father John was staying. They were to take with them the package on the table, which was clearly something very important, eagerly awaited at Lost Lake. What they intended to do with him, Jimmy did not discover, and he had an idea that they did not know yet themselves. Jimmy realised now, of course, that they were worried about him simply because they could not understand how he had so nearly succeeded in deceiving them, and wondered where an outsider had learned at least one or two of their secrets.

Then he heard Kaydick say, "We had better go down and telephone again," and there was a movement in the room. "You have your revolver, Joseph," Kaydick continued, in his own grim fashion. "Keep an eye on that man in there. He may be waking soon. And I leave this package in your charge too, Joseph. We shan't be long." And then he heard the two of them going out.

Jimmy thought quickly. This was his only chance. Joseph still imagined he was asleep and might possibly be off his guard. Even merely to look in, he would have to open the door, and once the door was open, anything might happen. Jimmy stared thoughtfully at that door, which was about three feet from the corner. He could stand behind it, and take a chance at surprising Joseph if he came well into the room. But that was unlikely. His best plan was to stand at the side on which the door opened, for there would be just a moment when Joseph would have to stare into the dim interior to see what was happening there. So Jimmy pushed his back against the wall, wedging himself between the door and the corner, and waited, wanting to breathe hard and not daring to, hearing almost with despair what seemed the loud thumping of his heart. And there he seemed to wait a long, long time, so that it seemed impossible that Kaydick and the other man would not return, to wreck his whole plan.

Just when it appeared hopeless, and he felt he could not stand there, all aching, another moment, he heard the key turn in the lock, and braced himself for instant action, bringing the shoulder farther away from the door, his right shoulder, round a little, and clenching his fist. Slowly, with agonising slowness it seemed, the door opened, and then Joseph's face looked in through the opening. Jimmy allowed it the fraction of a second to come in a little farther, and then, throwing his whole two hundred pounds of righteous indignation behind the upward swing of his arm, he gave it the most tremendous uppercut seen in this world since Jack Johnson left the ring. Joseph vanished, but Jimmy was in the other room in time to see him give a final quiver as he reached the floor. Jimmy hastily glanced round for his coat, but could not see it. No time to lose. They evidently considered that package on the table to be very important, so he would take that, just to make things harder for them. There was a key inside the outer door, so he took that too and locked the hut from outside, just to make things harder still. And now what? Where had Kaydick and the other man gone to? And where on earth was this place? He gave a hasty glance all round him.

Blinking a little in the bright sunlight, he saw that he was in the middle of the desert, but only about five hundred yards away from a junction of roads, where there were several buildings, probably a filling-station and a café and some auto-camp huts. He had no idea where it was, but guessed it to be somewhere between Barstow and the mountains. The road below reminded him of the one that went eastwards out of Barstow. The wooden building, little more than a hut, near which he was still standing, trying to get his bearings, was about fifty yards back from the side road, running behind the cluster of buildings at the junction. There was a rough track, just passable for cars, leading from this hut to the side-road; but the car that must have brought him here, last night, was nowhere to be seen. Perhaps Kaydick and the other man had gone along to the junction in it, though he had not heard it go. Or they may have left it down there, for some reason or other. Meanwhile, standing here, he was asking for trouble.

The only possible thing to do was to make for the junction, once he knew that Kaydick and the other men had left it, and trust to luck that he could get a lift from there. And this dodging of Kaydick was going to be tricky. You couldn't just cut and run anywhere across this desert stuff. Once away from the roads, you were lost and done for. The only course open to him at the moment was to get somewhere between the hut and the junction, somewhere from which he could see both of them, so that he would know when it would be possible to dodge along to the junction. He would have to think later what he could do when he arrived there. So instead of descending to the road, along which Kaydick was sure to come, he made roughly in the direction of the junction, across broken desert ground with a few dusty shrubs in it, keeping more or less parallel to the road. When he had gone about two or three hundred yards, still clinging to the package, which was fairly bulky but not heavy, he came to a clump of rock on a hillock, behind which he could see but not be seen, and there he stayed, breathless, excited, and now very warm. The sun was high, and it glared down on the shimmering empty scene. Jimmy had no watch, for he had kept it in his coat, and now the coat was gone, with all his money except what might be left in his trousers pockets. What had he left? He looked at it. A nickel and four cents. So there he was, with coat, pocket-book, cheque-book, watch, all gone, facing the desert and a good old stretch of road to anywhere with his shirt and pants and nine cents. And now he had time to feel hungry and thirsty and very grubby. And he had no hat, and the sun seemed to be stronger every moment. And if he did dodge Kaydick, and slip down into the junction, what then?

Well, they couldn't take him again down there, with other people all around? But couldn't they? They had managed, with some Dr. Johnson hocus-pocus, to get him out of that hotel at Barstow all right, hadn't they? Now that he no longer felt the exhilaration of uppercutting Joseph and of his escape, he saw that his prospects were not at all bright. All that was bright, blast it, was the sun, dazzling and burning and boring into him.

Two figures coming along the road? Yes, Kaydick and the other fellow. They had been along to the junction then. And they were not looking his way—why should they? He dropped behind the hillock, and stooping as he went, he began working his way towards the junction. The package was a nuisance, but he decided to keep it as long as he could, because he was curious now to know what it contained. Awkward, though, if Kaydick caught him at the junction, and accused him of stealing it. True, they had kidnapped him, but Jimmy, still making his way painfully behind rocks and over rocks and trying to dodge a lot of hellish prickly stuff, had an unpleasant idea that they would find it easier to accuse him of stealing—for there was the package and it certainly wasn't addressed to him—than he would find it to maintain that he had just been kidnapped. Trouble about this whole business was, he reflected, between curses at the cactus and sharp stones, that the truth about it, whatever that might be, was so fantastic that any nice little lie that Kaydick and Company brought out would obviously be believed. And so far, these hymn-singing brethren had beaten him—to say nothing of poor dead Phil—all along the line. Well, he could but try. And then, he remembered with a mixture of pleasure and self-reproach, there were the two young fellows, Darbyshire the Englishman, and the scientific chap, Booker or Tooker or Hooker, trying to puzzle it out, back there in Barstow, and also probably trying to puzzle out what had become of their new friend, Mr. James Edlin.

He had lost sight of Kaydick now, and there was no difficulty at all in cutting behind the buildings for the main road, then turning down to the filling-station and café there. He learned at once where he was, at Baker, with Barstow sixty miles away down that empty main road. Well, it might have been worse. But now what? Business at Baker this morning was not brisk. Not a car in sight.

At any moment one might come along, going to Barstow, and he could tell some yarn to get a lift, but how long could he afford to wait? The grim and resourceful Kaydick and his boys might be back at any moment too. What would happen, Jimmy asked himself hastily, if he set off as hard as he could along that Barstow road? He might get a lift sooner or later. On the other hand, he might wear himself out, hatless, coatless, hot and hungry, and at the end of ten miles or so, with nobody and nothing else in sight, find Brother Kaydick and friends bearing down on him in their car. And a hell of a lot of fight there would be in him then!

He knew there were many more important things to worry about, as he stood there, a tousled absurd figure in a crumpled pink shirt clutching a large package, but for the life of him he could not help dismissing them to wonder if he could buy a good drink of coffee for nine cents. It would be just his luck if coffee were ten cents. The place, of course, was decorated with all manner of tantalising notices, imploring him to step inside and be cool, to try a nice long drink, to devour ham and eggs and other delicacies, to consider himself Welcome at Baker. Enough to drive a man mad! He turned away, to see that he was being regarded curiously by a man even plumper than he was but looking far more comfortable.

"I'll toss you for a nickel," said Jimmy desperately.

"Sure!" the stranger chuckled, and then as Jimmy tossed his coin, sending a prayer after it, the plump jolly damnable fellow called "Heads." And so it was.

"If I'd been as lucky with everything else as I've been at tossing," said the stranger, pocketing Jimmy's miserable last nickel and then jingling a pocketful of them carelessly, "I'd sure be going places right now."

So that was that. Jimmy walked away, but found that even when he was well clear of the buildings, he could not see the hut he had left. He discovered from the signpost that the side-road near the hut went on to Shoshone and Death Valley Junction; and now he spent the next minute or two anxiously and alternatively looking along one road or the other, hoping that a car would arrive on the road from Las Vegas to Barstow to give him a lift, and trusting that he would not see Kaydick and the others coming down the side-road. Meanwhile, the morning was wearing late, the sun was rising higher still, and the very sight of the shimmering desert made him feel more and more uncomfortable. What a place! And what a fine figure he cut in it too, with his sweaty and dusty pink shirt, his aching feet, his aching head, his aching heart, and his four cents! So there he stood, looking first one way and then the other; and nothing, one of the blankest hot nothings he ever remembered, nothing happened. In fact, it didn't look as if anything would ever happen again in Baker.

That, of course, was the signal for life to get busy. On the road from Las Vegas there appeared one, two, three, four buses. On the other road there appeared two hurrying figures, and Jimmy knew at once they were Kaydick and the other fellow. Desperate men too, for not only had their comrade been knocked out but their precious package had been stolen. Promptly dodging out of sight, Jimmy asked himself hurriedly what was to be done about this package. If possible at all, he meant to keep it, but if Kaydick arrived before those buses or (horrible thought) if the buses didn't stop, this package was better out of the way. Not far from where he stood there was a depression by the side of the road, and he put the package down there, as if it were waiting to be taken away by bus. Then he hurried to the far side of the filling-station, watched round the corner there, saw Kaydick and the other fellow come hurrying up on the other side, then dodged round the back among the auto-camp huts. This was not an ideal place for hide-and-seek, but it would have to do. Kaydick would probably waste a minute or two, asking if anybody had seen him, and now the buses would be here at any moment, that is, if they were going to stop at Baker. If they didn't stop, his chances were not good. He might be able to dive into an empty auto-camp hut, and then again he might not. He worked farther round the back, taking all the cover he could, until finally he was near the side-road again, where Kaydick and the other man had just passed. Here were the buses, and—glory, glory!—they were stopping. Then a miracle happened.

In one instant, it seemed, Baker was transformed. From an empty place, asleep in an empty desert, it immediately changed into the corner of a roaring carnival town, for from those buses, swarming out like ants, yelling for Budweiser and ice-cream sodas, banging one another on the back, each man making the noise and seeming to take the space of ten, there descended a host of lively fellows all wearing red, tasselled, conical hats, that Turkish hat known as the fez. It looked as if Baker had been suddenly flung into a revolution in Stamboul. The red hats stormed the place. A crimson tide swept into the café. "Attaboy!" they thundered, charging towards the beer. Not all went in. There was a strong side-current in the direction of the men's wash-room. And there were red hats bobbing up and down all over the junction. Blessing this miraculous invasion, Jimmy saw that his one chance now was to clap a fez on his head, and to do it at once. Risking discovery, though the risk at the moment was not great for even if Kaydick or the other man caught sight of him, they could hardly do anything in the press of this roaring mob, Jimmy hurried along and joined the fourth wave that was trying to storm the café, and jammed himself in amongst them, happily mingling his sweat with theirs. Once inside, he enjoyed the felicity of catching sight of Kaydick, a tall fellow and unmistakable with his squint, completely hemmed in near the counter, where he must have been making enquiries. For an instant, he imagined that Kaydick must have seen him too, among the faces pressing in at the back, but he did not look long enough to make sure. What he had to do now was to obtain a fez. He pushed his way through at the side, until he found himself near a table crowded with thirsty invaders who had already given their order and, now relaxed, ready for beer, kidding one another, mopping their brows, had piled their red hats on the table. Just as he was wondering if he could safely snatch a hat from the nearest pile, he saw one on the floor, dived like a swallow for it, pushed towards the entrance again, and came out triumphantly wearing, towards one ear, for it was too small for him, a glorious, idiotic, crimson fez. And there, among the group just outside the door, he almost ran into the other man, who at the first sight of Jimmy opened his eyes and his mouth. But, Jimmy, making the most of his fez, bustled past him at once, feeling sure that the man would not have time to make up his mind. Jimmy did not intend to give him time. He threaded his way hastily through the remainder of his fellow fez-wearers, picked up the package, climbed into the nearest bus, the second of the four, and hurried to the far corner of the back seat, where he made himself as small as possible and pretended, with the fez as far over his face as the miserable little thing would go, to be asleep. "And now, for the love of Pete, boys," he cried to himself, "let's go."

How long he was there before they did go, he could not have told, but it seemed horribly long to him in that corner. He did not dare look about him, but every instant he expected to hear an unpleasant voice asking him what he thought he was doing there. He hoped he looked like a man trying to sleep off the effect of wearing a Turkish hat during a long wild night in Las Vegas, where he knew these fellows had been the night before; but he never felt less sleepy in his life. His right shoulder was taut, expecting to feel a heavy hand laid on it. "Come on, boys," he kept on imploring them silently, "come on. Don't stay in this hole all day." And never did he hear a cry so welcome as that of "All Ab-ooo-ard!" or feel so delighted to find a vehicle suddenly invaded with hot heavy bodies and shouts and perspiration and dusty shoes and the smell of beer. Yes, yes, they were off—and good-bye, Baker! He sat up, and looked out. Was that Kaydick over there, looking angrily about him? It was. Good-bye, good-bye, Brother Kaydick!

They were all hot, in that bus, but the hottest was Jimmy, who now began to fan himself with his fez. His neighbour, a small round man, who looked like a warm pink egg, if an egg could be made to wear rimless eye-glasses and a Turkish hat, and who wore a little label announcing that he was J. F. Hofelstanger, Los Angeles, now glanced curiously at him several times. Jimmy knew only too well that J. F. Hofelstanger had something to glance at. The boys had seen Boulder Dam and had had a fine night out at Las Vegas, that "wide open" Nevada town of gambling saloons, and so they were not looking their sprucest this morning, but Jimmy knew they were fashion plates compared to him, with his ruined pink shirt, his tousled hair, his filthy unshaven face. Thank God he was on his way, at fifty-five miles an hour, back to that hotel at Barstow.

"Well, brother," said Mr. Hofelstanger, "I'd say, by the look of you this morning, you'd had one big night in Las Vegas."

With an effort, Jimmy winked. "You're right at that, brother. That was one night I won't forget in a hurry."

"You didn't lose your coat, did you?"

"Sure! Lost everything." Jimmy spoke expansively—one of the boys.

"Say!" cried little Mr. Hofelstanger, not unimpressed, "you hit it pretty hard, didn't you?"

"I hit that town high, wide, and handsome," cried Jimmy. "And d'you know what I have left, brother? Four cents—just four cents."

Mr. Hofelstanger pursed up his chubby little lips and whistled. Then he looked down at Jimmy's knees, between which he was clutching the large upended package. Now he pointed to it. "You managed to get something out of it."

"Don't know how I held on to it," Jimmy confessed, solemnly. "But it's a present—you know—for Mrs. Edlin. Yes, sir, it's a nice present. Must take her back something, y'know, Brother Hofelstanger. Have to do it. Never get away if I didn't. Fact is, Mrs. Edlin isn't too pleased when I come away like this with the boys."

"Mrs. Hofelstanger's the same way. I've bought her a brooch. Got it in the Indian Store. Set me back six dollars, but it's worth it, I guess."

"Certainly it's worth it." Jimmy felt confident in the part now. "Gives the little woman a bit of pleasure, doesn't it? And makes it easier to get away next time. That's what I always say. How did *you* make out last night, Brother Hofelstanger? Burn it up all right, eh?"

"I hit the spots," replied Hofelstanger, with a modest cough that was not quite in keeping with his words. "Matter of fact, believe me or believe me not, Brother Edlin, but I pulled a jack-pot out of one of those fruit machines—yes, sir, a jack-pot. Only one of the nickel machines—though that's enough for any sensible man, I guess—but I pulled two dollars twenty-five out of it—and—say—you ought to have seen 'em shooting out. First jack-pot I ever made. Well, a fellow's got to cut loose now and again, I say. If he doesn't he gets into a groove, and that's bad for his business." He was very solemn now.

Jimmy could be solemn too. "You're right there, brother. A man's got to keep himself all alive and kicking, or where would his business be? And what's your line, Brother Hofelstanger?" This ought to keep the little man busy and prevent him from asking awkward questions.

It did. Mr. Hofelstanger was in the restaurant and caterers' supplies business, and some fifty miles of desert road flowed under them while he described, with a deep solemnity, the strange vicissitudes of this trade, the way it shot up and then as suddenly sagged and sank, the astonishing demands it made, the unique combination of strength and subtlety necessary for the man who would cope with it. By the time they were approaching Barstow, where a halt was to be made for lunch, Jimmy felt he could have filled any vacancy in the restaurant and caterers' supplies trade. He also felt a horrible vacancy in himself that asked for everything a caterer could do. He had had an early dinner last night, and since then not one crumb or drop of anything. Mr. Hofelstanger now confessed he was hungry. But Jimmy could almost have eaten Mr. Hofelstanger.

They crossed the bridge where Jimmy had done his hundred yards flat, the night before, and then drew up majestically—just as if the whole expedition was under Jimmy's command—at the side of the Harvey House. Nothing could have been more convenient. Still hugging his package, Jimmy filed out with the others, and silently blessed the Shriners or whatever they were for having brought him so neatly out of a very nasty situation. Here he was, back at the hotel, where those two nice youngsters must be wondering what had become of him, very little the worse—that is, once he had had some food and drink and a bath and shave and a change of clothes, and some more money had found its way into his pocket—and probably with some very important evidence indeed inside this package. The red hats, a little more subdued now than they had been at Baker, marched into the hotel, where the dining-room had been set aside for them, and Jimmy brought up the rear. He waited, very hungrily because there was a rich promise of steak and French fried potatoes in the air, until some of them had stopped milling round the desk in the lobby, and then when the desk was clear he approached the clerk, beaming upon him. For an instant, the clerk automatically smiled back, but then his face suddenly froze and into the stare he gave Jimmy there leapt a look of consternation.

Jimmy realised that he must seem a fairly grim spectacle, enriched perhaps but not really improved by the addition of a Turkish fez that did not even fit him. He snatched it from his head, and now tried to look as if it had never been there, as if the clerk was now making the mistake of seeing too many red hats. What Jimmy did not realise was that as he stood there, with one arm embracing a large package, soaked in perspiration, covered with dust and bits of straw, he made the perfect image of a man who had succeeded for the second time within the last eighteen hours in escaping from an inebriates' home. That is how the clerk, remembering last night and Dr. Johnson, saw him, and the clerk cannot be blamed.

"Had a bit of an accident," said Jimmy casually. "You'll have to give me another key for my room, unless the door's open. Twenty-two, I think it was."

The clerk shook his head, then looked round rather anxiously. He seemed to be muttering something about that room not being available.

"Well, give me another then," said Jimmy, rather impatient now. After all, he couldn't stand there, looking as if he'd just been dragged out of the ash-can, with the clerk merely goggling at him.

"We're full." Something desperate about that statement.

"Now, look here," said Jimmy sternly. "I booked a room here last night—and I'm entitled to it——"

"Yes, but you checked out," the clerk said, with the same desperate air.

"I didn't."

"Well, the doctor did for you—and he was responsible for you——"

"He wasn't." But Jimmy did not explain why. Ticklish, this doctor business. Could he say outright he'd been kidnapped? No, too many explanations, and nearly all hard to believe.

"I'm sorry," said the clerk, who did not look it, "but you can't stay here—and I'll have to ask you to go. Y'know, you're only making it worse for yourself," he added, in a not unkindly tone, which Jimmy found more maddening than the other, "breaking out like this. They're doing it all for the best. Why don't you give them a chance?" He was a decent, kind-hearted lad, wanting every-body to lead decent sober lives and be fit to enjoy the hospitality of the Fred Harvey Company. "It'll get you in the end, if you don't. Go back before you find yourself in trouble. They're doing their best for you. And we couldn't possibly allow you to stop here again. Go back to the home, to Dr. Johnson. What d'you say?"

"What do I say?" roared Jimmy, in a fury. "I say, don't talk like a Goddam' fool. Where are those two young men I met last night— y'know, Mr. Darbyshire and Mr. Hooker? Tell them I'm here."

"I can't," and the clerk was very stiff now. After all, he had tried to be kind.

"Why not? What's the matter with you?"

"I can't, because they've gone—they checked out this morning —and now you'd better go." He turned away, pretending to look at his book, then gave Jimmy a hard look, saw that he was still stand-ing there, so went to the telephone. And Jimmy did not like the look of him at all as he took up the telephone; he had the look of a man about to make further trouble, as if there hadn't been enough already, Jimmy reflected bitterly. And hundreds of steaks, delecta-ble mounds of French fried potatoes, apple pies by the score, were now being passed through from the kitchen to the dining-room. At this very moment little Hofelstanger was stuffing his already overstuffed little round carcass. "Hell's blasted bells!" said Jimmy, as he took himself and his package outside. If those two young men had been there, it would have simplified matters, but no, of course, they had to go running off, without giving him a chance to explain. A lot of use they were! Well, what next?

There was only one thing to do. Yesterday, he had left the Olds-mobile he had hired in Los Angeles in a garage up in the main street. He could not hang around Barstow in this condition, with only four cents in his pocket, and the sooner he got out of it, from every point of view, the better. So he walked as briskly as possible over the railway bridge to find the garage. There, the man who had taken over the Oldsmobile yesterday was still on duty, and a fine stare he gave poor Jimmy.

"You remember me?" said Jimmy, not considering it necessary or wise to try and explain his odd appearance to this fellow. "I left an Oldsmobile here yesterday, round about six o'clock."

The man still stared, and now he added a not very pleasing grin to his stare. But he made no comment on his customer's appearance. "Sure! Got it right here." He led the way inside, with Jimmy following. "There she is."

"Fine!" And Jimmy really felt it was fine. Here, at least, was the car. Nothing mysterious had happened to that.

"I filled her up, then checked the oil, like you said, and gave her a couple o' quarts, and looked at that starter. And the water's okay. She's ready now to take you anywheres."

"Fine!"

"You bet!" And the man fumbled in his pocket and finally brought out a dirty little bit of paper. "Gas, oil, garage—just three dollars twenty."

"Three dollars twenty." For the moment Jimmy had clean forgotten, and was about to put out a hand for a wallet that wasn't there, when he remembered.

"Three dollars and twenty," the man repeated. "Here—I'll show you, if you like. Gas——"

"No, that's all right. Reasonable enough. Cheap, in fact. The trouble is—well, I've had an accident—lost my coat, and with it my wallet and chequebook——" Jimmy's voice trailed away, and for the life of him he couldn't help feeling a bit of a crook. There he was with enough even in the Los Angeles bank to have bought the whole garage and everything in it, and yet he couldn't help feeling a twister. Enough to drive a man mad!

"Too bad," said the garage man, but with very perfunctory sympathy. "What happened?"

"Well," replied Jimmy lamely, "it's a long story."

"I'm not busy."

This wouldn't do. He decided to try another tack. "Now listen," he began, bluffly, boldly, "my name's Edlin—Jimmy Edlin—and I'm staying at the Clay-Adams in Los Angeles—they know me there all right—and I bank at the Californian Unity—and they know me *there* too——"

"Sure! But does anybody know you here? This is a long way from Los Angeles. Only been there twice myself—and didn't take to it neither."

"You've only got to ring up and ask them, either at the hotel or at the bank. They both know me—Jimmy Edlin."

The man was doubtful. The hotel and the bank, his expression plainly announced, might know a Jimmy Edlin, but was this the Jimmy Edlin they knew? "Well, there's the car, I guess," he said dubiously.

"Well, no—that won't tell you anything. I hired it."

"Oh—you hired it, eh?" The man scratched his nose. He did not appear to like the sound of this hiring at all. Then, his face cleared, as if he had arrived at a solution of the problem. Jimmy looked at him expectantly.

"We'll call it three dollars," said the idiot.

Once again, and now with every reason, Jimmy lost his temper. "I tell you—you—you—numskull——"

"No names, mister!" said the man sharply. He understood about names.

"But I've told you I haven't three dollars. I don't care whether it's three dollars or three dollars and twenty cents—or—for that matter, if it's ten dollars—but the point is, I've lost my money—and so you'll have to trust me, that's all——"

"I'll trust you all right—we have to trust a lot of people in this business—as long as I know who you are."

"But I've told you who I am," cried the maddened Jimmy, his voice nearly cracking with fury, thirst, hunger, heat, weariness, and growing madness. "For God's sake—use your wits."

"Use your own. You don't seem to be doing so well with 'em just now. Losing your coat and your wallet and what else——"

"Oh, shut up! I'm taking that car."

"Here, wait a minute, mister. There's three dollars——"

It was then, when they stood glaring at one another, not knowing what to do next, that the second miracle of the day took place. Into that garage, that dim hell-hole of stupidity and mistrust, tripped the neatest little figure of a woman, with the brightest eyes beneath the sauciest little hat you ever saw.

"Mrs. Atwood," roared Jimmy, and pounced upon her before she could escape.

She started back, as well she might do, at the sight and sound of this astonishing grimy fellow.

"It's me—you remember?—Jimmy Edlin."

"Mr. Edlin? So it is. But—but——"

"I know, I know, you needn't tell me. Please come over here a minute." She followed him into a corner. "Mrs. Atwood, I can't begin to tell you all about it now, but I've been having a hell of a time. I was kidnapped, last night. I escaped this morning, but I've lost my coat with my money and cheque-book in it—I haven't had a bite or a drink or a wash since early yesterday evening—they won't have me back at the hotel—I can't even get my car out of this garage because I owe them three dollars—and I'm rocking on my feet, I don't mind telling you, because they doped me last night——"

"Who did? Not those people?"

"Yes, that tall squinting devil, Brother Kaydick. This package here belongs to them. I gave them the slip at Baker. But ten to one they'll be coming after me."

"Mr. Edlin," she said earnestly, looking hard at him, "this *is* true, isn't it?"

"Mrs. Atwood, it is," he assured her, even more earnestly. "Every word's true—and a lot more there isn't time to tell now. You've got to help me out of this—please."

"But of course! I want to. I wanted to all the time. That's why I was so annoyed with you, on the telephone. Did you notice? I don't suppose you did."

"Yes, I did. Jerusalem!—but this is a lump of luck, coming across you again. Not just because you can help me—and believe me, I need it—but y'know, Mrs. Atwood—I've been thinking a lot about you."

Mrs. Atwood had the bright-eyed look of a woman who would return to that interesting topic later, but who realised that this was the time for other things. "Must you go back to Los Angeles, Mr. Edlin?"

"No—except I need some more money—and clothes. If it wasn't for that, it's a waste of time going back, because whatever that crowd is after—and it's something grim, let me tell you—this is the lively end of it. I'm sure of that now."

"You see, I have a ranch up here—just a little place——"

"You have? That's why you're here, then?"

"Yes, you didn't seem to be interested, when we talked on the telephone, so I didn't tell you. But I have. About forty miles from here. I've called for my car. I always leave it here, because I don't like driving down to Los Angeles—I go by train. Yes, I've a little ranch—and I was wondering if it would help—if you came and stayed a day or two——"

"Mrs. Atwood, that's a great idea," he cried enthusiastically. "I could telephone or wire the bank for some money—that would be easy. And I could work out the next move almost on the spot. Besides," he added, artfully, "having you there to explain it all to and have your advice."

At this she glowed and sparkled away in that dim corner like a little firework display. "But we mustn't go on talking here. You must be dying for something to eat—poor man."

"I am. Now there's just one thing I feel I ought to say, Mrs. Atwood, and you mustn't mind my saying it. You know my name and where I was staying in Los Angeles and that I believe these Brotherhood fanatics killed my brother—but that's all. I think I ought to tell you, right now, that I've done pretty well for myself lately—I was in China and then sold out—so don't imagine, because you see me in this mess, I can't look after myself or haven't plenty of money behind me. You'll have to believe that, because I'll have to borrow some money from you right away. Of course I can fix it up easily, if you've a bank here."

All this merely made her rather impatient. "Yes, yes, I understand. But never mind about that now."

"It's important."

"Yes, but don't you see, Mr. Edlin—and why are men so stupid?—I'd never have asked you to come to the ranch if I didn't believe you were all right. Now, come on—we mustn't waste time."

"That's true enough. Brother Kaydick, if I know him, isn't going to stay quiet at Baker. He'll be making a move, you bet."

Meanwhile, they made some glorious moves. In a corner of the nearest little restaurant, exhibiting a sound feminine pleasure in the spectacle, merry and rosy and bright-eyed, Mrs. Atwood watched him put away pot roast and baked potatoes and beans and apple pie and cheese and three cups of coffee. After that, a new man now, he bought a few necessaries for the visit. Then, after some discussion, they decided to go out to the ranch in her car and to leave his in the garage. She did a little shopping herself, but was very quick about it, being a very quick, deft, decisive sort of woman. It was still early in the afternoon when they set out for the ranch.

They crossed the railroad bridge again, and it was when they were slowly coming down on the other side that Mrs. Atwood, who was driving, was astonished to see her passenger suddenly slump down in his seat as far as possible and put his handkerchief up to his face. Being a sensible woman, however, she did not stop the car but began to accelerate, and looked about her to see what was wrong. On the other side of the road, a tall man in dark clothes was talking earnestly to a figure in uniform, one of the state patrolmen. The tall man looked across as they passed and she had just time to notice that he had a bad squint. It was the man she had seen at the meeting—Brother Kaydick. She pressed on, turning to the left at the junction of roads below, going along towards Mohave for about half a mile, then turning to the right up a steep side-road. By this time, Jimmy was sitting up again, and had looked behind more than once.

"That was Kaydick all right," he told her, rather reluctantly, "and, if you ask me, he was telling some fantastic yarn—about me and this package—to that trooper or whatever he was."

"That's just what I thought," she replied, looking ahead, because the road was narrow, rough and rather tricky.

Jimmy was apologetic. "You see what that may mean? They may be going to bluff it out and bring the police in, to try and find me. I'm sorry—but that's what it looks like to me."

"To me too," she cried. "Isn't it exciting?" And her eyes fairly danced.

"Mrs. Atwood, do you know what you are? And I mean this—by thunder! You're a peach. You don't mind me saying so?"

"Not if you really mean it," she replied, a trifle confused but showing no signs of annoyance.

Jimmy's whole being, with that lunch settling down to work nicely in it, now expanded. He had dodged Kaydick and Company. He still had the package. And now if he wasn't bumping up a mountain-side, on the way to her ranch, with the nicest little woman in California. He lit the new pipe he had just bought, and though it tasted more of varnish than of tobacco, he puffed at it luxuriously. Well, he had earned a piece of good luck, and here it was. This was the life.

"I don't know how you feel about it, but this Mr. Edlin business doesn't sound right to me. How about it? Just Jimmy from now on, eh?"

She agreed, and then, under slight pressure, confessed to being Rosalie herself.

"And you couldn't have a nicer name," he cried, repeating it once or twice, to her confusion. "Sounds just right."

As they went up the narrow winding track into a bright empty world of blue air and shining rock, he learned a good deal about his new friend, Rosalie Atwood. Her late husband had been told by the doctors to leave Philadelphia and to try California. He had been considerably her senior, and delicate. They had settled in Riverside, where he had bought a small business and had done well with it, until he finally broke down altogether. After his death she had sold the business, and, after clearing things up in Riverside, had let her house there, furnished, at a good rent, and since then had divided her time between travelling and staying with various relatives and this ranch up in the hills. It was a tiny ranch, she told him, and did not really pay for itself, but it was cheap to run, with only a Mexican couple there and an old-timer, a former cowboy, miner, sheep-man, guide, called Deeks. And she loved the life up there, so quiet and far away from everything. Sometimes a relative or two came to stay with her. Her husband's brother, much younger and a wild fellow, Charlie Atwood, who had been a stunt man in Hollywood for years, sometimes descended on her, usually when he was broke. He might possibly be there now. This was the only part that Jimmy, who had not missed a word, although he was sleepy, did not like. He could do without this Charlie Atwood. Women had a trick of talking disparagingly about "wild fellows" and, on the quiet, fancying them. So now he told her a few fine things about himself, gave her a picture of himself stalking like a conqueror through the mysterious East, just to show that he was as tough as any Charlie Atwoods.

Then he must have dozed off, for he was very tired and the afternoon, even up here, was quite warm, for when next he looked about him they were running down into a small valley, ringed round with blue-shadowed mountains. There were patches of green in the bottom of the valley, and water seemed to sparkle there. As they came nearer, he noticed some cottonwood trees and a small field or two of alfalfa. It was like an oasis held tenderly in a deep cup of blue air. Wire fences and some cattle and horses. Smoke from a low building. Jimmy looked looked at it all in delight. It was like Mrs. Atwood, Rosalie, herself, being small, cosy, clean, comforting. Then he saw, to his astonishment, a long level field, not far from the ranch-house, a stretch of ground with nothing growing on it and as smooth and flat as a brown billiard-table; and, what was astonishing, there was reposing on this ground an airplane, a small and battered-looking biplane of an oldish design but nevertheless an honest-to-God airplane.

Mrs. Atwood, as she turned in towards the ranch-house, regarded the airplane with neither surprise nor enthusiasm. "Yes," she murmured, "Charlie's here."

They were now running up towards the porch of the pleasant little ranch-house. "Oh—this is grand," cried Jimmy, who after all his troubles really felt at that moment that he had arrived at a haven of peace. "You couldn't want anything better than this. All on its own, and a marvellous situation, and yet as cosy as you like. It's a real home. Peaceful."

He had no sooner said this than out of the ranch-house came running and yelling, apparently in terror of their lives, two middle-aged Mexicans and three Mexican children and a very thin old man in patched pants and two dogs and a cat. Out they came, and from behind them came tremendous shouts and roars and the clash of broken glass, as if somebody in there was busy smashing the place to bits.

"Yes," said Mrs. Atwood, a little wearily but without any trace of surprise, "Charlie's here."

Blinking a little, feeling rather dazed, he followed her into the house. This looked like being a long day.

CHAPTER SIX

OUTSIDE THE GATE

It was rather late when Malcolm came down to breakfast, for he had not had a very good night's sleep and then had dozed on past his usual time. Barstow seemed to have been up for hours. The dining-room was deserted. He tried the lunch-room and there, with his long legs wrapped round a stool at the counter, was Hooker, cleaning up what looked to have been once a noble plate of ham and eggs.

"You see, Darbyshire," he observed with a grin, "why Science makes progress while Art stands still. Art has just got up, but Science has been up and out these last two hours, making enquiries. And if we're going exploring to-day, you'd better have a good breakfast. The ham's good."

"I'll try it." Malcolm gave his order, then apologised to Hooker for being down so late, and asked if he had discovered anything about the MacMichaels.

Hooker had. "I figured that if I went round early, before the fellows were busy, some of them would know something. Henry MacMichael's a multi-millionaire, and he's not the kind to live in a shack somewhere. He'll live in a big way wherever he is. And even if he gets most of his stuff in from the Coast, he must use this place now and again. Besides, those instruments from London had to be sent here, I knew that. So I went round with a packet of Luckies. Tried the railroad here first, then one or two of the garages, and the drug store."

"The MacMichaels are here, aren't they?" asked Malcolm eagerly.

With an air of leisurely enjoyment the other spread a map out on the counter. He pointed a long stained forefinger. "Up here somewhere."

Malcolm leaned over and stared not very hopefully at some grim shading on the map. *Lava Mountains. Quail Mountains. Granite*

Mountains. Copper City. Leadpipe Spring. Eagle Crags. Not a very promising lot of names. And he said so.

"I know," said Hooker. "But between the road here and this end of Death Valley there's a little valley, might be a miniature canyon, and there they are. None of these fellows has seen the place. If they had workmen up there, I think they must have brought 'em in from the Coast. But one fellow had a brother who'd done a job for them up there. Some miner who'd struck it rich started building a big place—like Scotty's Castle at the north end of Death Valley— you've heard of that, eh?—well, this miner seems to have died before it was finished, and then the MacMichaels bought it two or three years ago. It's called the *Castello*, and it's at Lost Lake. So what we're looking for is the Lost Lake Castello, somewhere about there"—he pointed again—"and if that isn't romantic enough for you, my romantic friend, I give you up."

"It's romantic enough," said Malcolm, "but do you think it's true? Why, there isn't even the ghost of a road marked here, and they'd have to have some sort of road."

"They've probably made one since this map was printed. This is three years old. Don't worry about that."

"Did you hear anything about the girl—Andrea?"

Hooker seemed to take even more time than usual before he replied. "Yes, she's here all right. Fellow at the filling-station at the corner knows her. Says she sometimes drives a big Packard, and stops there for gas. He described her—dark, good-looking girl— she'd taken his eye, I guess. She was through here only about four days ago."

"Going away?" And Malcolm's heart sank.

"This fellow thought not. Coming up from the Coast."

His heart expanded and rose like a balloon. "Are you game to go up there as soon as possible, Hooker?" he asked eagerly.

"Sure! I want an explanation from those two MacMichaels, and I'm going to have it. But listen, Darbyshire, are you ready to take a chance, and rough it a bit? You are? Fine! Because I've been think- ing we'd better check out of here, and take a chance on staying somewhere up there. If there isn't anything for us, then we might be able to push over to Death Valley—I was through there once, about four years ago—and even if we can't make that, well, I've got a couple of rugs in the car and we'll put some food and drink in—what do you say?"

Malcolm agreed with enthusiasm. What did he say, indeed! To charge into the mountains and find that girl again, perhaps to rescue her for ever from her deep mysterious unhappiness, to break the spell of Lost Lake and its Castello—and what did he say! They must be off at once.

"I'll get my car out and buy some stuff to eat and drink," said Hooker, now enjoying himself too at the thought of this very unscientific expedition, "while you pack up here." He unwound himself from the stool, and lovingly folded his map. "By the way, have you thought any more about that fellow who disappeared last night?"

"Yes, but I still can't make it out. I'd thought of asking that reception clerk a few more questions. It still doesn't make any sense."

"Never did. But the way I look at it is this. Whatever he was, we can't do any good by hanging about here. If he was just a crazy drunk, then we're obviously wasting time. If he wasn't——"

Malcolm cut in here. "And I think he wasn't, y'know, Hooker. He might have been the kind of chap who makes mountains out of mole-hills, but that's all. Sorry, go on."

"Well, if he really was on to something, and they got him away, then we're still wasting time hanging about here, because we'll know more by going straight to the MacMichaels and asking them what they think they're doing. Now, I'll be all set for going in half an hour. Can you make it?"

Malcolm could and did. He packed a small bag for the journey, and left his big one at the railway station. Hooker arrived in a rather dingy coupé, which had, however, a very efficient look.

"Matter of fact, she's really a very powerful little brute," Hooker explained, proudly, "and she's just right for this job because she isn't slung too low and can climb anything. Be ready for some rough going, though, because once we're off the main road we're liable to strike some very rough tracks. Now I've got enough to eat and drink for at least a couple of days, so that's okay. Gasoline's the real trouble, though. No filling-stations up there. I've got eighteen gallons in the tank, and we'll fill up again at the very last place we come to, and I managed to get three spare two-gallon tins for emergency. Best I could do. So let's go."

It was a glorious morning, not too hot yet, with something still left in the air from the chill of the night, and as clean and bright as a new knife. The Mohave Desert looked as if it had just been created. The mountains beyond, brown with faintly-blue folds in them, might have been just delivered from some vast cosmographical toy-shop. The heavily-tarred main road looked like a thin black ruler laid across a map. The distances were immense. Malcolm found himself glancing across empty spaces into which whole English counties could have been dropped. They rushed on at seventy miles an hour and yet hardly seemed to be changing their position. Soon, as the sun climbed and burned more fiercely, they began to see mirages: the road in front of them appeared to be flooded; miraculous pale-blue lakes glimmered in the distant desert and even reflected the mesquite bushes; and the far mountain ranges dissolved and re-assembled themselves magically: it was like a country in a faintly cruel fairy-tale. The air was even newer than the landscape; it had neither age nor weight; nothing, it seemed, had happened yet in it; history had not yet begun, to load it with the sorrowful rumours of man's perpetual unrest and unhappiness; it blew from a colossal Eden; and seemed to refresh not only the body but the spirit. Between the cruel yet enchanting desert country and the friendly magic of the air, and shaken by the vast trembling expectations of a lover, Malcolm was lost indeed. His own small green land, the gloom and sullen thunder of London, his two rooms and the office and the unbuilt cottage on the North Downs, his architecture and tennis and leathery sedate University Club all fled or were extinguished. He did not feel himself, but was not yet changed into anybody else. He was lost, but in a kind of happy madness. This was a dream, in full glaring sunlight.

Hooker, who liked driving his car and was nearly as anxious to have it out with Paul MacMichael as Malcolm was to confront Andrea again, talked cheerfully of this and that, the country they were passing through, his previous travels, his work and colleagues. Both young men were in tacit agreement not to discuss further the object of their journey, for each felt that there was more than a grain of folly in his own reason for being there, and hardly any reason at all, just a sort of pleasant lunacy, in the other's motive. Hooker could not see any sense in threading a way into these mountains merely to see a girl who had not, he gathered, been very encouraging when Darbyshire had met her at the other side of the world. Malcolm for his part could not understand what Hooker thought he was going to do when he met the MacMichaels again, for if they had behaved badly to him in London there seemed no reason why they should behave any better in this grim wilderness of theirs. And each knew the other thought this, and could see that it was not unreasonable, and felt too insecure to begin arguing about it. So nothing more was said about the most important topic, and they talked all the morning about other things.

Malcolm knew that on these occasions it is best for one man and one alone to read the map and decide on routes, and as Hooker knew a little about this region and was obviously a passionate map-reader, Malcolm left it to him. He left it to him so thoroughly that he dreamily accepted every turning and new bumpy climb, not knowing where they were going. They had now left the main road and were twisting and climbing and crawling on vague spectres of roads, dim tracks among rocks, ruts in the sand, more or less in a northerly direction. They had taken in a few more gallons at a shack that had told them firmly it was their *Last Chance For Gas*, just as if they were now making for the empty roof of the world. And so, it seemed, they were. They stopped finally at the very dead end of a track that Hooker confessed had been a mistake, for it petered out on a remote little plateau, uncovered to the sun and frizzling, which contained nothing but some fantastically-coloured rocks, some very unfriendly cactus growths, the ruins of a shack, and a mound of rusted old tins. A faded notice announced that this was—or had been—the Five Buzzards Mine. It might have been a mine on a lost continent. But the whole rocky surface of the plateau glittered deceptively, as if promising anything, chiefly with what Hooker declared to be mica—or fools' gold. At this dead end they ate lunch, canned beef and crackers and fruit from Hooker's store of provisions. Then they smoked and looked lazily about them, at the surrounding summits and long mountain slopes coloured like Eastern rugs, and far down below where the alkali deposits looked like a covering of hoar-frost. Hooker, who was a thorough traveller, had both a compass and a pair of field-glasses, and now he used them both, while Malcolm stared in dreamy astonishment at the wide scene. Hooker declared he had caught a glimpse of some electric pylons crossing the slope of a neighbouring hill, and gave it as his opinion that these might possibly be running power and light to the MacMichaels' place, for otherwise he could not understand how they came to be there. The MacMichaels, he said, in their opulence must have arranged to tap the electric power that ran from Boulder Dam to the Coast. If they followed the pylons, they had a good chance of finding their way to the Castello. But not only were the pylons some way off, but there was the question too of finding some sort of track along which they could take the car. So first they had to go back a few miles.

Eventually, in the strange dead middle of the afternoon, when everything has lost its colour and savour, they came to a track that was the twin of that which had led them only to the forgotten mine, but which Hooker thought was going in the right direction. This track ran along, in a dejected fashion, and with many a bad place in it where it crossed the steep washes, for about six miles, and then, just beyond a sharp rise, and just when they were beginning to think they had been deceived again, it joined a much broader and smoother track that, in this place and in this weather, could almost be considered a good road. It was not marked at all on the map, though it showed signs of much usage, and Hooker said that this was in their favour, because the MacMichaels must have had to make some such road as this, for their own traffic. It led them, with some sharp curves to avoid fallen boulders, round the side of a granite mountain, then down into a rock-strewn valley that was empty of all life; and it was here that they noticed the line of pylons curving down and then running up the farther slope, well above the road itself.

"This is it, I guess," said Hooker, after stopping and using his field-glasses. "The line goes over the top there, and I'll bet you ten dollars this Lost Lake canyon—or whatever they call it—is on the other side. I don't suppose this is the only way in. There's probably at least another road to it, from the other side, but, at that, they've used this quite a lot since the last big rains. Look at those tracks. They've had quite a few trucks along here—and not such little ones either."

"What's that up there?" asked Malcolm pointing forward at a

speck near the place where this road curved out of their sight.

Hooker examined it, then handed the glasses over. "Looks like a miner's cabin or a small ranch-house to me. Not their place, of course, not big enough. The fellow in Barstow whose brother had worked up there told me that this Castello of the MacMichaels was an elaborate affair, towers and what not, with room for plenty of people. But if anybody's living in that shack, they'll be able to tell us something. Let's get on."

They rushed through the valley at a smart pace, and then climbed the rather stiff gradient at the other side, where the road showed traces of the battles that the heavy motor-trucks had fought there. Towards the top of the road the slopes on each side were much steeper, until at the very top, where the road vanished from view, they were almost like the jaws of a gorge.

"If they do live somewhere on the other side," said Malcolm, "they've a fine natural entrance. Almost like a gateway. That hut there is bigger than I thought, and I think I can see smoke, so there must be somebody there. It's a little off the road."

As they neared the top, his excitement mounted too. Was this the enchanted place, the castle of the sleeping princess? Would he, in another minute or two, be looking down on the mysterious towers her father had built in this wilderness? Was this the end of so many, many hours, since they had stood together looking down on the glittering Riviera, hours of confused thinking and dreaming, vast vague hopes, self-reproaches, idiotic determinations?

"I believe we're here," he cried, in his excitement.

"Take it easy, boy," Hooker replied, with a grin.

Leaving the shack a little to the right, where it was perched above the road, with a fine look-out down into the valley, they swept forward to the summit of the road, but only to find the way barred, and barred just short of the summit, so that they could not see into the valley or canyon beyond. It was a thorough job too, and a recent one. A high and strong fence, made of both plain and barbed wire, came down at each side, descending from each wall of rock, and these fences met at a high and new metal gate, covering the width of the road. On this gate was a notice as new and bold as itself: *Lost Lake. Strictly Private.* And they soon discovered, on getting out, that the gate was securely locked. Standing there, they looked at one another in a mixed fashion, a trifle disappointed at being held up, but still triumphant at having found the place.

Hooker looked about him shrewdly, and Malcolm tried to follow his example, although he was still too excited to be very observant.

"There go the pylons," said Hooker, pointing. "There's a telephone line too. See it, just by the shack there. I suppose the fellow up there thought he might as well be on the telephone while they were about it." He went nearer the gate and fences, looked closely at them, and then turned. "If you ask me, they can electrify this little outfit, and give it plenty of juice too. If you walked into that on a dark night and they had the current turned on, you might be fried in no time. But they can turn lights on." And he pointed up to two powerful lights above the gate that Malcolm had not noticed before.

"I don't like this, y'know, Darbyshire," Hooker continued, returning from his inspection and lighting a cigarette, "I don't like it at all. Down there in Barstow—in fact, a long time before I arrived in Barstow—I'd begun to think I was imagining things, like our mysterious pal last night. Now I'm not so sure."

"Well, I don't know," protested Malcolm. "After all if they want to be private, y'know, Hooker—why shouldn't they keep people out?"

"If it was back East I could understand it. But they don't do things like this in the West. People don't shut themselves up and tell you to keep out. Why should they? A place like this isn't just off Main Street. And look at the expense and trouble they've gone to—I tell you, it's screwy." He looked thoughtfully at Malcolm.

The latter was not sure what "screwy" meant, but he could see what Hooker, not given to imagining things, was driving at. And now there came, not to subdue his excitement but to change its colour and flavour, a sudden sense of the inexplicable and sinister. This quality of things had been there, he had already felt dimly, in Andrea's mysterious background, and now that he had crossed the world and at last come within a mile or two of the girl herself, with the very country of that background piled up round him, he realised it very sharply and unpleasantly. And somehow here, standing in front of a fence that could easily annihilate an intruder, it did not seem absurdly improbable that their acquaintance of last night, Edlin, should have disappeared so mysteriously. Now there seemed to be nothing to prevent this and even stranger things happening. The dream through which he had moved all day was taking on something of a nightmare aspect. Rather impatient with himself, he looked round again, then pointed up at the shack.

"There's somebody outside now," he remarked, trying to be casual. "We'd better go up and ask him what happens here."

They ran the car up to the tiny porch of the shack, for there was an uneven but easily passable track up from the road, and as they covered the few hundred yards there, Hooker observed: "Looks like a typical Western old-timer. We'll go easy with him. They're queer, slow old cusses, most of these chaps. Comes from having spent most of their lives in places like this."

The old-timer, dressed in a faded maroon shirt and blue jeans, was an oldish fellow with an unruly thatch of hair, very white against his leathery brown wrinkled face, which also set in relief his clear-blue, candid eyes. He was enjoying a corncob pipe, with an immense sense of leisure. He appeared to come out of a deep and very agreeable reverie in order to observe their existence and address them; and both his appearance and manner suggested the Will Rogers type of homely philosopher and humorist. He was almost too good to be true.

"Well, folks," he remarked, without malice and quite simply, "you'll have taken the wrong road, I reckon."

Malcolm was about to reply, but felt a nudge from Hooker, who replied casually: "We didn't know this road was closed here."

"Shorely is. Then again it ain't, 'cos it don't go no place, bein' private." He said this very slowly, almost tasting his words, as if they all had unlimited time for this chat and might as well make the most of it. "But didn't you see the notice 'long there at Black-water where she turns off the public highway, tellin' you this don't lead nowhere?" There was nothing sharp, cross-questioning about this query: he seemed to ask out of mild curiosity.

"No, we didn't come that way," Hooker explained carefully. "We struck this road just over the other side—there was a rough track, and I'd lost my way before that, and had to take several of these tracks—so we never saw any notice. It must have been much farther along."

The old-timer thought a moment or two, then said slowly, keeping his candid blue gaze fixed on Hooker: "I reckon you must ha' been out Five Buzzards way." When he had heard that they had eaten their lunch near the old mine, he nodded in slow-motion, and continued: "You were smart, I'm thinking, not to have lost yourselves under Five Buzzards, but mebbe if you'd been smarter you'd not ha' been out that way at all. Ain't prospectin'? No, I figured you weren't prospectin'."

"Just looking round, that's all," replied Hooker.

"Easterners, I reckon?"

"I am. He's an Englishman."

The old-timer turned his candid blue gaze now on Malcolm, who felt he was being examined—though with no intentional rudeness—as a new specimen.

"That so? Well, I ain't seen an Englishman this long time. Worked with one once, though, out at Bullfrog." He paused, shook the mouthpiece of his pipe, wiped it on his jeans, then resumed. "So you're two young fellers just lookin' round, eh? And now you're at the top o' the wrong road, an' a long way to go back to anywhere. Well, I reckon that comes of bein' in a hurry—even when you don't know where you're goin', you young fellers now's in a mighty hurry—and comes of not lettin' her run just natural. That's what I'm always saying to Maw. 'Now then, Maw,' I says, 'just let her run natural, that's all.'"

As if waiting for her name to be mentioned as a cue to enter the scene Maw now came out of the shack. She was the feminine counterpart of her husband, a small leathery elderly woman, though younger than he was and grimmer, more suspicious, as if life under these conditions was harder for the female than for the male. She hardly glanced at the newcomers, and Malcolm felt that she did not need to because she had already had a good look at them through the window.

"What's this you're sayin', Paw?" she enquired.

Paw winked all round. "I'm just a-tellin' how I asks you to let everything just run natural."

"You and your run natural!" she replied, with scorn. "And have you come far?"

"From Barstow," said Hooker.

"Take a powerful lot o' gasoline to get back to Barstow," observed the old-timer.

Hooker replied vaguely that it would, and now changed the subject. "No, we didn't see the notice. Who does this belong to?" He tried to be as casual as possible, but Malcolm could not help fancying that he had not been quite successful.

The old-timers, however, did not appear to notice anything. Maw left the answer to Paw, but did not leave them.

"Some folks by the name o' MacMichael."

"MacMichael." Hooker repeated the name as if he had never heard it before. Malcolm tried to look uninterested.

"What's the idea—wiring themselves in like this?" asked Hooker, not disguising his curiosity in this matter.

"Eastern ways, I reckon. What would you say, Maw? Maw's folks came from back East, an' there's times when she lets me know it— eh, Maw?"

Maw did not reply and Malcolm, suddenly looking up, was rather disconcerted to find she was staring hard at him.

"That power line," said Hooker, pointing, "must join the one coming from Boulder Dam. The people here must have arranged to have a sub-station specially for them. That must have cost them something."

"Mebbe it did, but I couldn't rightly say. Seems you know more about it than I do, but then you might be in the electrical line o' business yourself, eh?"

Hooker replied that he wasn't, but knew something about it. There was now a long pause. Maw rocked herself vigorously in a little chair; Paw smoked peacefully; and the two young men stood in front of them feeling rather awkward. Around them the afternoon waned, with magnificent blue shadows.

"Jove—I'm thirsty," Malcolm announced, not merely to break the silence or out of policy but simply because he was thirsty.

"So am I," said Hooker, giving the old-timer a glance.

He responded amiably. "You bet! You can have a pitcher o' good water—cold as ice water it is, straight out o' the mountain—or Maw might make us all a cup o' coffee."

"I wish," said Hooker, not without tact, "you'd sell us a jug of good strong coffee."

Maw nodded, then looked at Paw, who also nodded. "What Maw means by that is that we ain't sellin' no coffee—but you can have a cup with us an' welcome—so long as we let it all run natural and put it on a proper straight visitin' footing. My name's Larrigan, which makes Maw Mrs. Larrigan, though she ain't none too proud of it, far as I've seen. And what may yours be?"

They were only too glad to humour the old fellow, and gave him their names and told him where they came from, and, when he asked a further question, what they did when they were at home.

"There, Maw," he announced, with a twinkling sort of humorous pride, very much in character, "you can set to makin' your coffee an' know who's visitin' with you this afternoon—Mr. Darbyshire, who builds houses over there in England, and Dr. Hooker, a scientific professor from back East."

Maw smiled and nodded. "Shorely, Paw! An' if you'll just show 'em what there is to see, I'll have everything ready when you come back."

Mr. Larrigan, in his own leisurely fashion, now joined them, while his wife went bustling indoors, and drawling away he took them at an easy pace up the steep ground at the back of the shack, past several outhouses, to a spot where he said they would have the best view. Here they stood and gazed at the distant shining peaks and down into the valley, already deep in shadow though there were one or two shafts of golden light still finding their way into it, and Mr. Larrigan carefully pointed out this peak and that, exchanged geological information with Hooker, who found him more knowledgeable than he had expected, and told them one or two mining stories. He said nothing more about the MacMichaels, and never even referred again to the road below, which to Malcolm had MacMichael traced all along it. Indeed, Malcolm found it hard not to keep his eyes fixed on that road, and once or twice Mr. Larrigan had caught him at it, when he ought to have been looking where Mr. Larrigan's finger was pointing, and Malcolm fancied that the old chap had then given him a sharp look. But then the old gossip probably didn't like to think he was not succeeding in entertaining his visitors. And Malcolm felt it a pity he could not explain that he was looking down there because every moment he hoped he would see a girl in a car; for he liked Mr. Larrigan and hated to hurt his feelings. Evidently Mrs. Larrigan was as leisurely as her husband, for she took a long time preparing that coffee. At last, even Mr. Larrigan himself had to acknowledge that.

"Maw don't seem to be lettin' things run natural down there," he observed, in his own vein of grave waggery. "Seems to me we bin waitin' some time for that coffee. But it'll be good when it comes. Maw's shore slow when she's in that humour, but she don't do no sloppin' an' messin' about, same as so many womenfolk, an' call it cookin'. An' I'm hopin' there might be a slice o' pie for us, the way things is goin'. Reckon we've all earned a slice o' pie waitin' this long. Now there she is—wavin' an' screechin' as if she'd bin doin' the waitin' an' not us. Come an' get it. All right, Maw," he called down, in his thin high voice, "just let her run natural—we're comin'. This way, folks, it's shorter by a step or two."

The shack faced west, and some of the gold piling up magnificently in the sky spilled in, to show them as they entered a neat cosy living-room, as unpretentious and homely as the Larrigans themselves, and a table rich with pie and cookies and the heavenly smell of good coffee.

"Everything runnin' natural, Maw?" asked Mr. Larrigan.

"Yes, Paw, but before you set down to your coffee, you better come round an' help me with the water—that pump's stickin' again. No," as Hooker and Malcolm offered to help, "you set right down an' help yourselves. Me an' Paw can fix this in no time."

The coffee was very good. The apple pie looked very good too: it was not one of those pies in which the crust and the fruit are still leading separate existences and continue being at odds inside the eater; you could see at once that in this artful golden confection the pastry had probably shared its essential fat goodness with the fruit, which had immediately responded by covering the hollows in the crust with its own jellied sweetness. Malcolm and Hooker looked at that pie, and then at one another.

"Have a piece of pie, Darbyshire?"

"Thanks, Hooker. But after you."

"No, here you are."

Mr. Larrigan had done only the barest justness to his wife's capacity as a creator of pies. There might be something rather grim and formidable about Mrs. Larrigan; she might be too little aware of the easier feminine graces, too contemptuous of womanly charm; she might be disinclined at times—in Mr. Larrigan's great phrase—to let things run natural; but she could make a pie.

"Hooker," said Malcolm, rather sternly, "we must insist upon paying for this."

"I doubt if they'll take anything. These old Westerners have their own pride."

"I know. And I appreciate it. But unless we agree that they must be paid, I don't like taking another piece of pie."

"We must pay them then, Darbyshire, because I'm going to have another piece."

After a further interval, Malcolm said dreamily: "I don't ever remember eating pie and drinking coffee at this time of day before, but there's something to be said for it. I believe I could stay here a week or two, just sitting out there, staring at the mountains and dropping a philosophical remark now and then, and coming in three or four times a day for more coffee and pie. Not a bad life at all. Nothing to worry about. That's what's the matter with us, Hooker. Look at these people. They don't care."

"Not a hoot, I guess. They've enough to live on, and plenty of space, and peace and quietness," said Hooker. "If I hadn't some work to do, this would be the kind of life I'd like to lead. Think of all these business men worrying themselves sick and silly, into the grave—and all for what? Pa Larrigan here is better off than any of them."

"Nice old boy, Pa Larrigan. I took to him at once."

"Typical old-timer. I've met lots of 'em."

"Didn't tell us much about the MacMichaels, did he?"

"No. Wasn't interested, I guess. And these Western folks, though they seem to say anything that comes into their heads, are inclined to be cautious really."

"I was amused at the way in which they insisted upon knowing our names and a bit more about us, before they'd ask us in for coffee." And Malcolm smiled.

Hooker did not look amused, but rather puzzled. "I didn't quite get that," he confessed. "That's not the usual thing with these people. But living right out here, I guess——" He ended with a shrug.

The two young men lit cigarettes, and ruminated. It was very peaceful in there. The Golden Fleece itself was now piling up in the western sky. This was not the moment to begin planning again. Let things look after themselves for a little while: let them run just natural.

But Malcolm, looking out to enjoy the magnificent sky, found himself remarking: "The old couple seem to be very curious about your car, Hooker."

This did not surprise Hooker, who knew that all good Americans have a deep and abiding passion for the automobile. Only the year before, one afternoon as he was going down Lexington Avenue during a brief visit to New York, he had noticed the unusual look of awed and reverent expectation on the faces of all the people approaching a large building and had then remembered it was the week of the Automobile Show. So he did not rise, but casually enquired what the Larrigans were doing.

"Poking round it," replied Malcolm. "Pa's inside now."

Hooker chuckled. "There are one or two little gadgets of mine on that board that'll give him something to think about."

"He looks thoughtful," Malcolm continued. "He's getting out now. He's coming back. So is Ma. She's looking grimmer than ever. I hope she won't mind about her pie. You've made it look pretty silly, y'know, Hooker."

"I have. Gosh!—you'd twice as much, Darbyshire. Not that I blame you. I tried pie and coffee over in England. You're right to make the most of your chances."

"Seems to me, Hooker," said Malcolm, falling into the same vein, "you were too busy in England going on switchbacks and wearing false noses and picking up shop-girls, to know what sort of grub we have."

Pa Larrigan stood in the open doorway, and surveyed them in his own easy candid fashion.

"Mr. Larrigan," cried Malcolm, "the pie was marvellous. You must let us pay for what we've had. It's not fair to come here and eat you out of your house——"

"Call it your supper," said Mr. Larrigan briskly. "Now then, young fellers, step outside."

There was such an odd change in his tone and in the look in his eye that first they stared at him and then at one another.

"Come on, step outside, before there's trouble. And you can have trouble, if you want it." And now he showed them, as he stepped back on to the porch, to allow them to come out, a very nasty-looking revolver that seemed to have seen much service.

They stared, wondering if this was some elaborate joke. But the genial, homely Western philosopher and humorist appeared to have vanished. There was a very hard and uncompromising look about Mr. Larrigan now. His tone was harsh. There was cold blue fire in his eyes—to say nothing of the revolver in his hand. They went out, still staring. Mrs. Larrigan appeared round the corner.

"Mrs. Larrigan," cried Hooker, protesting, "what's this?"

"This, young feller," said Mrs. Larrigan grimly, deliberately mistaking his meaning, "is a shot-gun, and if you think I can't use it, you don't know me. Jest do what Paw tells yer, if you don't want to get hurt."

"Got another key to your car?" asked Mr. Larrigan sternly.

"No," replied Hooker, not convinced yet that this wasn't their idea of a joke.

"Well, I've got the one that was in the car, so don't think you can get away. It's a long walk to anywhere. And you can't get that way." He pointed towards the wire fence. "Don't try it, young fellers. Did you open that door, Maw?"

"Shorely did, Paw."

"Mr. Larrigan," cried Malcolm earnestly. "I was just going to thank you both for being so kind and hospitable to a couple of strangers. But if you're serious about this, let me tell you I think it's a damned dirty trick."

"And so do I," said Hooker angrily. "I didn't know Westerners asked strangers in to have a bite and a drink, and then did this to them."

These reproaches had no effect upon Mrs. Larrigan, who told them to be quiet, but her husband looked a trifle shame-faced.

"My orders is to keep you here, boys, till I know what they want to do with you," he said, with some trace of apology in his tone.

"But you can't have had any orders," said Malcolm, bewildered.

"The telephone," said Hooker, out of the corner of his mouth. "After we told them who we were, she must have rung up the MacMichaels and told them. They gave the orders."

"Now come on, Paw, we're not going to stand here jest chattering."

"Move on, boys," Larrigan commanded. "We're puttin' you in that shack up there till you're wanted."

The two young men glanced at one another, then with a shrug walked slowly round the back, and, under the directions of Larrigan, who followed them, entered a small bare shack, which contained nothing but a couple of rough bunks, an old blanket or two, some sacking, a little tin stove and a little heap of wood.

"Here's your place for the night, boys, or till you're wanted," said Larrigan at the door. "And it's orders and can't be helped. If you're ready to take it easy—just letting her run natural—then that's okay with me. But if you try any tricks, you'll find we're good an' tough around here. So better make the best of it."

"And how long are we supposed to stay here?" demanded Hooker.

"Couldn't rightly say. Till morning, anyhow."

"Then you might let us have our things out of the car," said Malcolm.

Larrigan nodded. "Let you have some of 'em, mebbe. No orders sayin' I shouldn't." He locked them in, and departed.

They examined the shack thoroughly. There was a small window, and it would not be difficult to smash the thin wooden strips that held the panes, clear all the glass away, then climb out.

"No use to-night, though," said Hooker. "We couldn't do anything if we got out."

"Well, I wondered once or twice what we were going to do to-night," replied Malcolm, pretending to be more cheerful than he felt, "and now it's been neatly settled for us."

When Larrigan returned, with his wife behind him, he dumped into the shack the two rugs, some of their things, and the provisions that Hooker had bought in Barstow. If he had overheard their remarks, he could not have spoken more exactly to the point. "You might get out by smashing that window," he observed calmly, "but I've a dog out here, an' he'll bark, an' me an' Maw happens to be light sleepers. Then when I put you back in here, it won't have a window, that's all, an' it's cold up here nights. So I shouldn't try it, boys, jest for your own good. Light your stove if you feel like it, but don't call for no more wood because you won't git none—we're short o' wood in these parts. Let her run natural, boys, that's my advice," he concluded, with a slightly sardonic emphasis.

"You go to hell," said Hooker irritably.

Pa Larrigan only chuckled as he slammed and locked the door on them.

"Now do you believe that chap Edlin was only a crazy drunk?" asked Malcolm, as they sat on the edge of their bunks.

"No. And I wish he was here with us." Hooker stared at the little tin stove. "You see what happened. They just kidded us along, of course."

"I know that part all right," said Malcolm bitterly. "I thought that name business a bit queer at the time."

"While the artful old devil had us up on the hillside, well away from the house, his wife was telephoning to Lost Lake to say that that couple of saps, Mr. Darbyshire the architect from London, and Dr. Sap-brained Hooker of the Weinberger Institute of Technology, had come prying round. Old Larrigan knew, of course, from the word 'go' we hadn't simply got lost but were up to something. That's what he's here for—the nice simple old-timer."

"Yes, I can see all that. But why did they tell them to keep us here?"

"Search me! If they'd told us to get out and mind our own business, I could understand it."

Malcolm thought for a moment. "If Andrea's there—well, she knows my name, of course. But either she'd ask them to tell me to go away or she'd come out here herself. What I can't see her doing is telling them to take out their guns and have me locked up for the night. And the others—her father—and her uncles, if they are her uncles—I'm still confused about all that—don't know anything about me. So I can't make it out."

"I don't want to be egoistical, Darbyshire," said Hooker dryly, "but I must tell you that I think it's me—and not you—they're interested in. Both Paul and Henry MacMichael know my name all right, and they know very well I wouldn't be poking round up here if I wasn't on to them again. They tried to frame me over there in England, and now they're having me locked in for the night here. And my guess is this. Paul MacMichael is on the other side of that wire fence, and he's working at something very big. And either he's going to tell me himself to keep away and stay away or—and this is just possible—and—gosh!—it's an exciting notion—he's in some sort of jam with his experiment and wants me to take a look at it. I know that isn't likely—he's not the kind who wants to let you in on anything—but it's just possible. Gee!—that would be a break. I'd forgive 'em everything for that."

Afterwards, when it had been dark some time and they had the stove going and had made the shack as snug as possible, Malcolm broke a long silence by saying, "I've been thinking. We might as well try to work this whole thing out. I feel we've been dodging it rather."

"Dodging what?"

"Dodging the issue, I suppose. We're not really pooling our evidence, to begin with. We ought to put everything we know together, then try to deduce something from it."

"But—no, go on."

Malcolm waited, however, until Hooker, who appeared to think he was in for a long session, made himself comfortable by removing his collar and tie and shoes and then stretching out his long legs on the bunk. They both began smoking again. Fortunately, they had brought along plenty of cigarettes.

"Now then," said Malcolm, "I'll begin with my little bit. I know it's the least important, from this point of view, though I think it's more important than you imagine."

"The trouble is, there's a girl in it, as I told you before."

"Yes, I've heard all that," replied Malcolm, with some impatience. "But just listen. I meet this Andrea MacMichael and I feel there's something wrong with her. Obviously she isn't ill or anything. We know it's nothing to do with money. What is it?"

"Some love affair," the other gloomily suggested.

"No, I'm sure it wasn't that. You can tell. She wasn't—how shall I put it?—her real self, the sort of girl she ought to have been, and really was inside. She was repressed and unhappy, and she told me nothing was any use—which is dam' silly—and really meant it." He reflected a moment. "It was as if she'd been brought up to believe nothing was any use, that life was hardly worth living, and had come to believe it—in a dreary sort of way."

"She sounds a dreary girl to me."

"No—that's the point—she isn't, really. Underneath that cold covering, as if she'd been packed in ice, there was somewhere a grand girl—that's what I felt all the time. Now she's Henry Mac-Michael's daughter, we know. She never talked about him. She never talked about her life here at all. Why?"

"It's unusual, certainly," said Hooker. "The girls I used to know would go gassing on for hours about their families and homes. I thought all women did."

"Well, she didn't. You'd think a girl who was living in a fantastic sort of modern castle among these mountains, miles from anywhere, would have plenty to say about it—but she didn't. She was very secretive. Why?"

"If you're asking me, you needn't. I give it up."

"I'm asking myself, I suppose, seeing you're so useless. But, take it from me, there's a mystery there. Mystery Number One, which brings me here—like the chump I am. Now how does that connect with Mystery Number Two—yours?"

"I've told you what I think. Paul MacMichael, the late Professor Engelfield, cleared out, disappeared, changed his name back again, because he's on to something new in his—and my—field of work, atomic structure. He's money of his own, and now he has his brother Henry to back him up. Ten to one he has his lab. in this Lost Lake place. And whatever he's doing, he doesn't want me or anybody else to butt in. At least, he didn't. He may have other ideas now he's made me stay here until wanted. That's all I can tell you, Darbyshire. It may possibly be something that Henry MacMichael thinks he can exploit commercially—which may explain the secrecy—but knowing Paul and the sort of work he does, I don't think that's likely."

"Mystery Number Two, then," cried Malcolm, now warming up. "The first is—why is Andrea MacMichael so secretive and unhappy? The second is—what are Paul MacMichael and his brother up to here? And now we come to our friend Edlin. Let's assume he meant everything he said. I've been going over all he told us last night. Now he didn't know anything about my approach to this business, had never heard of Andrea——"

"And he knew nothing about Paul."

"Right. He said—unless I'm sadly mistaken—that his brother, the reporter, had probably been murdered by a religious sect called the Brotherhood of the Judgment——"

"Los Angeles is full of 'em."

"Yes, but the others don't go murdering and kidnapping people. Now he'd got some information from his brother's notebook, had gone to their meeting, gone behind the scenes, so to speak, because he happened to know their passwords, and arranged to go to Barstow, where one of their men—what did they call them?—wasn't it servers?—something like that—was to meet him and take him to their leader—Father John, otherwise John MacMichael, whom we know to be a brother of these other two queer fish. These brethren or whatever they call themselves are gloomy religious fanatics, and he told us definitely they were up to something. And before we could compare notes, they're on to him again, and he's whisked away—by some trick about a doctor."

"I wonder," said Hooker with a grin, "if he's somewhere on the other side of that fence?"

"If you remember," replied Malcolm gravely, "he said he was sure they were going to kill him, or that's what he thought when he was in that car with them. Mystery Number Three now—what is this Brotherhood doing, that it's ready to kidnap or murder people who seem to know too much? Remember, they're fanatics, who are looking forward—according to Edlin—to something grisly happening."

"I wouldn't take too much notice of that," said Hooker. "Those people always like the gloomier bits of the Bible. They're usually farmers who look forward to seeing the wicked city folks burning in hell. But—I'll admit one thing—if you could work on them properly, they'd make a thundering good bodyguard or something of that sort—they'd be completely loyal—and they're probably tough. Like these Larrigans. They'd be a darned sight better than hired gunmen, at that. Listen, Darbyshire," he continued, with more excitement than he usually displayed, "this is where it might all link up. John MacMichael, we'll say, is some kind of religious loony—the Hitler of the Brotherhood of the Judgment—and so Paul and Henry say to him 'Come and live with us, and we can use your big boys from Los Angeles, give some of the tougher ones a nice job.' Meanwhile they get on with the real work, keeping well out of everybody's way, and importing a lot of apparatus. I know for a fact they've done that. You see what that means?"

"No. What?"

Hooker sounded aggrieved in his reply. "It means it can't be some purely scientific experiment. There's a commercial angle to it, obviously, or there wouldn't be all this elaborate secrecy and flourishing of guns and what not. They're fooling about, trying to make a new precious metal or some rubbish of that sort. I'm surprised at Paul MacMichael, but I suppose the family spirit's been too strong for him." Hooker was quite disgusted. "That's the only possible explanation. And they think we're being employed by some rival commercial gang. It's disappointing, but there it is."

"There it isn't."

"What do you mean?"

"I mean, that may possibly explain your mystery, possibly Edlin's —though about that, I'm doubtful—but it just doesn't begin to explain mine. No girl is going to behave as Andrea MacMichael did at Beaulieu, merely because her father and her uncle are pottering about with metals. I don't care if it's the most tremendous commercial discovery of the age, that's not going to make a girl like Andrea so secretive and mysterious and unhappy. You'd see in a minute what I meant if you met her."

"I doubt it," said Hooker, shaking his head over the whole mysterious sex and its bewildering and inexplicable antics and tantrums, "but I do see your argument. If the whole girl angle isn't just your fancy, then my explanation won't do—I can see that."

There was a long silence, only broken at times by the howling of the wind through the passes and down the valley and by an occasional shake or creak of the thin wooden walls. Through his brooding, Malcolm was now aware of the strange remoteness of their situation here, and of the fantastic character of their position. What was he doing here, in a shack in the mountains above the Mohave Desert, a prisoner for the night at least, perhaps for longer, with a young American physicist, whom he had only known about twenty-four hours? And somewhere among these mountains, a prisoner like them or perhaps dead by this time, was a middle-aged adventurer from China and Honolulu, who had arrived on a similar quest to theirs. He remembered now what Edlin had said about their meeting at Barstow, that it could not have been a coincidence.

He looked thoughtfully across at Hooker's long lean face. "It *is* queer, y'know, Hooker," he began slowly, "that the three of us should have met like that, last night. Perhaps Edlin was right. I mean, that it wasn't a coincidence."

"I'd say it was. Careful, Darbyshire, don't start being romantic."

"But I was just thinking then how unscientific it was of you to suppose a thing like this is all pure chance. In the world of elements that you explore, surely you keep on finding that what was once thought to be pure chance isn't really chance at all, that it isn't a mere accident, for instance, when certain elements combine in a certain way to form certain compounds. Why do we assume— as most of us do assume now—that in human affairs it's always chance that rules, that there's nothing in our lives but accidents and coincidences?"

"Because," replied Hooker promptly, "we don't know enough about them to say anything else."

"You mean, we're mixed up in it, not standing well out of it, just trying experiments and comparing results. But I can't help wondering whether it really was chance that I decided, at the last moment almost, to go down to Beaulieu for the tournament."

"Otherwise, you wouldn't have met the beautiful Andrea," Hooker mocked, but good-humouredly. "All right, old son. You can go right on, telling me all about the lovely princess. I've had to go through it before, and I guess I can stand it."

"I wasn't thinking about that part of it, you ass," said Malcolm. "I was thinking that if I hadn't gone there, I shouldn't be here. And you—for all you're so damned high-and-mighty and detached and scientific—are pulled along by the same string, for here you are. So was Edlin, just at the time we were too. How do we know that's mere chance? Suppose we were *brought* here—by some power we don't understand—to do something?"

"What?"

Malcolm looked rather confused, shy. "I know this sounds idiotic," he confessed. "I can't justify it, though I feel it may be true. But we might have been brought here, the three of us, to prevent something damnable happening. Honestly, Hooker, I believe there *is* something damnable behind all this, and Andrea MacMichael knows it, and that's why she's so queer and unhappy. Now then!"

He rose and looked down defiantly at his companion, who answered him with a rather sardonic but not unfriendly grin. Then the grin vanished, as Hooker rose too, and gave Malcolm a slap on the shoulder.

"You may be right, at that," said Hooker, quite serious now. "I'll admit this much. I don't like those two MacMichaels I know— never did like Paul, though I admired him. Something wrong deep down. And it's a pity about the girl. I wish she wasn't one of 'em. And unless one of those guns goes off at a bad moment, I'm going to ask 'em what the hell they think they're doing round here; and I'm going to stick around, old son, until I find out. So I'm with you, whether it's chance or destiny or the ways of God or whatever you want to call it. And now, that pie seems a long way off, so let's have another bite and then get some sleep."

Although he was far less comfortable, Malcolm actually slept better than he had done the night before at the hotel, though when he finally wakened and found it was morning, he seemed to remember having had several long confused dreams. He told Hooker so, when they began to exchange sleepy remarks across the shack, still lying covered on their bunks.

"Don't go in for dreaming much," said Hooker, suddenly sitting up, "but I've just had a most peculiar dream. I wasn't quite out of it, really, when you first spoke. I was in a great tower, a hell of a thing, with all kinds of people I knew drifting round in it, and I had to fetch something from the top and then get out of it—quick!— it was that kind of dream, when you're under some mysterious compulsion—and finally I did get out—and, boy, was I in a sweat!— and then—wallop—the whole tower disappeared in a flash—as if it was a candle flame and somebody had blown it out. I tell you, that was some dream. I was still staring at the place where that tower had been when I woke up."

They were still leisurely exchanging remarks from their bunks when Larrigan looked in, bringing them a most welcome pot of coffee.

"What's the news this morning?" asked Hooker.

"Ain't heard a thing yet, boys, so take it easy."

"I'd like some hot water soon, please," said Malcolm firmly.

"My friend likes to be all spruced up when he's round here," Hooker explained, with a grin.

"You bet! Long as you don't make trouble, I'll do what I can for yer," said Larrigan.

"Just let her run natural, Mr. Larrigan."

"That's it. Well, there's your coffee, boys, to start the day with. Fine morning—an' everything runnin' natural."

"The fact is," said Malcolm later, over their coffee, "I can't help still liking that old scoundrel. I can't believe he's one of their fanatics."

"No, I'd say he's just on the MacMichael pay-roll. Probably he was here when they came."

"And they turned him into a new kind of lodge-keeper. This coffee's good, but—golly!—I feel filthy. Hope he brings some water. Did he bring our shaving kits out of the car?"

"Yep—think so, though I don't care. Might try a beard. I'd go big with a beard at the Weinberger Tech. It'ud look well at conferences too. What about an architect with a beard? Sounds just right to me. No? I believe you think that girl's coming running out to meet you this morning, and you're taking no chances."

"She may not even know we're here."

"May not be there herself, old son. In fact, by this time, she may be happily married to an oil man and be living at Long Beach."

"Oh—rot! Besides, didn't that fellow at Barstow say he'd seen her a few days ago, and she was heading this way?"

"But you don't expect to see her?"

"I don't know—better not talk about it."

It must have been about an hour later when Larrigan returned, this time bringing with him a pitcher of hot water and a bucket of cold. "You'd better be right smart with these, boys," he told them. "Let's see, you're Hooker, aren't you?"

"Yes. Anybody want me?"

"Shore! Mr. MacMichael just rung through. He wants you along there. He's sending a car up for you, in about half an hour. So better get spruced up, if you're that way inclined."

"What about me?" asked Malcolm, feeling clean out of it.

"You'll stay right here. Nothin' said about you, except by Maw, who says you're too good-lookin' though can't say I noticed it myself." And Pa Larrigan went off chuckling, though that did not prevent him from turning the key on them again.

They washed, shaved, brushed themselves. Hooker was eagerly awaiting his visit to the MacMichaels, was indeed quite excited by the prospect, but was good-natured enough to try and console Malcolm, who was obviously cast-down. Hooker assured him that he would attempt to have him released as soon as possible. He would also try to tell the girl, if he should see her, that Malcolm was there. And, for the time being, nothing more could be done. But when Larrigan returned to take Hooker away, Malcolm, left to himself and heartily sick of this miserable little hole, was very gloomy. He could see neither the gate nor the road from the little window, which told him nothing but that it was a fine morning and he was not out in it. After he heard the car go, taking Hooker away, he passed a few minutes moodily tidying up the place. After that he sat on the edge of his bunk and tried in vain to recapture the fine determinations, the sense of high destiny, of the night before; but now he was just a gloomy young man, still absurdly in love, who had allowed himself to be locked in a hut miles from anywhere, a chump and not even a free chump.

Then the door gave place to a bright oblong of sunlight, and the next moment, when he looked up, this sunlight framed somebody standing there. This was not old Larrigan again. No—his heart shouted. It was Andrea.

CHAPTER SEVEN

TWICE JIMMY SEES THE WHITE TOWER

As Jimmy Edlin had guessed at once, Charlie Atwood was very drunk. They discovered him in the living-room of the ranch, roaring for the Mexicans and Deeks to come back. He was a reckless-looking, battered fellow in his thirties, and he was not one of your flushed, sloppy, dribbling drunks, but that more dangerous kind which turns white-faced, glittering-eyed, and takes on an air of quiet determined lunacy. Apparently he had been attempting some elaborate balancing feat, which involved half the furniture and ornaments of the living-room and a corps of willing assistants. The result had been disastrous, but the breakages were not so serious as they had appeared to be from outside. A large china bowl and an empty bottle and a glass or two had been broken, and Charlie had cut himself; but that was all. For a moment Charlie stared at them wildly, as if he could not understand how a Mexican family, an old-timer, two dogs and cat had contrived to return in this guise.

"Oh—Charlie!" cried little Mrs. Atwood reproachfully, "you're drunk again."

Being no ordinary drunk, Charlie did not attempt to deny this. "Rosalie, glad to see you. Welcome home," he said, with a sort of desperate seriousness. "And you're quite right. I'm bottled, stewed. In fact, very bottled, very stewed."

"Then you ought to be ashamed of yourself. You know you've promised—over and over again."

"Over and over *and over* again," he said gravely, as if correcting a careless statement. "Given my solemn word, Rosalie."

"Yes, I know you have."

"Not worth a damn." He shook his head mournfully, then looked in a glassy fashion at Jimmy. "No, sir, not worth a damn. How are you?"

Rosalie, after pulling a little warning face at Jimmy, introduced them. "And now you ought to go to bed."

He appeared to think this over. "What do you say?" he asked Jimmy.

"I think I'd call it a day, if I were you," Jimmy replied gravely.

"Call it what day?" asked Charlie earnestly. "What day is it?" They told him, and this too gave him food for thought. "There's a day missing," he announced finally, and looked sternly at them both, as if he thought they had been up to some trick with the calendar. "Clean gone. How long have I been here?"

"I don't know, Charlie. You weren't here when I went away. I can ask Deeks when you came, if you like."

"Deeks? He wouldn't know. He's too old. Deeks—Deeks—old Deeks," he stammered, "why he's older than anybody. God's truth—he's a kind of mummy. If anybody has to be blamed—besides me, of course—for all this, I'd blame Deeks. Too damned ancient." He looked at Jimmy. "Would you like to see me go clean round this room without ever touching the floor?"

"No, Charlie, please, not again."

"Rosalie, allow this gentleman—your friend—to answer. Now would you? I go round the walls, see?"

"I'll tell you, old man," replied Jimmy, who had met these fellows before and knew how to deal with them. "I'd like to see you do that—it's a dandy trick—but to-morrow, to-morrow."

"Why to-morrow?" asked Charlie suspiciously.

"Because I'm tired—I've had a long day—and I'd enjoy it a lot better to-morrow."

"Surely, surely." Charlie nodded approvingly, then turned to his sister-in-law. "A nice fellow. Very nice fellow. Treat him right, Rosalie——"

"Now Charlie, don't be silly," cried Mrs. Atwood, somewhat confused. She was now trying to put the room to rights. "Mr. Edlin's only a friend—a new friend—we have—we have some business to do together."

Charlie, a man of sentiment, ignored this nonsense, and now turned to Jimmy. "You know how to pick 'em. Trust Rosalie. She's a peach. I don't know how to pick 'em. That's been my trouble. Isn't that so, Rosalie?"

"I must say, you haven't been very lucky, Charlie."

"Lucky? Did ever a fellow have such an eye for chromium-plated pieces as I've had? They've taken the very laces out of my shoes before now. All the same—studio extras, hospital nurses—I've had plenty of them because I've been busted so often—and fortune tellers, Gipsy Tea Room bits with ear-rings as big as your fist—and that manicure girl with a cork leg——"

"Now, Charlie, behave yourself," cried Rosalie anxiously, though she could not help adding: "I don't believe she had a cork leg either. You were drunk that time, I do believe."

"Not me. She was drunk. Didn't she stick a fork in it?"

"That's what you say."

"I saw her. Did it just to make me mad. Up to all kinds of tricks—all of 'em. Things you'd never dream of. Look at that one who ate nothing but nuts and oranges, down at Malibu. There was something to look at. Eyes like lamps, and black hair that came down to her knees——"

"Stuffy!" cried Rosalie, in a disgusted tone.

"And she'd slip that fancy robe off—you could never stop her—and there she was, a Venus——"

"That'll do, Charlie, we don't want to hear about these awful women——"

"Just what I'm saying. Crazy as coots or tough as hell, once they started to work on you. I just couldn't pick 'em."

"I must be thinking about supper," Rosalie murmured.

"Did you bring back anything to drink?" asked Charlie, with the finely assumed casual air of a man who had not had a drink for some time and rather fancied one. "That's the point."

"No, I didn't. And I'll bet you've finished up everything here, haven't you?"

"There isn't anything left, Rosalie. You'll have to watch Deeks and that Mexican. I've told you before."

"Deeks! What have you had to eat to-day? Do you want any supper?"

Charlie shook his head, and gave himself the appearance of a disdainful ascetic. "Couldn't face it. All the same, women, even Rosalie, Mr. Whosit. Always want to pack food into you—great lumps of greasy food—soup—stews—hash—ugh!"

"Then you can stay and watch us eat," said Rosalie briskly. Artfully too, because she knew her man and realised that by this time he would do anything but what was suggested to him. "Then we can have a nice long talk."

"That's another thing," said Charlie mournfully, out of his deep despair of the sex. "That nice long talk business. Always want a nice long talk. About what? About nothing. They've said it all and yet they want to go on saying it. No, sir, not for Charlie. I'll go to bed. Yes," he added sternly, looking from one to the other of them, as if defying them to stop him, "to bed." And off he went, there and then, and must have fallen asleep immediately for they saw and heard no more of him that night.

"There isn't a bit of real harm in poor Charlie," Mrs. Atwood explained, an hour or two afterwards, when she had completely restored order, brought back the Mexicans, shown Jimmy his room, and was now setting before him an excellent supper. "He really can't help it. I've done everything I could for him, but there isn't much I can do, beyond keeping him here now and then to build him up a bit. You see, he went into the War when he was only a boy, and became a pilot. Then afterwards there wasn't anything much for him to do—and he was very wild—so he came out here to Hollywood and became a stunt man—you know, he jumped out of airplanes and drove cars just in front of locomotives and rolled over precipices and all that—oh!—you wouldn't believe the things he did for them—and he's had his arms and legs broken I don't know how many times. And, of course, he always spent every cent he made, helped by all those awful women you heard him talk about—and then when the talkies came along, they didn't want so many stunt men—they hardly use any now, Charlie says—and of course he's tried other things—he was with a sort of flying circus one time—but he can't settle to anything, and gets terribly discouraged—poor Charlie!—and so he drinks. He must have excitement, you see. An ordinary life's no good to him at all."

"I can see that," said Jimmy, who now realised that he had been foolish to feel even vaguely jealous of the wild brother-in-law. "But where does this airplane come in?"

"Oh—that! Well, it's a terrible old thing really, and Charlie had it given him years ago by a man he was working with. And Charlie, who's clever with things like that, has kept it—through thick and thin, you might say—because now and then he makes a few dollars out of it, doing stunts with it or taking people up—he's often asked me but I won't go up in the awful old thing—I'm sure it's falling to pieces. Charlie says he's fixed it so that it doesn't take much gasoline—he couldn't afford to run it if it did——and he comes out here in it—and wanders round. Poor Charlie! I hope you didn't mind him, Mr. Edlin?"

"Jimmy," he corrected her.

"All right then—Jimmy? You didn't mind him being like that, did you?"

"Not me. I've seen plenty of 'em. Matter of fact, I rather took to him. And—I've been wondering, Mrs. Atwood—Rosalie, I mean. Most certainly I mean Rosalie."

"Go on."

"You and I will have to do some talking about this Brotherhood business, won't we?"

"Yes, and that reminds me—Jimmy. I want you to tell me all about it, right from the beginning, because I'm still muddled."

"Right! But I was wondering about Charlie. It'll be a bit difficult if we leave him out. On the other hand—well, you know what you said about him yourself—he's wild—and I don't want to say too much at this stage of the thing."

"No. I understand." She thought for several moments, leaving her food untasted, and cupping her chin in her hand. In this cosy domestic setting she seemed to him more delicious and desirable than ever. He had never seen her before without a hat, and now he had a clear view of the grey curls framing the round face, the cheeky little nose, the friendly soft mouth, the clear bright eyes, and making it all reasonably contemporary with his own middle-age and yet delightfully youthful too, and somehow more genuinely youthful than half the young girls you saw about these days. He stared at her appreciatively, in the soft lamplight, and felt he was ready to go on doing it for a good long time. Now she looked up, smiled to see him there, then looked serious.

"I think you ought to tell Charlie. Not just because it might be awkward—and not very nice, anyhow—hiding it all from him, but because I think he might be very useful. About some things—well, you've seen him and heard him—he's no sense at all, but about other things he's really quite smart. And he's knocked about all over the place, here in Southern California, and he might be able to tell you some things you don't know. Yes, please, Jimmy, do tell Charlie."

"I will," said Jimmy, and now he began from the beginning and told her all that had happened to him since he landed and all that he knew about the Brotherhood of the Judgment. He had a grand time doing it, too. She was a perfect audience. Sometimes she looked startled, sometimes angry, and sometimes, of course, she laughed, and then he had to laugh too, though he had not been much amused by the actual events; so although in the main it was such a grim and serious business, they did quite a lot of laughing. After the table had been cleared, and the varnish in his new pipe was frizzling nicely, he brought out the package, and together they stared at it.

"Of course it isn't ours," he remarked. "No getting away from that. I've stolen it."

She dismissed these qualms at once. "Didn't they try to kidnap you? It isn't stealing from people like that, up to any kind of horrible wickedness. And it isn't as if you *wanted* whatever's in there. You—we, because I'm in this now as much as you, Jimmy— we want to see what they're up to. And I know too they're up to something. Didn't I say to you, that very night—and I didn't know you at all, hadn't I a nerve, but I had to say something to somebody and you looked all right—but didn't I say then they were all mad? I saw it in their faces. I hate those sunken eyes, and big noses, and tight mouths. Now let's open it, shall we?" She laughed then at her curiosity, and was as flushed and eager as a child. "Isn't this exciting?"

Whatever was inside that package, the people responsible for sending it had been most elaborately careful to ensure that it would arrive intact. They had done a most thorough job of packing. It took Jimmy and Mrs. Atwood about five minutes to unfasten and clear away all the various inner wrappings and layers of packing. But at last the table was bare of everything but the one important object.

"What is it?" asked Mrs. Atwood, with a touch of disappointment in her voice.

"Looks like some sort of scientific apparatus," said Jimmy, still staring, "but God knows what it's for."

It was some kind of long and fat glass tube with metal attachments of various shapes, all bright and beautifully made, at each end. It made no sense to Jimmy, who did not pretend to have any scientific knowledge.

"But what could those people want with a thing like that?" she demanded, looking at it with some disgust.

"It's my belief," said Jimmy slowly, for he was still thinking hard, "they were taking it up there for the other brother, the one that young scientist mentioned. But they weren't just acting as delivery agents, I'm sure of that. I mean to say, the Brotherhood and Father John and the whole works came into this business. I know that by the way they talked about it. They'd had word this thing was tremendously important, whatever it is."

Involuntarily he glanced across at the window, which was open. They had not troubled to draw the curtains. Outside was the vast impenetrable darkness of night in a remote place. Jimmy frowned at it, then went and drew the curtains.

"Nobody'd come here, you know." She had guessed his thought. "It doesn't lead to anywhere. We're very quiet out here. And we'd hear the dogs if anybody strange was near."

"Yes, it's a good place, from one point of view. And a bad one, from another. If somebody *did* come, they could do what they liked right out here. Is there any chance, do you think, of Kaydick finding I'm out here?"

She thought a moment. "If he went all round Barstow asking if they'd seen you—he could easily describe you, especially as you looked rather a sight—and somebody told him they'd seen us together, then it might be awkward, because of course there *are* people in Barstow who know I live out here. But even then they'd have to take the chance of wasting a lot of time, coming out as far as this."

"It doesn't sound likely, does it?" He was more cheerful now. "Well, we'd better put this object carefully away. Perhaps Charlie might know what it's for. I'll try him to-morrow. How long does he take to recover from one of these blinds of his?"

"He's usually all right by the middle of the next day," she replied.

The next day proved that she had shrewdly guessed Charlie's form. He made no appearance at all during the morning, when Mrs. Atwood interviewed her employees and attended to the ranch and the house, while Jimmy smoked his pipe and explored a bit and pottered about happily in the sunshine. It was early afternoon when Charlie appeared, looking more battered than ever, but fairly spruce, and quite sober.

"Jimmy," he began, holding out his hand. "Jimmy's the name, isn't it? Well, Jimmy, I'm glad to know you. Rosalie's been telling me a few things. You look all right, a good guy. I'm a louse."

"No, Charlie, that's all right. How do you feel now?"

"Like a louse with a big head. Got out here and Rosalie'd gone —say, isn't she swell?—so started feeling sorry for myself, got the willies, and drained the ranch. Sorry, don't seem to have left you a drop."

"I can do without it—for once."

"Fine! I lay off for about three years one time—when I was making good money too as a stunt man—but what the hell! I went and busted myself so many times in so many different places, I just had to relax. Half the pictures you saw, one time, when the leading man had to drop from a plane into the cab of a locomotive because the bridge was down in front and the villain had switched the signals, that was me, but when it was all over and the beautiful blonde was twining her arms round his neck and he was saying, 'Let's begin a new life together, Mary', that was the leading man back on the job again and I was back in hospital and plaster of Paris. And now they don't even want mugs like me, to risk our necks for fifty dollars a time, because all the leading man does now is to sing to her, unless she's too busy singing to him. Let's walk round."

As they walked round, Charlie, whose powers of speech had certainly not been impaired, gave a picturesque sketch of his career, with some incidents, professional or amorous, narrated in full; and Jimmy, amused, was quite content to listen. Towards the end he found himself less and less amused, however, not because Charlie was a bore, for he was not, but because Jimmy could not help feeling sorry for this younger man who was no longer young enough, who had risked his life so often, anonymously and for a poor reward, for the idle entertainment of the crowd, and who now, beneath the superficial appearance of ease and cynicism, was broken, bitter, despairing. He had struggled back to life so many times—and for what? This he more or less admitted himself. Rosalie had said to him several times, "Really, Charlie, I don't know what's to become of you?"

"And she asked something when she asked that," Charlie now confessed. "Though she didn't mean it badly, take it from me. I tried to get out to China—like you, only I was going out as a pilot—but I couldn't make it. The things I haven't made! I ought to have conked out long since—saved a lot of trouble. They put you together again, only to throw you out. I'm about through. You can't see me—after the life I've had—filling your gasoline tank and

wiping your windshield and hoping you'll come again very soon—
even if they'd have me, which they wouldn't, not with a lot of nice
polite college boys to choose from. Or wiping the counter in an
all-night joint and serving hash to truck-drivers. Or calling with
my hat in my hand asking some frozen-faced wife of a drug-store
assistant if she'd like to see me demonstrate the new dish-washing
machine. I couldn't even hold a gun steady enough to make good
as a stick-up man. I don't know why I'm telling you all this, Jimmy,
unless it's the hang-over and because I let Rosalie down last night.
Didn't know she was bringing a friend, of course, though I guess
it would have been all the same if I had have known. All I really
know, most of the time now, is that I'm all washed up. I wouldn't
be sorry to pull one good stunt—a really good one, some use to
somebody too—and then call it curtains."

As he heard this, Jimmy, not usually aware of such things but
somehow feeling more sensitive than usual this afternoon, had a
strange premonition, as if there came suddenly from the blue a
whisper of sudden disaster, sudden glory; and he looked earnestly
at Charlie almost as if to discover some confirmation of this
written on him, there in the sunlight. And for long afterwards he
was to describe this moment of queer revelation, which came as
if a trumpet had suddenly sounded through the quiet little valley.

"What's the matter?" asked Charlie. "Am I talking too much?
Are you wondering whether I always talk too much? You needn't. I
can keep my mouth shut, I've had to sometimes. Rosalie said you'd
something to tell me. I'd like to hear it, Jimmy."

Jimmy was in no mood now to hide anything from his
companion, and once again, as they walked slowly back to the
ranch-house, he told the story of his adventures with the Brotherhood and revealed the maze of vague speculations in which he
was now wandering. What were they after, what were they up to?

Charlie didn't know, of course; indeed, he had never heard of
the Brotherhood. He had heard of the MacMichael family. And
there was something he definitely knew, and was jubilant about it.

"Yes, Jimmy, you're talking to the right man. I've seen that place
of the MacMichaels."

Jimmy stared. "*You* have?"

"I have. It's—wait a minute—" then he pointed a towards the

north-east—"over there, perhaps sixty, eighty, might even be a hundred miles, in more or less a straight line. I don't know how far by road, because I didn't go by road. You see I flew over it, one time. Yes, that's how I came to see it. I was cruising over it, and came right down to have a good look, took Bendy—that's my old plane there, Bendy—as far down as I dare go to have a look."

"Where is it?"

"I'll show you on the map. Lost Lake, of course, but then you said that. But I'm not kidding you, Jimmy. I saw it all right. Quite a place, I'll tell you, all set out towards the top of a little canyon. Trees and some small houses, then a big house—Spanish style, it seemed from the air—and then a tower, a white tower. It's the queerest set-up to be in a place like that, farther away from anywhere than even this is. They must have spent a fortune on it. I wondered what the idea was, at the time. Here, Jimmy, listen—" and he stopped, and halted the other promptly by seizing him by the arm—"now listen, we'll go and have a look at it together. I'll fly you over. My tank's nothing like empty, and Rosalie's got plenty of gas she can spare. Take you any time you like."

This was tempting. "Is this plane of yours—what do you call it?—Bendy?—all right?"

"All right? Of course she isn't all right. She's all wrong. There isn't a disease that planes suffer from that Bendy hasn't had for years—she's a worse crock than I am—she's thousands of years old—she's shaking herself to bits, and one of these days the whole damned engine'll drop out of her, unless the wings go first—but she can fly—I'd take her anywhere, and take anybody in her. Hell!—let's go."

But Jimmy had no intention of going there and then, and even Charlie admitted that the middle of the afternoon—or even late in the afternoon, for they could hardly set out that very moment— was not the best time to start a journey over the mountains. However, Jimmy half-promised to make the trip the next day, if conditions were favourable; and this delighted Charlie, who said he was longing for something to do. On their way back to the ranch-house Charlie decided that the MacMichaels had built their tower over a huge secret gold-mine, which the brethren of the Judgment for some reason he did not trouble to specify were busily and grimly engaged in protecting against discovery. He had not yet seen the strange piece of apparatus, and now Jimmy showed it to him. Charlie spent a long time examining it from every possible angle, and finally declared that it must be some kind of instrument used in testing the gold they were bringing up, which he obviously imagined to be in the form of great shining nuggets. In short, Charlie knew nothing whatever about the large glass tube, and under a severe double cross-examination from both Jimmy and his sister-in-law had in the end to admit as much. But he stuck to his secret gold-mine theory, and half-succeeded in convincing Rosalie, who was more than ready to welcome any glittering marvels of this kind.

It was when, after much talk, they had settled down to play rummy, between supper and bedtime, that Charlie again mentioned the idea of flying Jimmy over Lost Lake. Rosalie was at once alarmed.

"Don't go, Jimmy," she cried. "I told you what that awful old plane of his is like. It's terrible, all falling to bits. Don't go."

"Poor old Bendy's all right."

"Poor old Bendy!" cried Mrs. Atwood scornfully.

"Well, she brings me here quite safely, doesn't she, and takes me back again? And that's a whole lot farther than just flipping over to Lost Lake. Don't take any notice of her, Jimmy. This is your great chance to have a peep at 'em. Don't miss it."

Jimmy looked apologetically across at his hostess. "I think I ought to take the chance, y'know, Rosalie. It might give me some idea of what they're up to there, and we agreed we ought to know."

"I knew you'd say that," she told him, without a smile; then to Charlie: "Oh!—you are annoying, Charlie. Sometimes I could—I could slap you—yes, slap you hard, you and your ridiculous Bendy!" She left the table, throwing her cards down, marched away, then turned accusingly on both of them: "I suppose it doesn't matter you both going away and leaving me here alone, does it? What am I going to do if those awful men come? You've never thought about that, have you?"

"They won't come here," said Charlie, dismissing them airily. "Why should they?"

"They might. And Jimmy knows they might."

Jimmy was silent. She had a nice little temper of her own too, this nice little woman, but then, why shouldn't she have? Also, he couldn't help feeling flattered by her concern. He didn't believe she really minded being left there alone. She was only trying to make them put off the trip.

"If they find out that thing's here and that Jimmy's here," she continued, reversing their reasons in her haste and annoyance, "they'd be up here in no time. And then what am I to do?"

"The fact is," said Charlie, with some penetration but a complete want of tact, "you're only finding excuses, so we won't go. And not to prevent *me* going either, because I've been coming and going in poor old Bendy for years and you haven't objected. Jimmy, she thinks I'm going to smash you up among those mountains, and she's all against it."

"Anybody would be against it," she retorted, very pink now, "and I've never said anything about you flying because you're used to it and you're crazy anyhow—and if you're going on making idiotic remarks—I'm going to bed."

"It's far too early," said Charlie.

"Not after the way you upset me last night——"

"Why, you said this morning, when I begged pardon——"

"It doesn't matter what I said this morning," the unscrupulous female retorted sharply, and then, suddenly catching Jimmy's eye, she had to laugh. "But I'm cross with you both," she announced, as she sat down again.

And somehow the life had gone out of the game. Jimmy caught himself several times wishing Charlie were not there, and once or twice he fancied that Mrs. Atwood, who was now very severe upon Charlie if he tried to evade the more stringent rules of the game, felt the same thing too. They went to bed early.

The next morning was fine again, and good for flying, Charlie declared at once, on making a rather late appearance. Now Rosalie did not press her objections again. She quietly accepted the fact that they were going, and as they would not be back until some time in the afternoon, she gave them some sandwiches to eat in the air. She seemed to Jimmy oddly subdued, almost sad, and while Charlie was putting some more gasoline into his Bendy, Jimmy took her to one side and asked what was the matter.

"I don't know," she answered, looking troubled. "I didn't want to say anything. You'd think me silly, going on again, after last night. But this is different. And I wouldn't have said anything if you hadn't asked me. But I feel—oh!—I dunno—queer and rather sad inside. Not like me either, but I must be honest and tell you what I feel. But I'll be all right, don't worry. And just see that Charlie doesn't do anything silly."

He looked at her solemnly, then took her hand and held it a moment, and astonished her by saying: "I wonder if you're fond of pictures."

"Pictures?"

"Yes, pictures—paintings—my paintings I'm really thinking about."

"Why, do you paint pictures, Jimmy?"

He nodded solemnly. "My great hobby, painting pictures. And I'll tell you something. Nobody thinks I'm any good at it—but me."

"Oh—what a shame!" She sounded honestly indignant. A good start, but she hadn't seen any of the pictures yet.

"I'd like you to see one or two."

"I'd like to, Jimmy."

"Yes, but this is specially important."

"What do you mean?"

"Can't tell you now, Rosalie." But he pressed her hand and looked for a moment as if he was about to kiss her, and Rosalie was deciding like lightning that he could if he wanted to. But he didn't, only gave her another solemn searching look, over which she speculated for many an hour before they talked again.

"Now look after yourselves, you two," cried Rosalie, as she drew back from the plane, and Jimmy climbed into the open cockpit beside Charlie.

"Careful where you put your foot, Jimmy," said Charlie. And Jimmy saw that he would have to be very careful indeed. There was a horribly improvised, boys' magazine, canvas and lath look about this airplane. It had looked a very dubious vehicle even from the outside, but on a closer view, from the inside, it set Jimmy quaking.

"And what in the name of Pete," he asked himself anxiously,

"have I let myself in for this time?" He had only once been in a small plane before, and even that had looked a miracle of safety compared with this dilapidated little old monster. It was difficult to feel any confidence in Bendy. And then there was Charlie. He might be a most experienced and brilliant pilot, but the fact remained that he was also a reckless devil who confessed that he was getting tired of this life. Curtains indeed!

"Charlie," he roared, for now the engine was being warmed up and the propeller whirring, "just remember that if you're tired of life, I'm not. Take it easy, boy."

"You leave it to me," replied Charlie, now in high delight. "Look out. I'm letting her go."

A last wave to Rosalie, standing there, an anxious little figure, and they were off into the blue. The ranch went huddling down into a few tiny roofs; the whole valley contracted into a narrow greenish slit; and now they were over the mountains, and bumping about horribly, so that Jimmy felt terrified. Charlie yelled that it was always bumpy over these mountains, and Jimmy wished he had thought of that before he agreed to come along. Every time Bendy dropped, she seemed to creak and groan and flap and shiver as if her last moment had arrived, and it was small consolation to Jimmy that Charlie did not appear to mind at all but continued in the highest spirits. Give him the air, he cried; and Jimmy felt ready to make him a present of the entire element.

They were still climbing, though not steadily, for Bendy still kept bumping and suddenly dropping. "Ride her, cowboy——" roared Charlie, handling the controls, which had a home-made look about them, with a dash and abandon that failed to bring confidence to his passenger. Now they might have been flying over the dead face of the moon. They were above desolate mountains, and ringed round with desert. Jimmy could see innumerable wrinkles and folds below, as if some old brownish fur rug had been hastily kicked into position down there, and not a sign of man. Any green places there might have been there were lost to view. No water gleamed. Where the rocks ended, the sand began. Nothing stirred, except an occasional vulture or buzzard. Far off, on their left hand, to the north, were higher mountains, shining remote peaks. But it was the grim desolation below that caught and held Jimmy's imag-

ination, for it was as if a world had died there. Beneath the first
fear, the fear of an immediate disaster, a sudden drop that Bendy
would not shiveringly come out of, a crash on one of those pinna-
cles of rock, he discovered now a deeper and darker terror, born
of this ancient desolation, this dead face of a landscape, and not
to be put into words and reasoned with, a terror that came in full
sunlight and yet seemed to belong to midnight and bad dreams.

No nonsense of this kind about Charlie, who seemed to prefer
rocketing about in mid-air to a sensible existence on the ground.
He was in great form. He began to play with Bendy as if she were
a kind of monstrous flying kitten; they had the jolliest romps
together up there above the rocky spears and bludgeons of those
mountain tops; and as he cavorted with her he shouted and sang.
Jimmy hoped the madman was really making for their destina-
tion, but doubted it. He had an unpleasant notion that they were
just playing about in blue space. He had just opened his mouth to
say so, at the top of his voice, when Bendy's nose went down and
the whole earth suddenly tilted. So Jimmy decided to reserve his
energies in order to cope with these startling phenomena. That
tilting earth, now, those mountain peaks all askew. Charlie seemed
to want to have a closer look at them; but Jimmy closed his eyes.

"No," roared Charlie, "that's not right. Try again."

This time they went very high, and Charlie stopped playing the
fool—if he had been playing the fool, for Jimmy was never quite
sure—and now looked about him soberly, carefully. Finally, he gave
an exclamation, pointed Bendy's nose down again, and descended
in a vast skimming curve. Jimmy noticed they were losing speed,
and beginning to spiral down.

"That's it," shouted Charlie. "I'll take her nearer—but—not
easy—get very near."

Sheer curiosity now conquered all Jimmy's mixed fears. He
looked and saw a steep and narrow valley, almost like a gorge,
and nearly at the head of it was a cluster of roofs among trees.
Bendy went nearer, and now he saw the white tower, which was
just behind the main house. A road ran the length of the valley,
and another went back, through a little pass, almost as sharp as
a cutting, in the mountain wall behind. Now Charlie was circling
round steadily; but though Jimmy stared hard all the time, he did

not learn very much more. The buildings had white walls and red roofs, of curly Spanish tiles; all, that is, except the tower itself, which appeared to have an open platform instead of a roof. A line of pylons approached the buildings from the rear, running not far from the road that went out at the back. Apart from the main house and the tower, there must have been ten or twelve smaller structures. It was a most impressive-looking establishment, and there was obviously room in it for all three MacMichaels and a small crowd of friends or employees. Clearly, they might be up to anything in a place like this, but there was nothing to throw any light on what they actually were doing.

Charlie shouted something about trying to get nearer, and suddenly roared down, bringing out several people from the main house and one man out on to the tower platform; but Jimmy could not discover anything more of any importance. He appeared to have seen all there was to be seen from the air. He yelled this in Charlie's ear, and Charlie nodded, and sent Bendy careering up again, leaving the valley behind. Jimmy could not help feeling a trifle disappointed. He could not imagine what he had hoped to see; but what he had seen had really told him nothing. They were no wiser than when they had left this morning. He did not even understand how the place was reached by road. In fact, he understood exactly nothing.

The return journey, however, was much pleasanter. Jimmy was now fairly familiar with most of Bendy's playful antics, and could believe that each repetition of them did not mean the beginning of the end. They ate their sandwiches too, which made him feel more at home in this rickety machine. The desolation below was no longer so startling and terrifying; it began to take on the appearance of a vast relief map; and Jimmy tried to take an intelligent interest in its topography. Reluctant to leave the air, Charlie took a wide sweep round, and Jimmy was able to observe the Mohave Desert curving away like a yellowish sea. At last a faint thread below, dropped among the black or glistening rocks, was declared by Charlie to be the very road along which Rosalie had brought Jimmy from Barstow. They could follow it, Charlie said, straight back to the ranch; and Jimmy was all for doing this. So Charlie brought them down several hundred feet, remarking casually at the same time that it was a risky thing to do, and they went swooping and roaring above the road.

Farther along there was a moving blur of dust. Jimmy looked at it anxiously. "Isn't that a car going to the ranch?" he shouted.

"Must be," said Charlie, and swooped down to get a better look. As they came nearer, the car arrived at a point where another track, going to lose itself in the hills, left the road to the ranch, and now it stopped, and two men climbed out presumably to decide the way and after a moment they were joined by two others. Jimmy could plainly see the four of them pointing and gesticulating, and then he saw them look up.

"Can we get closer?" he yelled to Charlie.

Charlie swung the indignant Bendy, who tilted and creaked and strained horribly at being wrenched from her former course, round in a circle, and then, returning towards the men, sent her roaring down, sharply, sickeningly. But Charlie seemed to know exactly how to handle his machine, for he brought her down in such a way that although they were bumping along at a great speed and it was not easy to look down over the side, Jimmy was able to catch a reasonably good glimpse of those men. One, taller than the others, wore no hat. Yes, it was Brother Kaydick again.

"All okay?" asked Charlie.

"No," shouted Jimmy. "Get back to the ranch."

Charlie shot them up and swung them out again, and as they turned Jimmy saw that the car was moving again, and had taken the right turning, straight to the ranch.

"Four of 'em," he shouted to Charlie.

"They're travelling too," said Charlie. "Doesn't look it from here, but they're going hell for leather."

Bendy might be old and battered but she was still more than a match for any car, though Charlie could not let her full out and had to be careful because, he explained, there were some particularly nasty air pockets above the little patch of mountainous rock between them and the ranch. As it was, they bumped horribly, but now Jimmy did not care, so long as they got back to the ranch in time. Once it looked as if they would never return at all, for Bendy behaved very badly and Charlie cursed and sweated at the controls. And the landing was not easy, for there was not much room to spare and Charlie shouted that the wind, which curled sharply, almost spun itself, in that narrow little valley, was unusually bad. But at last they did land.

Charlie had been so occupied handling the machine that Jimmy had felt it impossible to discuss anything with him. Now he had to talk fast.

"There's only one thing to do, Charlie," he cried urgently. "Get Rosalie out of it."

"This won't take three, y'know——"

"I know. But I'll stay——"

"Hell, I don't like that, Jimmy," Charlie began protesting. "Let's fight it out with 'em."

"We can't—only two of us—and with Rosalie here—and four of them, ready to use guns. Honestly, it's the only thing, Charlie. Now keep her running, and be ready to take off. I'll fetch Rosalie."

As he turned and ran forward, he saw her come out of the ranch-house and wave. He ran as hard as he could go, but once he had left the flattened ground where Charlie landed and took off, it was soft going and he was a heavy man, so that it took time to cover the two or three hundred yards and when he arrived near the house, yelling as he came, he was hot, breathless and nearly exhausted.

"What's the matter?" she was saying.

"Kaydick—and three other men—coming along in a car. Be here any minute. Only thing to do—you go off in the plane with Charlie."

"Why, Jimmy, certainly not."

"I tell you, Rosalie, it's the only thing we can do. You'll have to believe me. And we haven't a second to lose."

"But are you sure? I mean, that it's those men?"

"I distinctly saw them. Come on." And he grabbed her by the arm and began hurrying her away from the house. At first she was taken by surprise, but after a moment she tried to free herself.

"I don't want to go. You're the one who ought to go. It's you they're after."

"They'll think now we're all in it together," he replied, still pulling her along. "Look! There they are."

His own startled tone and the actual sight of the car racing up the road combined together to make her afraid now. She offered no more resistance, but hurried along, with his hand at her elbow. Charlie must have seen or heard the car too, for now he had his engine running again and had turned the plane round. He was leaning forward to help Rosalie in. Now she was hesitating again.

"It's all right," said Jimmy gasping, "quite safe."

"I wasn't thinking of that," she flashed at him, reproachfully. "I was thinking of you."

"I'm all right," said Jimmy, who felt anything but all right. He could hardly get his breath, and there were fifty knives in his side— to say nothing of Kaydick and the others bearing down on them. But he made a great effort and fairly lifted Rosalie into the plane.

"Jimmy," Charlie shouted, "you're a great guy. I'll take her to the coast. Here," and he flung out a folded scrap of paper, "that's my phone number, if you want me and Bendy in a hurry. Or shall I tell the police?"

"Not yet, Charlie, give me a day or two. Goodbye, Rosalie," and he staggered back out of the way. She was saying something, but he could not catch a word. There was just time, however, to notice that she seemed to be crying a bit.

As Bendy shot forward, Jimmy saw that the big car had stopped, and now the men came hurrying towards them. But they were too late. Bendy was off, tilting badly, protesting against it all, but nobly taking to the air again. Jimmy just gave himself time to make sure she was up, and then, with the knives at work inside him and his heart nearly bursting out of his body, he made for the ranch-house again, as fast as he could go. And as he went, he cursed himself for a thrice-damned fool. While he was persuading Rosalie to go, he could have easily rushed inside, taken out that piece of apparatus that Kaydick thought was so important, and put it in the plane. Now it was hopeless, but with some vague idea of reaching the house before they did, he staggered on, almost blindly, with the sweat streaming down his broad puckered face.

He arrived at the doorway only to find himself confronted by the bleached young man he had knocked out in the hut at Baker. And once more that young man was pointing a gun at him, and this time he looked as if he were only too anxious to use it. There he had to stay, sobbing for breath, until the others came up. No sign of Deeks or the Mexicans, but Jimmy felt they would be useless in such a crisis.

"You stole a package, friend," said Brother Kaydick sternly. "What have you done with it? No, before you begin to lie or evade the question, I will tell you this. We are not ordinary men going about our ordinary business. We do not work for gain. We have been set apart from other men because we have been given a little insight into the mysterious ways of our Lord. We are his faithful servants. In a little while all things known to you will come to an end. Therefore it is nothing to us if we should have to make an end of you now, or if, to make you speak, we should be compelled to give you a foretaste of what you will soon suffer in Hell. Nor would it seem hateful to us to destroy everything here, leaving not a stone standing, because it would only be going the way of all worldly things. Friend, you have heard me combat your lies with lies of my own invention. But now you hear the solemn truth. Where is the thing you stole from us?"

Jimmy had not led an easy and sheltered life; in many rough places he had been compelled to listen to many rough speeches; but he could not recall one that had impressed him as this of Kaydick's did now. The man might be living in some mad world of his own, lit by the gleams of hell-fire; but he was terribly in earnest and was not making idle threats. Jimmy knew that so far as that piece of apparatus was concerned, the game was up. These cool madmen were desperate. He was glad Rosalie was out of it.

"I opened it," he told Kaydick, "and all that there was inside is in there."

They took him into the living-room with them and he showed them the large fat tube with the curious metal fittings.

"Is that all there was?" demanded Kaydick sternly.

"Yes. Nothing else at all."

"Where are its wrappings?"

Jimmy was not sure but thought they might have been dumped into the shed at the back. Fortunately, one of the men found them there, all but some of the straw and stuff; and this seemed to convince Kaydick that Jimmy was telling the truth. They made another secure package of the apparatus, while one of them began to make a second secure package out of poor Jimmy, who had both his hands and feet tied. They sat him at the back of the car, between two of them; and then after Kaydick, who took charge of the apparatus, had made Jimmy swear again that they had all that was in the package he had taken, they drove off, without carrying out their threat to destroy the ranch-house, much to Jimmy's relief.

They drove quickly over the rutted and rocky tracks, and Jimmy, so trussed up that he could not adjust himself to all the bumping, had a horrible time of it. Nor was it long before the thin rope began to cut into his wrists and ankles. Where they were going, he did not know, and it was difficult to see out from where he was at the back; but he had an idea, not very carefully considered because his misery was too absorbing, that they went back along the road to Barstow and then turned off, up a steep side-track, to avoid the town and the main roads. The pain was becoming unendurable, and Jimmy implored them to untie him. For a weary long time they ignored his outcry, but then, just as he was about to faint, Kaydick gave the order that he should be loosed. In the vast relief of this freedom, and in spite of his chafed and aching wrists and ankles, Jimmy, leaning back and vaguely seeing the sunset glow all round them, began to nod and droop, and finally in his utter weariness fell fast asleep.

It was dark when they shook and roused him, though there were lights coming from somewhere. He crawled out shakily into the delicious cool air of early night, saw deep indigo hills against the stars, and high in front many lighted windows; and he knew without being told that they had brought him to the very place at which he had stared from the plane about six hours before; for this could only be the secret headquarters of the Brotherhood, the home of the MacMichaels. Yes, dimly rising there, ghostly beneath the stars, was the white tower.

CHAPTER EIGHT

ANDREA REVEALS THE SECRET

Yes, it was Andrea. Malcolm rose and went slowly towards her. She was wearing a black sombrero, a coloured shirt, trousers and boots, as if for riding. She stepped back, staring, and he came slowly out, and they looked at one another, standing there in the sunlight. Her face was heavily shadowed under the broad brim, but he fancied it went suddenly white, and she certainly put up a hand, as if to stop her heart pounding. And it seemed quite a long time before they spoke.

"I didn't know until this morning," she said, speaking with some difficulty, "and even then I couldn't believe it was you." She waited a moment. "Oh!—why did you come here?"

"I came to see you again."

"Yes—but why, why?"

"You see," he explained carefully, "I managed to get that job—of seeing our client out in Hollywood—I think I told you about that—and then I felt I had to find out where you were and to try and see you again. As a matter of fact, that's why I came to America at all. To see you again, and if possible to talk to you and to try and find out what's the matter."

"Why should there be anything the matter?"

He seemed to know a lot of reasons now, but this was not the moment to bring them out. He hesitated a moment, and lost the chance of replying.

"I didn't ask you to come here." And she gave him a sombre reproachful look, out of eyes that now he saw he had not remembered properly at all.

"No," he replied, trying to keep a careful level tone, "you didn't. In fact, you discouraged me from ever finding out anything more about you. In spite of that telegram."

"I shouldn't have sent that," she said quickly. "That was silly. I was sorry afterwards."

He waited a moment, still looking at her. "Probably you're not interested now, but I might as well tell you that since that telegram, or since that night at Beaulieu, I don't think I've spent three waking hours together without remembering you, thinking about you."

She swung away, and stared—or appeared to stare—down into the empty valley.

"That's why I came," he went on, not pleading, not giving his tone any more warmth. "I've probably made a fool of myself, but that can't be helped."

She did not reply to this, did not even turn to look at him for a moment or two, then said frowningly: "I still don't understand. I—tore up—in such a hurry. You were with some other man, weren't you, that my uncle wanted to see?"

He explained, briefly, about Hooker, and pointed out, to bring her back to where they really left off, that Hooker had nothing to do with them. "We happened to meet at Barstow, that's all," he concluded.

"You needn't have gone on thinking about me," she said, with a very feminine lightning dive into the very heart of the real topic. "Need you?"

"No, and I tried not to. After all," he added, so grandly that he suddenly realised he was simply being pompous, "I don't particularly want to spend all my time thinking about mysterious young women from California."

"Oh—young *women*?"

"Well," stiffly, "one young woman then."

She regarded him calmly. "You're very silly, and very British, and somehow rather sweet, when you're like that," she announced, to his astonishment. "I remember you like that—before."

"You haven't been thinking about me too—by any chance—have you?"

She nodded. "Once or twice." She had a dimple in her cheek. Why had he never remembered that? Had he never seen her smile before? Was she going to be quite different, here among her deserts and mountains?

But no sooner had he asked himself these questions than her face clouded again; all the fun died out of it; and she was the strange sombre girl he remembered so well.

"I ought," she said very slowly, "to tell you to go now—this very minute——" She stopped.

"I ought to point out," he put in lightly, "that last night I was very definitely prevented from going—by Pa and Ma Larrigan, who, I take it, besides being a couple of artful old ruffians, are also under the orders of your father and uncle—or uncles."

"You seem to know a lot about us."

"No, not much. But I've done my best."

She returned to her previous theme and tone. "You ought to go.

I ought to send you away—now. It's so useless."

She was back talking the sad stuff he had heard from her that night at Beaulieu. Everything useless indeed! And here she was, and here he was, and the sun smiling down on them.

It was as if she caught his unspoken thought, "It's a lovely day," she remarked, rather wistfully, as if there might not be many more of them.

"It's a glorious day," he told her enthusiastically. "And I'll tell you another thing. I wouldn't be anywhere else in it but here for the world. I'm sorry to say so, but you still seem to me as puzzling and wrong-headed and mysterious and miserable and idiotic as when you left me in front of the Bristol Hotel that night, but you're here—at last you're here—I'm not just thinking and wondering about you—you're really here, a solid girl——"

"Solid is right," she murmured. "And if I didn't take plenty of exercise, I'd soon be an awful lump."

He looked at her appreciatively. "You're just right," he exclaimed, "that is, so far as your appearance is concerned—these new things, new to me, I mean this Western outfit of yours, suit you too—but as far as behaviour is concerned, with one or two staggering exceptions, you're all wrong."

He smiled at her, but she did not return his smile. She was very serious again now, but rather hesitant, indecisive, as if she couldn't make up her mind what to do or to say next, but knew that something important must be done or said quite quickly.

"If you knew that everything was coming to an end for—for you," she corrected herself hastily, then hesitated a moment, "what would you do?"

Was she serious? Yes, she appeared to be, and was looking at him quite solemnly.

"Would you do—something—you wanted to do?"

"It would be easy for me," said Malcolm, smiling at her. "I'd go wandering round here with you, all day, and try to shake that moodiness out of you. By jingo!—I'd do it too."

And now the surprising girl was suddenly alight, all decision, energy, fire, a magnificent creature. "Can you ride a horse?" she asked quickly.

"Yes, after a fashion."

"Wait, while I telephone," and away she flew down to the Larrigans' house, leaving him staring. What a girl! What a frightening, bewildering, quick-changing, entrancing girl! And if she drove him away, he would never look at another.

He fell into a reverie, and was only startled out of it by the sudden appearance of Ma Larrigan, who looked searchingly at him as he had remembered her doing once or twice the previous evening.

"I wondered last night if it might be the same," she began at once, "and said so to Paw. 'Now why should it be?' he said. 'Well, why shouldn't it?' I said. 'Because it's not likely,' he said. 'Just let everything run natural, Maw, and stop fancyin' things,' he said. But now I said 'Well, Paw, look at the way she's tearin' round now—an' don't tell me it's not the same feller she told me of—she met in France or England or one of them countries last winter—because I know better. Use your eyes, Paw,' I said. 'I used mine last night,' I said. An' that left him no answer—him an' his running natural!"

"Wait a minute, Mrs. Larrigan," said Malcolm. "Do you mean she—Miss MacMichael—said something to you about me? That is, before to-day."

"D'you think she's nothing better to do than talk about a feller like you?" demanded Maw, grimly, as if disgusted by his impudence.

"Well, from what you said——"

"What I said's nothing to do with your conceit an' impudence," cried the unscrupulous Maw. "Gracious sakes! A straight nose an' a bit of wave in your hair, an' you think girls has nothing better to do than be gassing an' gabbing about you. An' specially one like that—not one of your little blonde fly-by-nights—why—she wouldn't look twice at you."

"All right, Mrs. Larrigan," said Malcolm, "you've won. She's a grand girl, though, isn't she? I suppose you know her very well."

But this didn't work. "Yes, young man," she snapped, "very well." And away she stumped.

It was several minutes before Andrea returned, looking defiant now, not defying him but defying the whole scheme of things in order to protect the little happiness she had decided to enjoy; and it gave her a deeply feminine, almost maternal air, as if Malcolm and the bright day and that happiness were her helpless cubs and she herself a dark bristling lioness. She was almost curt with him, giving him orders; but he did not object because he understood vaguely that this very manner admitted him into a closer intimacy than he had known before. He felt he was nearer to her than when she had so suddenly and dramatically kissed him at Beaulieu, for that had only been a recognition of what-might-have-been, a kind of despairing hail-and-farewell in the dark, whereas this was conspiring comradeship under the sun. Her car was waiting outside the Larrigans'; the gate was open; and she took him over the hill and then slowly part of the way down the steep road into Lost Lake, so that he could see a white tower, some tiled roofs, and the yellow-greens of cottonwoods and Joshua trees. Then she turned sharply to the left, crossing by a very rough track at the back of the buildings and continuing until they were at the other side of the head of the valley, where there was no pass or fence or gateway, only this rough track circling round the hill-side and now joining another that came sharply up from the floor of the valley. Here, awaiting them, were two horses and a Mexican in a faded pink shirt and blue jeans.

"Did they give you some lunch for us, Joe?" she asked. And he nodded and pointed to a saddle-bag on one of the horses, her own evidently, for it stirred when it saw her and then nuzzled against her caressing hand. "Take the car down then," she told him. "But wait until we've gone."

Following her example, Malcolm hoisted himself into the unfamiliar deep Western saddle with its great pommel. His own horse was a rough-looking bay, too small by English standards for a man of his height; but Joe, after inspecting him critically, adjusted the stirrups; and Malcolm realised that he was expected to ride with a long stirrup, not gripping the horse but merely balancing himself. Andrea turned to have a look at him too, and seemed satisfied by what she saw. "That's Beany," she told him. "He's a bit lazy, but he'll do. And don't imagine these Western ponies will slip on the rocks or be afraid of the steep slopes—they're not like your English horses, and they're as sure-footed as cats. Thanks, Joe. And if they ask where I've gone, tell 'em you don't know."

At a walking pace, with Andrea leading, they followed the

track, which was stony and twisted, for ever avoiding boulders and menacing clumps of spiky bushes and stunted cactus, until it left the valley altogether. They were now on the other side of Lost Lake, facing a high wilderness of peaks, the nearer ones multi-coloured in their fantastic rock strata and those far away tinted violet or deep amethyst. Again Malcolm noticed how clear and light the air was, as if newly created. Nobody, it seemed, had ever breathed this air before. It had not been thickened and corrupted by man and his melancholy histories. It belonged to the time previous to man's appearance, to some golden age of sun and rock and winds whistling over an empty world. The sky was a silken blue, and there were one or two small clouds in it, their shadows wandering delicately over the faces of rock. The trail, very faint now but obviously familiar to Andrea, dipped into another valley, not as deep as that of Lost Lake but sprinkled with the dusty green of greasewood and creosote bushes and here and there glimmering with mirage water. No sound at all except what their horses made, ringing the rock with their hooves or occasionally grunting. Andrea led the way in silence. But when a pair of mirac-ulous birds, bright-blue when the sun caught them, flashed out of a bush, to Malcolm's astonishment and delight, she turned and said: "Mountain jays. Aren't they marvellous?"

They were. But so was everything else. It was to Malcolm a jour-ney in sunlight through an Arabian Night. Even the very rocks, so curiously veined in crimson and black and bronze, sometimes glittering as if they were crammed with precious stones, often so shaped that they looked like giants and monsters petrified at a stroke, were rocks in a fairy-tale journey to or from some enchanted castle. He told Andrea so, and she turned to nod and smile. Then, the trail being easier towards the end of the dip, she broke into a canter, he followed, and together they thundered nearly half-way up the opposite slope, where the trail became steeper and stony again. They climbed to the top at an easy walk, and then suddenly Andrea, who was then some fifteen yards ahead, turned and seemed to disappear into a tall black face of rock, as if she had cried "Open Sesame!" to it. He came up bewildered, then saw that the trail turned sharply through a cleft so narrow that one of his legs rubbed against the side of it. Night still haunted this tiny narrow gorge; the air was chilly; there was a trickle of water among the shadowy mosses; the horses rumbled and grumbled as they slipped upon the loose stones or were forced to scramble up or climb over barricades of small boulders; and they seemed to wind their way for a long time through this cavernous gloom, lost to the bright world above, like ponderous lizards moving through the rock. Andrea kept calling back, telling him to be careful in this place, to avoid that, and though her voice echoed strangely there, sometimes arriving as a shout, at others creeping along as a dying whisper, he thought he detected in it a gaiety he had never heard before. This, so far away from those crowded tennis courts, the Bristol Hotel, the hard lights strung along the Riviera, it appeared, was her own place: she was now at home. And he followed, not dissatisfied, but still wondering.

At last they came out into the open again, a whole dazzling world of sun and bright air and blue distance, and now what remained of the trail, for Malcolm could see few signs of one, went down at an easy slope on the top of a long ridge, a glistening spur of rock. Nothing moved in the whole wide scene; even the cloud shadows had vanished; and the solitude, the vastness, the silence, were immense, and had a quality of their own, were not accidental and immediate, but seemed to have endured there since the beginning of time. Or it might have been that time was not known to them, had not even begun because it could not make a beginning there, or lay along a dimension of things that either they could not recognise at all or saw in its entirety, with yesterday, to-day, and to-morrow spread out and flattened before them. But Malcolm did not lose himself in this calm and timeless immensity. To his own surprise, he found his outlook narrowing to a single glowing point of passion, his feeling for Andrea. It was as if here, where man was not known, his humanity must assert itself, but all that it could express at this moment was his passionate need for this girl, which claimed him now with astonishing force. As they went ambling down, with Andrea still in front, leading the way it seemed into blue air, he babbled silently but madly at her back, bombarding the space between them with extravagances of desire and devotion that surprised himself. In this state of mind, far removed from the dreamy consideration he had given her during these past six months, he remained until they halted, on a little platform of gravel at the very end of the spur, a look-out point sheltered on two sides by overhanging faces of iron-grey rock.

No sooner had they dismounted than he put his arms about her, feeling her warm and trembling within the thin shirt she wore; and though she cried out against it, he persisted and held her closer, and at last she relaxed within his grasp, and the kisses they exchanged had both passion and tenderness. When at last he released her, she looked at him a moment glowingly, then turned and attended to the horses, handing him the saddle-bag that contained their food. Then, still in silence, she led the way a little farther down to a still smaller sheltered platform, where she had clearly been many times before, put one hand on his shoulder, half leaning against him, and pointed with the other. "That's the beginning of Death Valley," she told him.

The ridges below them, running in fold after fold, were bare as a bone, but in their elaboration of light and shadow and varied rock formation they wore a thousand subtly-graded hues; far away, as before, were shining naked summits of rock and violet- or amethyst-tinted peaks; but now far below, quivering and glimmering, were the first reaches of the deepest valley in the continent, waterless miles crusted with salt, the sullen hot floor of the world. But now it seemed to lie there smiling in beauty. There was life, not death, in its vast quivering distances, its prismatic colours trembling and melting in the windless bright air, its antique stillness and silence. It was—or so it seemed to him, standing there with his love—expectant, part of a planet newly made, warm from the oven of God, eager not for more death but for life, ready to welcome eager, struggling, dreaming, foolish, love-haunted humanity. If no fruit or flowers bloomed, light itself did, light blossomed there, creating a million semi-transparent and dissolving roses, violets, daffodils, between salt-sand and the miraculous sun; yes, light itself, the first great creative principle, the beginning of all things, flowered there triumphantly. Malcolm stared down in happiness and wonder.

"You're glad we came here?" she asked, rather shyly, as they sat down.

He told her he was, thanked her gravely for bringing him, and said how strange and beautiful it was, all of it.

"Yes, and why, why is it so beautiful?" she demanded passionately, surprising him again. "Can't you see? Because it's itself, just the world, just sun and air and rock and sand, and no people to spoil it."

He sat up, regarding her wonderingly. "Do you really think people spoil the world?"

"Of course they do. Look at this, and then think of the places where people are, millions of them, your London, and New York, and Los Angeles, all crowded together, screaming and squabbling and thinking dirty little thoughts and all getting ready to murder each other again. And the more there are of them, the worse it is. Long ago, when there were only a few people—and perhaps thousands of places like this—it was all right. But now there are more and more people and ugliness and dirt and horrible things happening, and there isn't much like this left. That's what I believe," and she looked at him defiantly, "and that's why I don't mind."

"Don't mind what?" he asked, astonished by this sudden outburst.

She shook her head, then brought out their food and a thermos filled with hot coffee. Determined to respect her moods until the right moment arrived, for sooner or later to-day he must ask her point-blank what lay behind all this, he ate in silence, and succeeded in setting aside his bewilderment to enjoy their picnic.

"Have you thought much about that house you're going to build for yourself in the country?" she suddenly demanded.

He was delighted that she had remembered. "Yes, of course. But I didn't think you'd remember."

"I've tried living in it once or twice," she told him, rather like a little girl enjoying a solemn fancy. "Only in the summer, of course. I was back here for the winter." The dimple came and went; an enchanting glimpse.

"You often come here, I imagine, to this place—don't you?"

She nodded. "It's my favourite ride. Especially lately. I've been down here nearly every day lately. By myself, though sometimes a man comes along and talks to me—he's camping somewhere down there"—she pointed vaguely downwards—"he brought his car up Jubilee Pass, then ran it as far up there as it would go and camps near it. He's rather odd, with a beard—I think his name's Mitchell—and he knows a lot about geology and stuff, and tells me all about it. He's a nice man, though I hope he doesn't turn up to-day."

"So do I," said Malcolm fervently.

"You've a funny sort of little crinkle near your right eye. I used to notice it when we were playing in that tournament."

"Good lord! I never thought you noticed my existence then—let alone little crinkles." He was genuinely amazed.

"I noticed everything about you," she said calmly. "Naturally. Why, I wouldn't have come out to dinner—and—everything—if I hadn't already decided I liked you a whole lot. And you've never told me how you found out who I was."

So he told her about his mournful last day at the Bristol, after she'd gone, and how that blessed old gossip Bellowby-Sayers had shed light in his darkness in the dining-car of the Paris train.

"It's hard to believe out here—and up here—that old codgers like Bellowby-Sayers exist, but he did me a marvellously good turn."

"Me too—though I didn't think so this morning, when I heard you were here. I didn't know what to do."

"But you came straight up to see me."

"I know. I couldn't help it. Gosh!—I'm giving myself away," she cried, not at all mysterious now but a very nice ordinary sort of young woman.

They had finished eating, and were putting the remains together.

"Look here, Andrea, I warn you. I'm going to get to the bottom of all this," he told her sternly.

For a moment she looked frightened and said nothing but busied herself finishing the clearing up. Had he spoken too soon, he asked himself anxiously, watching her.

"Malcolm," she began, looking at him with wide dark eyes.

What was coming now? "Yes, Andrea?"

"You can kiss me, if you like."

He did like, and, mystery or no mystery, the next ten minutes went flashing by like those blue birds. At the end of them they were disturbed by the sound of a stone clattering down some-where below, but not very far away.

"Oh phooey!" cried the dark goddess, annoyed. She peeped over, then whispered. "Yes, I thought so. It's the man with a beard—Mr. Mitchell. He must have noticed the horses. But perhaps he won't stay long."

"Well, don't encourage him to," he told her severely.

"I will if I want," she retorted, but then made a little face at him. She was becoming more ordinarily but deliciously human every minute, he decided.

"Hello, young lady, you've got company this time. Well, I'll just smoke a pipe with you," said Mr. Mitchell, arriving somewhat breathless. He wore a wreck of a hat, a tattered tropical coat, and torn trousers, and yet contrived to have an air almost of distinction. His face was darkly tanned, as if he had been out in the open like this for years; he wore a short pointed beard, streaked with grey; his hair was nearly white but he had thick dark eyebrows; and he had a fine twinkling eye, which seemed to Malcolm to rest on Andrea with surprising interest and affection. After being introduced to Malcolm, he proceeded to ask that young man several sharp questions about himself that he ought to have resented from a total stranger, even here in the free-and-easy West, but somehow didn't. He and Andrea appeared to be on the friendliest terms and spent some time chaffing each other, after which Mr. Mitchell, slowly pulling at his pipe, produced some queer specimens of rock from his bulging tattered pocket and explained their significance. After he had been with them about half an hour, Andrea, perhaps in the hope of breaking up the party, said she must take a look at the horses and left the two men together.

"That's a fine girl," Mr. Mitchell remarked, as soon as they were alone. He looked curiously across at Malcolm, as the latter warmly assented.

"Is she happy, d'you think?"

This took Malcolm by surprise. "Well—I don't know really—in a way, I don't know an awful lot about her——" he stammered.

"You looked to me," said Mr. Mitchell coolly, "as if you were deeply interested in each other. All right, you needn't reply. And please don't take offence either. I'm genuinely interested too—as I hope you can see."

"Yes, I can see that. But why?"

"Well—she's a fine girl—and we've had several little chats up here. She listens to my geological yarning, and doesn't tell me I'm an old bore."

Malcolm looked hard at him. "I'm sorry, Mr. Mitchell. But you started this." He lowered his voice. "And that won't do. I mean, there's more in it than that."

"Think so?" He lowered his voice too.

"I'm sure. You might tell me."

The older man took his pipe out of his mouth, slowly blew out a shaft of smoke, stared sombrely into the distance, and said quietly: "She doesn't know this. But I—well, I knew her mother—long ago—before she married MacMichael—when I was about the same age and in the same state of mind, I guess, as you are now. I'm a mining engineer—or was. Been out of the country for years and years." He lowered his voice yet again. "One of the reasons why I came here was—well, just to have a look at this—daughter of—somebody I once knew very well. Now listen, young man, that girl isn't happy—oh!—she's happy to-day sitting up here with you, I could see the difference in a minute—but she isn't happy—and you know it."

"Yes, I do," Malcolm admitted.

The other leaned across and tapped him on the arm. "She'll be back in a moment," he whispered sharply and with great earnestness. "Don't you mind me talking like this. You look a fine fellow and you've got a good profession. If you feel it's the real thing between you, marry her, quick as you can, and take her out of this, right away. There's something wrong here."

"I know there is," said Malcolm. "And I'm here to find out what it is."

They could hear her returning now.

"Good luck to you!" whispered Mitchell, giving him another tap, then scrambling to his feet.

"The horses say they want to go," Andrea announced.

"Did they say they wanted me to go first," said Mitchell smiling, "because I'm just off." He looked hard at Andrea, who seemed slightly confused standing there before him. "Good-bye, young woman. And good luck, young man."

They watched him slowly descend and saw him turn and wave

once, a small friendly figure. "I'm afraid he guessed we didn't want him," said Andrea. "And I like him really, though I don't quite make him out."

"I do," said Malcolm promptly, then went and sat down with his back against the rock.

"I'll bet you don't. What do you mean?"

He beckoned. "If you'll come here and be quiet," he said softly, "I'll tell you."

"Why should I come there? Besides, it's time to go."

"It isn't, and you ought to come here because then you'd make me very happy, and I've brought myself a long, long way, after much misery, and I deserve to be made happy."

"Old Mrs. Larrigan warned me against you," she told him, as she stretched herself by his side and allowed herself to be kept there.

"Old Maw Larrigan was quite right, because she's a kind of old witch, one of the gang of witches and wizards here, and she knows I'm going to break the spell."

"You're cheating now. You see, you don't know anything about Mr. Mitchell—do you?"

"Yes," replied Malcolm softly and slowly, "because he told me while you were away. He comes here to have a look at you and to talk to you and see what sort of a girl you are, because he used to know your mother. I think—in fact, I'm pretty sure—he was once in love with her. Yes, that's what he meant, of course, when he said he'd been in the same state of mind."

"My mother," repeated Andrea, at once astonished and troubled. "She died years ago. I hardly remember her. And Father won't talk about her. I think he was terribly in love with her—and it was all horrible, I believe, the way she died. I heard my uncle, John it was —say something about it once—and it sounded frightening—he can be very frightening."

He felt her tremble, and gathered her closer to him and comforted her, so that nothing more was said for several minutes. Then, as she stayed quiet with her head resting against his arm, she asked: "Is that all he said?"

"No, there was something else."

"What was it?"

"He was very serious, and said that if I felt it was the real thing between us, I must marry you as soon as I could, to take you out of this, right away, because he felt there was something wrong. And I told him that I knew there was something wrong, and that you weren't happy—he'd said that he knew you weren't happy, except to-day. He knew you were different to-day as soon as he saw you, happy for once. You are, aren't you, Andrea?"

"Yes, I think this is the only happy day I've had since I've been grown up," she replied slowly. "Only bits before. There were some bits that week at Beaulieu, especially the last day. But to-day I've been really happy—I meant to be—and now you're spoiling it." She was almost ready to cry.

But he continued doggedly, for he felt that it was now or perhaps never: "I told him I knew there was something wrong, something, I meant, that was making you unhappy, and that I was here to find out what it was."

She struggled away from him, and looked at him reproachfully. "I thought you were here—because—you cared for me—and wanted to be with me."

"It's because I feel like that, I must know what's wrong. I knew from the first, from the very first time we played tennis together, that there was something wrong, that you weren't your real self, that you were wearing a sort of mask, and behind it were very bewildered and unhappy. And then you talked such bitter stuff, about nothing being any good."

"But I believe it, can't you see?" she cried.

"You *can't* believe it," he told her, almost angrily. Then he caught her to him, fiercely. "Is this no good? Is what I feel about you no good? Don't you really care anything about me?"

"You know I do," she flashed at him. "I shouldn't be here if I didn't. Look!" And she kissed him as fiercely as he had pulled her towards him. "Do you think I'd do that to any man? If you want to know, this is the very first time I've behaved like this. And do you think I *wanted* to go off like that at Beaulieu, when you looked so puzzled and miserable, poor darling? I don't care now, I'll admit it. I've been thinking about you too ever since that time. I've talked to you for hours and hours. I've written dozens of long letters to you and torn them up. I've stared at the miserable little map of

England trying to find you. I had the London *Times* sent up from Los Angeles, just to read the tennis reports to see if you'd been playing. And if it could be any use, if this world was all different, I'd go anywhere with you—now. How can you ask if I care about you?"

It took him a moment or two to recover from the effects, very mixed, confusing, rich, of this tremendous outburst, which revealed to him at last, in flashing full-length, the deeply feminine, fiery-hearted girl he had thought must exist behind the mask at Beaulieu. She was almost terrifying, yet still delicious, adorable.

"But then, don't you see, if that's how you can feel, that it's absolutely crazy to talk as if everything were useless, no good, better done with? It doesn't make sense at all, Andrea."

"Yes, it does." And he noticed, with an odd pang of remembrance how she reverted to the very same quick harsh tone she had used in that restaurant at Beaulieu. "We've been happy to-day— yes—and might be happy like this for some time———"

"But of course. And with a place of our own. And children— don't you like children?"

She gave a quick shiver that told him in a flash what he wanted to know, and he guessed at once that here was no girl who would try to avoid motherhood, that there was in her an immense, deep, dark well of maternal feeling he could not even begin to understand. But any sudden gleam of delight and tenderness soon died out of her face, and she looked at him and answered him bleakly.

"Yes, we could be happy for a time. But it wouldn't last. You'd fall out of love with me. Or one of us would be ill—suffer pain— perhaps die young—as my mother must have done. We'd be sorry then it had gone on. We'd wish we'd had this day and no more. Even if there were children, there'd be a war or something, to take them away, or they'd grow up to dislike us. There's always something wrong. People can't live in peace and happily together— there's nothing but misery in the end. You remember what I said about this view, how good it was simply because there were no people to spoil it, as they spoil everything, even for themselves. It isn't that I hate people—I know I'm just one of them myself—they can't help it—we all can't help it apparently—it's just the wrong way we've been made. There's good in us, wanting to love, to look after helpless little things, to enjoy the sun and the mountains and the sea, books and music and painting and fun, but it doesn't get a chance, because there's too much bad in us, and though we may try and try, all that happens is that there's more ugliness and pain and misery and fear and hate. You can't deny it, Malcolm. Look at what's happening all over the world. You know more about that than I do, for I don't care any more; I haven't time to waste even reading any more about their armies and navies and bombing planes and spies and executions; but I know everything's getting worse. Oh!—can't you see how useless and wicked it all is—just more and more pain and misery? And I love you so much."

And she pressed her wet cheek to his, passionately, groped for his hands and squeezed them, staring out at a sunlight she could no longer see. And never in his life before had he felt such a terrible tenderness as he did now, holding her close, and trying in vain to calm his mind, so that he might reason with her, not angrily, but calmly, gently. For now he felt that she was like a child who had been carefully taught a dreadful evil lesson, though there was still about the way she repeated it a certain nobility of her own, for the ugly ways of life, the pain and misery, against which she protested so fiercely, these were not hers, and she had only seen them from afar.

"You are telling me things you have heard over and over again," he said to her quietly. "It isn't really you talking. Deep down I doubt if you believe it."

"I do. Really, I do."

"No. And whether you do or not, it's only half the truth. It's one side, the darker side, of something that has to be two-sided, to have day as well as night. I too hate the way the world's going—that is, in some directions, and I think we hear more about the wrong tracks than we do about the right ones. We're not in Paradise, and have no right to expect to be. People fall out of love, children die, there are bestial wars, and everywhere there's ugliness and pain and misery, just as everywhere the sun goes down and the night comes. But people also fall in love, as we've done, and children grow up happily, wars come to an end or are avoided, bits of ugliness disappear—and it's our job not to whine that these things exist but to help them out of the world, and people have fun together, help each other in need, try to soften pain and drive away misery. Even now, in many ways, people are better than they were, and even if they aren't, we can't just sit about and moan that it's all hopeless. It's good—it's grand and glorious—for us to sit here together—as you admit yourself——"

"Yes, my duck, I do," she replied dreamily.

"But to imagine this is the only good thing in the world, where there are millions and millions of people just like us, all with their own particular bits of happiness, their own hopes and dreams, honestly, Andrea, that's so self-centred and egoistical—why—it's diseased—sheer megalomania—a sort of madness. And don't tell me that's really you. Never! You'd never have thought like that, left to yourself. You're quite different, really. This is just a foul lesson you're repeating. It was taught you by your father—and your two uncles."

"What if it was?"

"Andrea," he said solemnly, "you've got to tell me what those three are doing."

She gave a sharp exclamation, and then was silent, determinedly silent.

"I'll tell you this. I'm not the only one who's worrying about them. There are two other men—one of them is that scientist, Hooker—who have been trying to puzzle out what they're doing."

She shook her head.

"That's not why I'm here," he continued, trying to make her look at him. "You know why I'm here, because I fell in love with you. I don't care tuppence about your father or your uncles— they can do what they like, so long as it doesn't interfere with our happiness. But then it seems it does. They've made you believe life's hopeless. You talk as if this were the only time we could have together. You know something, and you won't tell me what it is."

"I can't," she gasped.

"If it didn't affect us, I wouldn't ask you," he went on, pressing her. "But it does, and you know it does. It makes all this—I mean, everything between us—a mockery, a bit of faked-up happiness snatched-at for a day——"

"No, it doesn't," she protested. "Just the opposite. Something perfect that nothing can spoil."

"That's not true. How can it be perfect when you're thinking one thing and I another, when you have a secret, big enough to cast a shadow over all your life, that you hide from me, when we're not really sharing our thoughts, when I regard to-day as a beginning and you talk of it as an end? That's just playing at love, just pretending for a few hours——"

"No, no, no, Malcolm—please!" And she wept, clinging desperately to him.

He waited, then asked quietly: "What is it, Andrea?"

She looked at him very earnestly, took his hand and put it against her cheek and then kissed it quickly. "This is real, isn't it? I mean, you and me?"

"Yes," he replied, rather sadly, "I know it's real with me. Nothing like it before, and there'll be nothing like it again."

She nodded. "Same here," she said slowly. "And you're right—I see it now—I must tell you. My father—and my two uncles—are planning—something."

"I thought they were. But what?"

"They want to end the world."

He stared at her. She looked perfectly serious, even tragic. "Wait a minute," he stammered in his bewilderment, "you don't mean, literally, they want to end the world?"

"Yes, I do," she replied hastily. "They want to destroy everything, *everything*—and you know why, because I've told you already—they believe life's hopeless, that it's gone all wrong, that it would be better if people were no longer born, just to suffer pain and misery—so they want to end it all. They'd destroy the whole earth, if they could——"

"I dare say," he retorted grimly, "but that's simply ridiculous. And I don't see what they can do."

"They think they can destroy every living thing," she told him gravely, "almost in a flash. I don't understand it, but I know they think they can wipe out all the surface of the world, even if they can't blow up the whole earth. And they've been working at it now for several years."

"But, Andrea, it's—it's—preposterous."

"I knew you'd say that, but you don't know them. And don't forget that Uncle Paul is a great scientist."

He was busy now remembering things that Hooker had said, and was silent for several moments. When he spoke again, they had reversed the roles in which they found themselves that morning, for then he had been uncertain and indecisive, rather helpless, and she, in her deeply feminine, maternal, urge and will towards their happiness, had known her own mind exactly and had been sharply decisive; but now she was uncertain and rather helpless, not knowing what should be done next, whereas he was now sure, curt, commanding, and she found herself compelled to accept his decision without protest.

"We must go back," he announced. "And I'm going there with you."

Never in Malcolm's experience had there been—and he felt there could never be again—a sunset like that they saw on their return to Lost Lake. It was as if the world was already ending. The whole western sky was swept with brooms of fire; the furnace doors of Heaven were flung open; the horizon was one huge conflagration; red-gold castles flamed and melted on burnished peaks of gold; islands of violet and palest green came through a dissolving fiery mist; the clouds to the north were like black guttering torches; the eastern sky had been sprayed with rose and amethyst; the south glowed orange and then paled to an egg-shell green; and at last the west forgot its anger and streamed out into blanched and tender night; and that was the end of the day's vast heroic death. When they were riding down the last slope the earliest stars were twinkling, though faint light from beyond the horizon still caught the pale stretched silk of the sky. The hills huddled down, their edges blunted, and the valley's length was lost in soft shadow. Angry little lights, like angry little questions, spluttered from the grouped buildings and the white tower, but above them the night arched itself, immense and ancient and still at peace. Without another word Andrea and Malcolm rode through the gateway, side by side.

CHAPTER NINE

THE THREE DESTROYERS

The room they had given Hooker was perhaps the most handsome and costly apartment he had ever owned, even if only for a day; although it was only one of many guest rooms, and of no importance in the establishment. The floor was covered with coloured and highly-polished tiles, with two fine Oriental rugs over them; the chairs and the bed were old Spanish, carved in dark wood; the curtains were of the best Italian weaving; there were some valuable pictures on the creamy walls, and a well-stocked scarlet bookcase; everything there was pleasant, instantly gratifying, to the sight or the touch; a sumptuous and staggeringly expensive room. And Hooker had hardly noticed it, though he had already spent some time within its charming walls. Outside, reached through the two long windows, was a broad balcony, running the length of the front of the house and looking down the valley; all tiled and polished and artfully coloured too, with magnificent fat lounging chairs and convenient low tables scattered about on it. Hooker had spent most of his time up there either wandering round and round his room or going out on to the balcony and moving restlessly between his window and the stone balustrade. He was trying to put his thoughts in order, to collect and weigh evidence, to make reasonable deductions from the evidence, to arrive at some conclusion. It just couldn't be done.

Ever since his session with Paul MacMichael that morning, when MacMichael had asked him to run his eye over some calculations, had then made various strange remarks, boastful in tone but mysterious in content, and had promised to show him a certain curious experiment before the day was out, Hooker had been trying to make up his mind about his fellow scientist. It amounted to this. Either MacMichael had resigned and disappeared and finally settled himself in this remote place because he was now so far ahead of his colleagues in physics that he could only work independently, had, in short, outdistanced the rest of them completely. Or MacMichael was going quietly mad, and had taken himself away, or had been removed by his wealthy brother, in order to play at being the greatest physicist on earth, here in this wilderness. Hooker was convinced there was no other adequate explanation of his behaviour and talk. Either he had left them all standing, or he was mad; though it was just possible, if not at all likely, that he had kept his scientific wits and was losing all his others, in short, that he was a great man going mad.

On arriving this morning, Hooker had been taken straight up to Paul MacMichael's study, and had begun to talk by asking his host what the devil he meant by playing him that stupid dirty little trick in England. But MacMichael had instantly pooh-poohed all such talk, and not like a man trying to rid himself of an embarrassing topic but quite genuinely, as if they had no time to waste on such trivialities. Indeed, he said as much. He was in a queer, nervous, jerky, excited state, as if he had been working too much and sleeping too little for months, a condition Hooker had encountered before in men who were at the end of a long piece of close hard research. But he had never seen any fellow scientist in quite the state of mind MacMichael appeared to be in now. One minute he would be biting his nails, muttering doubts, and cursing to himself; and the next minute he would be striding about and shouting, gleefully and boastfully, like a conqueror crazy with victories. The vast and intricate piece of calculation that he had allowed Hooker to run an eye over, the greatest privilege, he declared, that young man had ever enjoyed, was a sound mathematical edifice, as Hooker acknowledged; but the formulas and symbols had no reference, so meant nothing. And Hooker had not liked the way MacMichael had looked when he had told him so. Either the fellow had really something tremendous that he was keeping to himself, or he was going off his head. Then there was the experiment, which Hooker would have the supreme privilege of witnessing. It could not be performed yet; something was missing, some essential piece of apparatus, Hooker gathered; and MacMichael was dancing on red-hot pins and needles, it seemed, because the apparatus had not yet arrived. Several times during the morning he had called his brother John on the house telephone to ask about this missing apparatus. What brother John had to do with it, Hooker could not imagine. Finally, Hooker had been told, rather peremptorily, to go up to his room and wait there until he was wanted. MacMichael had also hinted, rather grimly, that if Hooker had so little genuine scientific curiosity that he would rather not wait, would rather leave the place altogether, he might find it difficult to get away. It was annoying, of course, being talked to and treated in this high-handed fashion, and Hooker had been annoyed, but unless he could prove to himself that MacMichael was simply going mental, he had not the least intention of leaving the place, would not for the world have been anywhere else.

So he had had a late lunch served up in his room, and there he had stayed ever since, trying to make head or tail of the business. He remembered Malcolm Darbyshire's talk of the previous night, and wished now he had not taken it so lightly. This was Mystery Number Two with a vengeance! He had decided then, rather reluctantly, that what these MacMichaels were up to here, with their secrecy and guards and guns and nonsense, must be something that had a commercial value, they were fooling about with gold or with the idea of a new precious metal; but now, after talking to Paul MacMichael again, he could not believe it even possible. The brothers, of course, might have their separate whims or lunacies, so that Paul knew nothing about John's murderous fanatics; but that too was hard to believe. What, then, was the answer? He covered a mile or two round his room and out on to the balcony and back again, trying to find that answer. Even when he stood outside, leaning on the balustrade, watching one of the most gorgeous sunsets he ever remembered seeing, he was still attempting to come to a decision about Paul MacMichael. He remained where he was, even when the light had faded, trying to recall every encounter he had had and everything he had ever been told about MacMichael, and was still in a maze when he heard the clatter of horses below, and looked down. The lights at the front gateway had now been turned on. There was a girl, probably the one Darbyshire had raved about. But who was this, coming along with her, now on foot?

He leaned far over. "Darbyshire, Darbyshire," he called. "I'm up here. Hooker."

"Stay there," the girl called up, softly but clearly. "I'll bring him." There were one or two men down there, but not one of the brothers came out. They were probably conferring together, up in the tower, Hooker decided. He knew they were all here, but so far he had only actually seen Paul.

The girl did not bring Darbyshire along the corridor but along the balcony, and there they all met in front of Hooker's room, and Hooker was briefly introduced by his friend to Andrea MacMichael.

"Andrea," said Malcolm, speaking very quickly, "I think you'd better keep out of this, and the less you know about us the better. So I'll stay here with Hooker. Where will you be?"

She pointed to the end of the balcony. "In that little sitting-room we just came through. I think my father and the others must be in the tower. If you're still up here in two hours' time I'll have some dinner sent up. And—please——" But whatever she was about to implore him to do or not to do, she suddenly changed her mind about saying it, and giving him a rather wan little smile, she nodded, then hurried away.

Malcolm hastily dragged Hooker indoors, and closed the long windows.

"I've found out what it's all about," he began hurriedly, "though it still doesn't make any sense. These people must be quite mad. But Andrea told me what they're planning to do, and obviously she believes it, and they must believe it themselves. Hooker, they're trying to bring the world to an end."

Hooker had to laugh. "Is that all?"

"Oh—I know, it sounds absolutely barmy. But let me tell you what she said." And Malcolm, omitting the more intimate and tender passages, recounted what he and Andrea had said to one another, dwelling carefully on her revelation of the secret. "And whatever you may think about it all," he concluded earnestly, "I do assure you of this, Hooker, that Andrea was dead serious—as a matter of fact it completely explains her; you remember, my Mystery Number One—and she knows what she's talking about, and I believe that whether these three brothers are sane or mad— and I suppose, anyhow, they can't be quite sane—that really is their plan. It can't be done, I suppose."

"What? Bring the world to an end? Of course not," said Hooker easily. "You might manage it if you could steer a comet this way, but I don't imagine they think they can do that. This planet may be a comparatively small and insignificant celestial object, but nevertheless it's a tidy lump of matter."

"But supposing it wasn't a question of destroying the whole earth, but only its surface, where there's life—could that be done?"

"Quite impossible. Of course, if you could make the earth crust shift everywhere, that would make a mighty nice wreck of us. Or if you contrived a simultaneous explosion of interior gases everywhere, like the one at Martinique, we'd soon be done for, but that's not on the cards either. If you brought the moon down, as the cosmic ice people argue—they say an earlier one did come down—we might soon be all tied in knots." Hooker was enjoying himself. It was a pleasant change from his recent bewilderment.

Malcolm still looked and sounded unconvinced. "Didn't they used to say something about splitting an atom?" he ventured.

Hooker laughed again. "You've been reading the back numbers of Sunday supplements, old son. We've been splitting atoms for years. Nothing happens that you'd be interested in. You don't even get a Nobel Prize for it any more. No, you'd have to do a bit more than that, to be dangerous. Now if all the electrons took it into their heads to be positive instead of negative, then there would be an almighty crack-up."

"That couldn't happen, I suppose?"

"Not a chance!"

Malcolm was persistent. "Look here, I'm completely ignorant about this atom and electron stuff. I can't imagine how you even start knowing they're there at all——"

"You can photograph their tracks. I could show you dozens of 'em."

"All right. I'll take your word for it. But isn't it just possible that this uncle of Andrea's, Paul, who's a scientist, and you say yourself a good one, isn't it just possible that he's got on to something you don't know about, something"—he gave a vague wave in the air—"that if you let it loose, full blast, might make a mess of everything?"

Hooker suddenly looked grave. "Quite apart from the sheer damned lunacy of the idea itself," he said slowly, "he'd certainly have to know a lot more than I do about atomic structure and behaviour even to dream of such a thing. Curiously enough, Darbyshire, that's just what I've been wondering all afternoon—whether he's just going quietly off his head or he really has something."

"It might be both, y'know," said Malcolm. "That would explain it."

"I've thought of that, but he'd have to keep pretty sane and have all his wits about him to work out a really long jump like that in atomic physics, though I don't say one part of him couldn't keep fairly steady on the job and the other part be going mad."

"That's what I was thinking. Hooker, you've got to find out about this. Why did he send for you?"

Hooker described his morning with Paul, the calculations and the promised experiment. And all this seemed to Malcolm a confirmation of Andrea's wild statement, and he told his companion so.

"The ironical thing is, of course," he added, "that we haven't the least chance of persuading anybody else—say, the authorities, if we told them—that we're not simply off our heads ourselves. They simply wouldn't believe a word of it."

"Sure thing!" said Hooker. "That fellow Edlin told you that, if you remember, when you asked him why he didn't try the police. Say—his yarn fits in pretty well with this stuff you're telling me. I wonder what became of that fellow. If they brought him up here, they're keeping him pretty close."

Malcolm suddenly shuddered. "Do you suppose—they might have killed him? My God!—we sit here, coolly talking it over—and we don't know what's happening. Hooker, we've got to do something. I know—I swear—there's some kind of evil madness here."

"I believe there is," said Hooker gravely. He waited a moment. "Listen! There's a car."

Looking over the balustrade, they saw five men getting out of the car. One of them, the tallest, was carrying a bundle of some kind. "I wonder if that's what Paul's been waiting for," Hooker whispered, as they continued to stare down. "Hello! Who's that? The fellow who's limping and cursing. Is it Edlin?"

Jimmy Edlin did not see them. He was far too busy now, limping and cursing and groaning. So they were going to take him to Father John, were they? Father John couldn't understand how one of his brethren could have given away secret information to a stranger, couldn't he? And he wanted to ask Jimmy all about it, did he? Well, Jimmy decided, Father John would get a piece of his mind if it was the last thing he ever did. And he went limping into the house, guided by the bleached young man. Kaydick had hurried off at once with that precious piece of apparatus. Told to wait in the entrance hall, Jimmy looked about him, with grudging appreciation. Some money had been thrown around here! A small fortune just in tiles and rugs and curtains and furniture and carved woodwork! Like a little Spanish palace. And a lot of damned fine games they were up to inside it, weren't they? Pretending to be religious, probably pulling gold like mad out of the hill-side, and cheerfully kidnapping and murdering! A nice crowd! And wouldn't he tell the reverend Father so!

Meanwhile, above on the balcony, before they could decide how to get into touch with Edlin, who had plainly gone into the house under escort, Hooker had received a message from Paul Mac-Michael asking him to go to the tower at once. Left alone, Malcolm at once thought of Andrea, only to find her standing farther along the balcony, outside her room. These two were now in that highly-magnetised state which irresistibly draws two persons together, compels their eyes to meet, instantly entangles their hands; and now they came together on the balcony, and Malcolm explained what had happened to Hooker and what had been said before he went. They were still whispering, standing outside the little sitting-room but in the light from its open window, when they were disturbed by a heavy, fierce-looking, oldish man, whom Malcolm guessed at once, before he was hastily introduced, to be Andrea's father, the fabulously rich Henry MacMichael. Like Andrea, he was dark, and in his older, heavier, masculine fashion, he had something of her square build, but otherwise Malcolm in that light could see no resemblance. He was undoubtedly a formidable personage, obviously used to command, but Malcolm made up his mind to stand up to him. But would Andrea stand up to him? This, he felt instantly, would be the final test of her feeling.

It came almost at once, just after Andrea had hurriedly intro-duced them. "Well, Mr. Darbyshire, it's interesting to know that you're one of Andrea's friends, but as I've never given her permission to bring her friends here—as she's never even asked if you might come along—I don't quite understand why we're having the pleasure of your company." He said this in a rough, heavy tone, as formidable as his whole weighty personality.

"I appreciate that, sir," said Malcolm steadily. "And I feel I ought to explain at once. Is that all right, Andrea?" And he looked at her.

"Yes, Malcolm," she replied, very quietly.

"Just a minute," said her father. "We'll go inside for this. Can't see out here."

This made it much harder, of course, and probably he knew that, but as Malcolm followed them both into the little sitting-room, he kept his courage tightly strung.

"Well?" enquired Mr. MacMichael looking curiously at them both, for involuntarily they had drawn closer together and now stood facing him. He did not appear any the less formidable in the light, with his heavy-jowled brooding face, like that of some ancient and incredible despot, some conquering emperor who had watched a thousand enemy cities sacked and burnt and was weary of all such spectacles, weary of everything.

"You see, I'm not just one of Andrea's friends. I'm—well—I'm in love with her."

"You might easily be that," said her father, shrugging his heavy shoulders. "It's of no consequence, but I might point out that at one time it used to be quite a habit of good-looking young Englishmen, with not very bright prospects, to find themselves falling in love with rich young American girls——"

"This is different, Father," Andrea flashed at him. "And I love him too."

"How long's this been going on? All news to me."

"It started when I went down to Beaulieu, you remember," she explained rapidly, not blushing but very bright-eyed, "and Malcolm and I played together—and I knew, of course, it was useless—and I tried to discourage him—and myself too—but that wasn't any good, for either of us, because we've both been thinking the same things all the time, as we discovered to-day. If people possibly could be happy together," she ended wistfully, "we'd be happy, I know."

He shook his head, but the heavy hard look softened a little as he regarded her eager young face. He was clearly very fond of her in his own fashion. "If this had come earlier, it might have been troublesome," he said, it seemed more to himself than to them, "but now—what does it matter—what can it matter? A day or two, to be happy in, young, and thinking that love's everything and lasts for ever. Perhaps this is a good thing in its way, Andrea, if Paul's in such a hurry as he seems to be. I shan't have to wonder what you're doing and thinking, if this young man is what he says he is. Young man," and he looked hard at Malcolm, and his tone was very grim, "if you're not as good as gold to this girl, if she's not happy with you every minute, if she's one complaint against you, d'you know what I'll do? I'll have you shot."

A little white-jacketed brown servant appeared, to say that Mr. Paul wished to speak to Mr. Henry at once in the tower. At the door, Henry MacMichael turned and looked again at Malcolm. "Or I'll shoot you myself. And don't take that as a joke, because it isn't one."

Left to themselves, the lovers looked at one another with pride and joy and moved out again on to the balcony, entirely forgetting for the moment that the world might be coming to an end.

In another part of the house, in a small room, closely-curtained, hung about with mysterious signs and symbols, a room that had nothing to do with the American South-West and the Twentieth Century, Jimmy Edlin stood and glared at the other MacMichael brother, known to his followers as Father John. They were alone; though Jimmy had a shrewd notion that the bleached young man who had brought him along here had only retired to the other side of the door, where he waited, with his gun handy.

John MacMichael was a man about Jimmy's own age, but there all likeness ended. He was dark, and his longish hair, with one lock falling across his right temple, was streaked with grey. His nose was rather long and pointed. His face had the dull flabby look of those who spend too much time indoors. He was a naturally slender and small-boned man now rapidly putting on unhealthy weight. He wore a dark-blue kind of blouse. His hands, Jimmy noticed, were quite unusually small, with the thin pointed little fingers of a woman. But his eyes were more remarkable; they were much lighter than his hair and eyebrows, almost yellow; and they had a strange blind look, as if they were not used to observe the world but only to see with in dreams and visions. They made Jimmy feel as if he were not quite there, solid and real, standing in front of them. On the other hand, a great many other things, invisible to him, were there, he felt, to those eyes.

"Kaydick reports," John was saying, in a small precise voice, "that you had information that could only have been given you by one of our servers, who are bound by a solemn oath of secrecy. It is necessary for me to know which of them it was who broke that oath, so that I may pray and demand his eternal damnation. And do not foolishly imagine we have neither the means nor the will to make you speak. We are the instruments of the divine vengeance."

Determined as he was to put on a brave front and to take this opportunity of telling Father John what he thought of his murderous Brotherhood, Jimmy could not avoid feeling the cold grasp of fear as he heard these words, which reminded him unpleasantly of what Kaydick had said, that afternoon at the ranch. They had the same cool, considered and total inhumanity. Jimmy felt that if ants or spiders could make speeches, they might be in a similar vein to this. No ordinary human contact at all. It was like trying to have a chat somewhere on the moon.

"I can soon settle that," said Jimmy hoarsely. "The information I had—the password about the clock striking, and all that—I didn't get from any of your fellows. It came from my brother."

"And who and where is your brother?" the other enquired softly.

"He's dead," cried Jimmy, more boldly now. "He was found murdered in the back room of a little café down-town in Los Angeles. Yes, and the people who killed him were these big-nosed retired farmers and tight-mouthed warehouse hands that you've roped in and talked out of their senses. And don't tell me that you—a man of your education and position—really believe this old-fashioned Bible-belt dope you've handed out to these poor brainless louts. I went to a meeting, and know what the stuff's like. And it wouldn't go down any longer even in a tent in Arkansas. If you ask me, you're not even an honest fanatic."

John MacMichael smiled, but only with his mouth, not with those yellow blind eyes. "You are wrong. I have an honesty that you have never dreamed of. But the people must be taught according to the reach and grasp of their understanding. That was always the way, and in this our time is no different from other times. What matters is not what the intellect can perceive but in what the soul may believe and rest. As for your brother, he died not because we delight in the shedding of blood, but because the divine spirit has its plan and chooses its instruments and workmen. Across the road by which you came here to-night, some little creature of the desert, perhaps a rat trying to return to its nest, may have scurried, only to be crushed by one of the wheels, set in motion by a plan, a scheme of things, far away from and unknown to the little creature. So your brother died; and so too, very soon, may you, and indeed all of us die in this corrupt body, a little of which dies every moment."

"But God's truth!" cried Jimmy, exasperated by this calm dismissal of downright murder, this lofty disdain of all ordinary human values, "who are you to talk as if you were God's right-hand man, in all His secrets?"

"Who am I?" He smiled again, then his strange eyes seemed to contract and his tone grew sharper. "I am the one who has listened and so has heard, who has looked and seen, who has asked through hours and hours of silence for a command and has at last received it. You have travelled far. I know that, you see, though you are a stranger to me. I have some powers almost lost now in this Western world. So, you have travelled. What would you say if you were describing the distant places you have seen to a man whom you knew had never left his village, and he refused to listen, denied your knowledge, and asked who you were to talk as if you had seen all the earth?"

"That's not the same thing," Jimmy growled, though he found himself oddly impressed. "Not the same thing at all——"

"It is. For I have spent my time travelling too, not along the surface of things, as you have, but penetrating them, moving into another world altogether, that of the enduring spirit. And what I have seen and heard there, what has been taught me, what I have received as a command, these give me the right to talk as if you were a child, which indeed you are——"

"I may be a child according to your twisted way of thinking," cried Jimmy, with some violence, "but I happen to know the difference between right and wrong, and it's my opinion you don't any longer. You've spent so much of your time sitting by yourself in rooms like this, with everything shut out, just imagining things and talking to yourself, that you've got all mixed up, and fancy God's talking to you——"

"Be quiet," the other commanded sharply, not because he did not want to hear any more from Jimmy, though there were distinct signs of that too, but because the house telephone on the table beside him was now ringing. "Yes, Paul," he replied, and then as he listened to what followed his face lit up and the strange yellow eyes seemed to glow.

"And whatever this is," Jimmy thought grimly, "I'll bet it's damned bad news for everybody but this gang of loonies."

"You see, Paul," John was saying, "that is how I told you it would be. I knew." He was triumphant. Then he listened again, frowning a little. "But why such haste?" he enquired, at length. "You are certain? Well, that's your concern. But I will send out the messages to-night, and tell Kaydick to summon all who can make the journey out here. There's one thing more. We've no time now to do as we planned originally, to justify ourselves before the world. Yes, too dangerous now, you may be right. But I still feel compelled towards that justification, and there is at least one man here, with me in this room now, and you have another with you, I think, and we may take these to represent that world. . . . Yes, later, of course. . . ."

Jimmy stared and listened hard, and suddenly found himself in a sweat of anxious bewilderment. It was the triumphant tone and look, and above all the wild visions flaring in those eyes, that frightened him. What in the name of hell-fire was brewing here?

Near the other end of that telephone, where Paul was still talking, Hooker wandered about restlessly, looking dumbfounded. They were in the laboratory, immediately beneath the platform of the tower, and a very fine little lab. it was too, as Hooker had admitted at once. The experiment had just taken place; hence Paul's triumphant and urgent messages to his brothers, and Hooker's bewildered dismay. While Paul was still talking, Hooker examined everything again, feeling a fool, not like a fellow physicist but rather like one of those open-mouthed fellows from the audience

who gape at the trick properties on the stage. Yes, the heavy lump
of granite, which he had handled himself, had gone. The thick
lead screens, the thickest if not the largest he had ever known,
were unbelievably scarred and blasted. A little more force, and
that would have been the end of those screens, perhaps the end
of everything and everybody in the lab. itself. He looked around
as carefully as he could, for he did not trust MacMichael, too
dramatic altogether, too queer, too conceited, to be a completely
trustworthy experimenter; but he was still feeling dazed. Gee—
what an experiment! More like a little volcanic eruption! And what
an eruption, what an earthquake, unless there was some catch in
it he couldn't see, it was going to cause in the world of physics!
Boy—oh boy! But he still couldn't make head or tail of it.

"No deception, Dr. Hooker," cried Paul, now coming across the
lab., "no deception at all, dear doctor, I assure you."

That emphasised "doctor" was just a sneer, of course, and
Hooker wished to heaven he could put his finger on some flaw or
trick that would wipe the sneering smile off MacMichael's dark
face, now alight with triumph.

"I don't get this at all," he grunted.

"Quite a small voltage. Get that?"

"Yes, I know."

"A mere speck of the bombarded element, the tiniest possible.
You saw it?"

"Yep. I saw it all right. But what is it?"

"One that we seemed to have carelessly overlooked, Dr.
Hooker. Of course it has no commercial value, and we live in a
world that cherishes commercial value. But oddly enough, it's also
been overlooked by all you fellows experimenting in transmutations, perhaps because you're all so busy instructing the young
about spectra and isotopes. But of course I've been busy some
time myself on transmutations, and I hardly need tell you that
this is an artificial element, very difficult to produce. It happens,
however, that tunnelling under this tower, deep down, we found
a rich deposit of a certain heavy mineral, also of no commercial
value—what a pleasure it is to say that, Hooker, in this greedy
world!—that was of great assistance to me. I don't feel inclined
at the moment to give you the atomic number of my element—

it's very high, of course, though curiously enough this element is only unstable under certain conditions, but then it can behave very queerly—but let's give it a name, shall we? I wonder if you'd think me egoistical if I called it, just for reference, paulium?"

"All right," grumbled Hooker, who disliked the tone of all this. "Go on."

"And I have another new name for you to learn, if you don't mind, Dr. Hooker, another little coinage of my own. I know you're well acquainted—I remember one or two little discussions we had——"

"So do I, MacMichael," muttered Hooker, angrily.

"Well, what about them?"

"Only that you were just as damned high-hat then as you're being now. Can't you drop it, and talk like an honest-to-God scientist?"

"When I first began to have a few ideas of my own, Hooker— oh, much younger than you are now—I did talk, as you say, like an honest-to-God scientist—talked straight out of my mind and heart, for I think we fellows sometimes have to use our hearts too—and what did I get in return? You ask some of those pompous old frogs still drivelling in their professorial chairs what they tried to do to me. And I'd even changed my name, so that people wouldn't think I was trading on the old man's fame and fortune. I received too many neat slaps on the face, Hooker, so I stopped showing it to them."

"Well, I didn't do it," said Hooker, speaking abruptly. "And I've had to take it—even from you—without getting sour. But let's get back to the subject."

"Willingly. I was talking about my other little new coinage, and I say that I know you're well acquainted with electrons, neutrons, deuterons, photons, but this, I think, will be quite new to you. And you saw it in operation here. Shall we call it a dynatron?"

"That doesn't mean anything to me."

"I know that, Hooker. But it meant something round here— didn't it—a few minutes ago?"

"Alpha particles?"

"No, that won't do, quite. In fact, we'll have to reconsider a good deal of that radioactive theory, in the light of what I've recently discovered. I can't explain the result of five years' intensive research in five minutes, Hooker, but you can take it from me that what I'll call my dynatrons have a very respectable kinetic energy indeed—hence the name. I suspect all the radium compounds are releasing them, but you know how difficult they are to handle, whereas this tiny group of peculiar unstables, of which paulium is easily the best for my purpose, are comparatively easy to handle. Now bombard, even mildly as we did just now, this paulium, and it starts to disintegrate at once, releasing the dynatrons—only a few, of course, if you treat it gently. Even then, as you saw, the fun begins. And if you don't treat it gently, if you're really rough with it——"

"Listen, MacMichael," Hooker broke in, earnestly regarding him, "I've just heard some ridiculous talk here about ending the world. Now quite apart from the sheer God-damned wickedness of the thing, you're not cracked enough to believe you could do it—are you—just because you've discovered one or two things ahead of anybody else?"

"Foolish idea, isn't it?"

"Yes, and you know it is. Handing 'em out that stuff—and you call yourself a scientist!" Hooker made the taunt quite deliberate.

"Why, you young lout, I not only call myself a scientist, but I'm a better scientist than you could prove yourself to be within the next five hundred years, not one of which you're going to live to see."

"World ends to-morrow, I suppose?" Hooker jeered.

"That's exactly what I'm planning, my dear doctor," said Mac-Michael, in a quiet but deadly tone, "and later I'll let you know the exact time."

"Boo! You can't kid me, MacMichael, even if you can play about with your precious paulium, and your dynatrons, which ten to one will turn out to be heavy electrons——"

"I knew they weren't that, nearly two years ago," said Mac-Michael, still quiet but very angry, which was precisely what Hooker intended he should be. "And I'm not fool enough to imagine I can explode this planet, for even you know what its density must be near the centre. But I can peel it like peeling an orange, only faster."

"Talk sense!"

MacMichael's gigantic conceit, amounting to megalomania, responded at once to this further jeer. "Just come this way, Hooker," he said, in the same quiet but very angry tone, and went to the other end of the laboratory and opened a door there. Hooker was not slow to follow him. A short flight of curving metal stairs led down to a small platform, inside the body of the tower. They reached the platform, and MacMichael switched on a light or two. Hooker, peering down, exclaimed in surprise. The few lights that had been turned on were not enough to illuminate clearly the great shaft, but Hooker caught sight of vast metal bulbs and other apparatus that suggested an electrostatic generator of unusual size.

"Yes, there's the generator," said MacMichael complacently, "but of course that's not all. I've combined that with a cyclotron of an entirely new type, and much, much bigger than the ones those boys at Cal. Tech. are playing about with. In fact, you may say that most of the tower itself is a kind of cyclotron. Which ought to make you think a bit, Hooker. And not only that," he continued, motioning his companion back up the stairs, "but as you may have guessed, I'm going to use a very high voltage indeed, something quite prodigious."

"You're on that power line from Boulder Dam, aren't you?" said Hooker bluntly.

"Yes, my brother arranged that for me, and though of course it's been an expensive business, it's going to be worth it. But you're still looking puzzled, though I notice not quite so incredulous as you were a few minutes ago."

"Then I'm not looking what I feel," said Hooker, in the same blunt tone. "I still feel you're cracked. You've got one hell of an apparatus there, I'll grant you that—it makes anything else I've seen look like a toy from a ten-cent store——"

"Oh, the whole thing, I can tell you, is very impressive, and I'm sorry I can't show it to you in detail. But you know the size of this tower—and that'll give you some idea of the scale I'm working on."

"All right. It's a honey. And so what?"

Paul MacMichael put his hands together with a little clap. Oh!—

he was enjoying himself all right! Hooker concluded that probably the real reason why he had been brought up here was that
MacMichael couldn't resist showing off to a fellow physicist. His
brothers, though probably sympathetic, weren't really interested;
and his colossal vanity demanded at least one scientist as a final
audience. And now he clapped his hands together and looked
delighted with himself. Hooker could not imagine what was
coming.

"According to my calculations, Hooker, and I've given the
matter very careful and long consideration—I'm very thorough,
though I may not look it, because I don't happen to be a dull little
professor—when that little instrument you've just had a glimpse
of is set in motion, the structure of the world's surface will not
stand the resulting strain."

"Because you can bombard a pinch or two of your paulium, I
suppose?" said Hooker, still trying to jeer hard.

"Not a pinch or two, my friend. I told you we'd been fortunate
in our situation here. I've been working hard and I've managed to
manufacture—a vulgar word for it, but you know what I mean—
and accumulate far more than a pinch or two, or even a pound
or two, of this most dangerous element. And I've worked out a
very severe treatment for it—it's quietly waiting down there—and
unless my calculations are very faulty, the instantaneous and prodigious flight of dynatrons—I must use my own term, if you don't
mind—will be very disturbing to the structure of the upper levels
of our earth, which was never devised to withstand such a sudden
release of energy, energy gone mad, instantaneously breaking all
decent bounds. What may happen to the earth's core, I neither
know nor care, but for everything outside that—unless, I repeat,
my calculations are all wrong—I think I can promise instant disso-
lution. I've taken science as far as it will go in the life of mankind,
Hooker. You're listening—now, I'm glad to say with that oafish
grin off your face—to the last and greatest of its great scientific
figures."

"I'm listening," said Hooker, rather painfully, "to a madman.
You wouldn't do such a thing."

"I would," and he glanced at his watch, "and in an hour's time,
after we've all had some food, I, along with my two brothers, will

explain why. Yes, we've agreed to justify ourselves. We'd hoped to do it on a much bigger scale, but that won't be possible now. I'll take you down. I must tell you, by the way, that there's no possible chance of your getting away from here to-night, and that we have guards all over the place, who, reasonably enough, as I think you'll agree, wouldn't hesitate if necessary to kill you here and now. After you. No, no, that's not politeness. You go first. And here, you see, waiting for us, is one of our men. You'll find them all over the place, I'm afraid."

Once back in the house, they separated, Paul joining his brothers, and Hooker being taken into a small room just off the entrance hall. Here he found both Malcolm and Jimmy Edlin, and food was brought for the three of them. While they ate, with no great show of appetite, Hooker grimly explained what he had recently seen and heard from Paul. He was still sceptical about the total result, he told them, but admitted that with such vast unknown forces being used deliberately to achieve the maximum of destruction, any horror might happen.

"But—but—hell's bells!——" stammered Jimmy, who had listened open-mouthed, "we can't just sit here and let three madmen blow everybody to smithereens. We must do something—now." And he banged the table.

"Yes, but what?" asked Hooker.

"Oh—jumping Moses!—I dunno—but there must be *something*, and you ought to be the fellow to tell us what—you know about this electron business."

While Hooker meditated, Malcolm remarked: "It seems to me the only possible thing we can do is to bust up the apparatus in some way, so that he has to postpone his attempt, and then meanwhile we'll persuade the authorities——"

"I don't believe much in those authorities," said Jimmy. "While we're trying to persuade them these MacMichaels are dangerous lunatics—and, mind you, from what I've seen and heard of 'em, they'd have us taped from the start, probably jailed before we'd begun our persuading—these three madmen would have time to take California to bits even with a pick and shovel."

"It's not as bad as that," said Hooker, who was all seriousness now, "because I believe I could get some federal people to take my word for it that something was all wrong here. But that would take time. And in order to give ourselves time, the only thing we can do, as Darbyshire says, is to try and wreck his apparatus. We can't cut off the electric power."

"Why not? That's an idea—if it'll stop it."

"It would cramp his style all right," said Hooker, "though of course he's probably storing up the juice right now. But how are we going to do it? We have to get outside first, and even then— those pylons are high and the cables are thick and tough. No, our best chance is to get inside that tower, with an axe or two."

Jimmy sighed. "I wish we'd a few shots of dynamite. I'd show those boys something."

"Whatever we do," said Malcolm, looking rather pale and desperate, "we must do to-night. I believe it's our last chance."

"Brother John—and there's a happy-go-lucky pal, believe me, Brother John—he told me they want to have a little chat with us, a nice cosy little party after dinner and a nice cosy little talk about why and how they're going to blow hell of everything. Great suffering catfish!" Jimmy bellowed. "Can't we do *anything*? I'm getting as nutty as they are, just trying to think about it."

Their presence was now demanded in the music room upstairs. It was, as Jimmy had said, quite a little party, and Malcolm thought as he surveyed it that the world could hardly ever have known a stranger party than this. The setting was nearly as odd as the people. Here they were among the Californian mountains and desert, but they might have been somewhere in Thuringia or Bavaria, for in this music room the MacMichaels had departed from the excellent old Spanish style and had attempted the old German or Austrian, a sort of Gothic with a touch of baroque, and a perfect background for one of Hoffmann's wilder tales. It was a long room with many heavily carved rafters, a great Gothic fireplace, pointed tall windows, some carved wooden screens, and high-backed chairs covered with dark-brown hide. In the wall opposite the fireplace was a wide and richly ornamented alcove, with its floor raised about a foot above the rest of the room, and here there was a fine concert grand piano. Opaque, golden-tinted bulbs in the two wrought-iron chandeliers, together with the red-gold flickering of the great wood fire, gave the place a dim soft light and made it look even more mysteriously Gothic. There ought to have been green-coated foresters in attendance, and a miller's beautiful daughter and a witch or two somewhere in the immediate neighbourhood. Malcolm stared at it all in amazement, and began to feel once more that ordinary reality was vanishing, to make way for fantastic dream stuff.

Andrea was there, thank goodness, to drown him in her great dark glances. Her father was there, coolly smoking a cigar, as if this really were a party. And now Malcolm saw her two uncles for the first time: Paul with his thick eyebrows and dark short beard, a kind of brooding brilliance about him; and the strange John with his falling lock of hair and his queer visionary's eyes. All three brothers were quite different, and it was as if they represented three different qualities of our species, for Henry seemed the embodiment of ruthless power, Paul of searching mind, and John of intuitions and dreams and visions; yet there was also a definite likeness between the three, something dark, twisted, remote, they had in common, like the branches of one sinister tree. And it caught at Malcolm's heart to remember that Andrea too had flowered from this same tree. He stared at her as if to discover where it had flawed her, and it seemed as if she knew what he was thinking and wondering, for suddenly she looked deeply troubled. Meanwhile, as if to give the scene its crowning oddity, John was stormily improvising at the piano. He played well too, though there was his own quality in the music, now despairing in great descending chords, now rising and clashing into some disturbing triumph. Malcolm, busy with his unspoken commerce with Andrea, only half-heard him. Hooker, who like many mathematically-minded fellows was extremely fond of music, listened carefully. Jimmy Edlin stared about him, and moved restlessly and impatiently, and appeared to be on the point of interrupting at any moment.

Then John came down from the piano, and stood near his two brothers. It was he who opened the fantastic proceedings. "You three men," he began, looking at them in his queer blind fashion, "are here because you may be said to represent the world of men we wish to destroy." He spoke in a careful, soft but clear voice that was peculiarly intimidating. "We intended to justify ourselves before the whole world, for we are not criminals——"

This was too much for Jimmy. "Why, you're the biggest crimi-nals who ever lived."

"Keep quiet, you," said Henry MacMichael sharply. "If you don't, you'll be taken outside, where a lot of things might happen to you."

Before John could resume, there came a knock. It was Kaydick, who stood just inside the door.

"All the messages have gone," he reported to John respectfully, "just as you commanded. All the broadcasting systems will now have received them. To the two here in America, I spoke myself over the telephone. The messages were received as you said they would be, in a spirit of mockery. They laughed," added Kaydick bitterly.

"I had already heard, in the depths of my mind, the fools laughing," observed John calmly, while Malcolm and Hooker and Jimmy exchanged quick glances. "You can do no more. You have told all those who have served us faithfully to be present here early in the morning, to receive my final blessing?"

"I have. And you have their prayers to-night, Father. But you have not told us what will be the exact hour and the final signal."

"Wait," said John, and turned to his brothers. They withdrew into the alcove, to talk privately. Kaydick waited with his back to the door, so that the remaining four, who had now risen and were all grouped near the fireplace, were left to themselves.

"If only one of us could get near a telephone," Jimmy groaned softly.

"I could," Andrea whispered, "but what use would it be?"

"I don't know," said Jimmy, whispering too, "but it's the only thing I can think of—and for God's sake, let's try it. Here, when we know the time and the signal business, for the love of Pete make an excuse and slip out, and telephone this fellow here—" he pressed a slip of paper into her hand "—his name's Charlie Atwood and at least he's got a plane and he knows me and knows there's some-thing wrong—and tell him from me what's happening and he's got to try and stop it some way or other——"

"Please, Andrea," said Malcolm urgently, trying to repeat in one deep glance all that he had said to her that afternoon.

She nodded. There was no time for more. They separated as

the three MacMichaels came out of the alcove. Andrea, whom Malcolm was watching anxiously, now leaned back in her chair and he thought he saw her tremble slightly. But now, at least, he knew that the long spell was broken, that she had come out of the evil dream, had turned from death to life; and even though he was terribly anxious, and could believe now that this dreadful lunacy might soon sweep them all away, underneath that anxiety there was a kind of deep solemn joy.

"Ask two of your men to come in here," John said to Kaydick. They must have been waiting on the other side of the door, for now he brought them in at once, and Jimmy recognised them as two of the men who had been with him in the car. And now they were not only armed with revolvers, which protruded from their pockets, but also with short powerful shot-guns. Kaydick stationed one of them near the door, and the other not far from the wall opposite, commanding the group round the fire from another angle. Then he looked enquiringly at his leader.

"At ten o'clock exactly," said John, "and from nine-thirty onwards we three alone will be in the tower. I shall be on the platform, praying, and when all is ready and the hour comes, three times I shall raise my hands. You will station the brethren on the hill-side, where they may watch and pray, but the servers must remain on guard until the very end, and from nine onwards you will station them round the tower. These two will remain here until we have done, and then take these three men away and keep guard over them until the morning. You have done well, Brother Kaydick, and will find your reward in a life more blessed and enduring than this."

"And I hope you burn and freeze in hell!" muttered Jimmy, as his old enemy prepared to depart.

"And now," said John, turning after Kaydick had gone, "you shall hear us. Will you speak first, Henry?"

The sombre heavy figure stirred, then put down the cigar, almost as if he were performing a symbolic act. But Andrea spoke first, rising hurriedly.

"Father," she said faintly, "may I go? I'm sorry—but all this— now when it's really here—I feel——"

"Yes, Andrea my dear," he told her, "off you go."

"Wait," said John, rather sharply for him, turning his queer blind gaze on her. And Malcolm, his own blood stopping, saw her falter and blench. "What is in your heart, Andrea?"

"Oh!—let her go, John," said his brother impatiently, and then waited until she had gone, the man stationed at the door opening it for her carefully. Malcolm breathed again.

"You think we're mad," said Henry heavily, addressing himself chiefly to Malcolm, probably because it was not long since they had talked together. "Well, we're not. And we're only doing what we are doing after many years of careful consideration. But I'll speak for myself. I'm a man of business, of affairs, of action, and a very successful one. I began with many advantages, as you probably know, and I've improved on those advantages. There aren't many things I couldn't buy, even in these times. I can look at life not from the bottom, as a poor failure, but from the top, as a man of wealth and power, not kicked about the world but treated everywhere with respect. I don't know what life's always been like—I don't pretend to have much imagination and I've never been interested in the past—but I say that as it is here and now life's not worth having. It isn't even for me, let alone the millions of poor devils who wonder where the next loaf of bread's coming from, who sweat their guts out just continuing to exist and feel more misery. I've struck many a balance, not only with my own life but with hundreds of other people's, and there's always a debit, way down on the side of anxiety and disappointment and suffering and despair. They talk a lot about love, for instance, but even that only takes away your guard, leaves you wide open, to suffer not only for yourself but for somebody else, as I've seen twice in my own life. Then again, we may be inventive but we can't grow up fast enough to use our inventions properly. I've gone over all the systems of production and distribution they try or clamour for, and not one of them represents a single grain in contentment and happiness. There's always a snag that was forgotten. There's always the iron law of diminishing returns. And the more there are of us in the world, the more anxiety and discontent and fear and misery. I pondered for years how to make the best use of my money. Patching people up in hospitals so that they'll have more pain later on? Colleges where they teach the poor young devils to want more than they can ever get? Then I saw that the best thing

I could do was to help put an end to it all. Why, there are millions and millions of poor fools now wondering when next they'll have a good night's sleep. Now, with luck, we'll all sleep well to-morrow night." And he gave a final shrug of his heavy shoulders.

Malcolm stared at him, his mind racing but finding no exact words to utter in protest. "It's all so twisted," he stammered, "so wrong—deep down—not mad in the ordinary way perhaps—but—but——"

John made a gesture to stop him. "Paul?"

Paul's brooding clever face kindled with a sort of bright malice. He gave a mocking glance towards Hooker, to whom he chiefly addressed his curt sentences. "I'm a scientist. A good one, an honest one, who's given his life to pure knowledge. I agree with with what my brother has just told you. And of course I have my own angle too. I have a chance of performing the last and greatest experiment known to science. To release the earth's energy to destroy—I hope in a flash—the life on it. That life, in my opinion, was an accident. Here I differ from my brother John, who has mystical views, though fortunately we agree about what will happen, must happen, to-morrow morning. I'm a materialist. What we call life is matter so arranged that it begins to think and feel. And it has no business thinking and feeling. That's the mistake. Man or any being like him is doomed from the start. He can't possibly find a lasting place for himself in this universe, which if it has plans are not plans for us. Out of the eternal dance and changing patterns of light and energy," he cried, now suddenly losing his curt cold tone and speaking with passion, "mind has somehow emerged, to acquire knowledge but also to understand its own noble despair. But it can still use that knowledge for one last triumphant stroke, one supreme act of defiance, refusing to wait until its long dreary death sentence is carried out, but deliberately timing its exit, with all humanity like a Socrates, grandly destroying itself, leaving the mindless cosmos to its own damned dance of blind energies, for ever."

Malcolm looked across at Hooker and was startled to see that long, lean, sceptical face suddenly wet with tears. Hooker did not speak but continued to look down, twisting his big capable hands, as if there had been something in this speech of Paul's—and something, too, that deeply stirred him—to which he could find no reply.

It was Jimmy, snorting and nearly purple with suppressed indignation, who found his voice. "Do you know what's the matter with you?" he cried, glaring from one to the other of the three dark brothers. "Partly conceit—thinking you know it all, not admitting most of it's above your head. And partly staying in too much, shut in a room, thinking round and round. One sharp morning's walk, with the sun shining, would teach you more than you all know put together, if you'd only keep your mind open and let it."

They ignored this outburst. Paul had clearly finished. John had still to begin, and apparently was in no hurry. But he made a sign, and Jimmy stopped fuming and grunting.

The strange John turned on them his unseeing amber gaze, shook his head so that the dark lock trembled on his brow, then smiled. "My brother does not realise," he said quietly, "that he himself is but an instrument in the grasp of a power whose very existence he will not acknowledge. This universe of his, with its blind dance of atoms, is only an illusion, and all our life here is only a kind of dream, a shadow play. And we can only be bewildered by the dream and the shadows if we imagine that science can give us any true vision of reality. The measurements of a house are not the house. The reading of a man's weight on the scales does not give you the man himself. My brother looks out through his eyes and is in despair because nowhere can he see himself, forgetting that he is behind and not in front of his own eyes. But I have looked the other way—and found God. Now all that is happening in the world has long been foretold, for God warns us. But all the nations, one by one, are turning away, some to this idol, some to that, and like the men who built Babel or mocked at Noah, in an age not unlike ours, they imagine they can live without God. But God is not mocked. And this world is now the great Babylon that was foretold in the *Book of Revelation*. I have prayed that no more souls of men may be born into this later and greater captivity, and as it has happened many times before, by the divine irony, my prayer has been granted and the instrument of destruction and salvation placed in my hand by the errors of my own brothers. They go to seek death. I go to seek life. And we cannot be judged by such as you, who are not proud enough to prefer death, nor wise enough to know where life is. Mad?" concluded John MacMichael calmly. "Are we, who know what it is we seek and take the shortest road to it, to be called mad, by such as you, who, like all true madmen, live in an uneasy dream of life, pursued by and pursuing shadows? I tell you——"

"You'll tell me nothing else, you crack-pot," bellowed Jimmy, jumping up and looking as if he were about to charge like a maddened bull. John stared calmly, but the two men, at a quick signal from Henry, came forward, pointing their guns. And even the furious Jimmy shrank from being immediately minced by those point-blank wide charges of heavy shot.

"Well, we've had our say," said Henry wearily. "Take 'em away—shove 'em in one of those little end rooms—and don't leave 'em until morning."

Without another word from the three brothers, they were roughly hustled away, Jimmy still shouting protests, Malcolm and Hooker subdued and silent. As they were marched along the corridor, Malcolm had no sight of Andrea, and felt it dangerous to enquire for her. Hooker looked grim, and said nothing. Jimmy muttered curses on the three they had just left. The room they were given for the night had no window in it, was not properly furnished, and appeared to have been used as a minor store-room. In the sharp light of its two naked white bulbs, they looked at one another, seeing in each other's eyes a growing and deepening despair, a dread of the coming hours of night, and a mounting vision of mountain peaks and desert valleys, of fields and gardens, rivers and forests, little towns and great cities, the whole familiar, stupid, beloved world, already passing away; and now they did not want to talk, but sat down, huddled together, on packing-cases and piled sacks, listening to their hearts, like time-pieces of rich curdling blood, registering and ticking away the moments of Doomsday Eve.

CHAPTER TEN

DOOMSDAY—AND AFTERWARDS

It was a morning no different from the others they had lately enjoyed. Some great shadow, left over from a night of terrible dreams, ought to have darkened the earth; but there was no sign of it. Lost Lake valley lay smiling under the bright sun and the flawless azure of the sky; the peaks to the west, in full light, glistened and shone, as if crammed with precious stones and metals, and those to the east, not yet facing the sun, wore plum-coloured shadows; the yellow cottonwoods trembled a little in the breeze; the distant sandy floor of the valley began to shimmer; and the air was very sweet and fresh, still with a cool sparkle in it. A few horses and cattle stirred in the narrow pastures. Now and then a red cardinal or a blue jay turned and flashed above the mesquite or among the grim tangle of the Joshua trees. Very high, one of the great birds of prey lazily circled in the blue. The place looked almost the same as usual. There had been no invasion from a terrified world; no cars filled with armed men tearing up the valley, or warplanes roaring down from the distant sky. If the messages to the broadcasting offices, last night, had been handed to the people in charge, then those people had merely laughed too, and may perhaps have passed on the information to the editors of the news service as a possible humorous little fill-up if they should happen to be short of items. If any outsiders had heard the news of the attempt and had taken it seriously, then they had not heard it in time to set out and arrive before the hour; which is not surprising, because Lost Lake was very remote and hard to reach. But a number of the brethren from the Coast, driving all night, were already here, and were now congregated on the hill-side, in small prayerful groups, like others of their kind before them, in this Western land, who had gone out to the hills to await the end of the world. The only difference was, as Hooker grimly pointed out to his two companions, as they too were taken up the hill-side, that whereas those other groups of fanatical believers had vainly looked for some miraculous piece of destruction, these were privileged to be on the spot where it was to be attempted. The two men who had been told to watch Malcolm and his two friends had been most formidably zealous, and even now, within half an hour of the appointed time, were still watching them, ready with their shot-guns. There had not been the smallest chance of escape, and there was none now. Other men, perhaps twenty altogether, and also armed, were posted round the tower.

Malcolm, staring out of heavy hot eyes, saw all three brothers now make their appearance on the platform of the tower; and though it was several hundred yards away, he could see that John was wearing some kind of white robe. But where was Andrea? He had not seen her, nor had any word from her, since she left the music room last night. Jimmy thought she must have been caught telephoning, and have been locked up somewhere. Malcolm kept staring from the tower to the house itself in the hope of catching a glimpse of her. He now saw that Henry and Paul MacMichael were no longer on the tower platform, and Hooker muttered that they must have gone below, where the great electrical apparatus was housed. John, a clear figure in his white robe, was now standing higher than he had been before, and had obviously mounted a small rostrum. To Malcolm's astonishment, John's voice suddenly came booming out to them all on the hillside: he must be using a powerful loud-speaker.

"Kneel down," the voice commanded, "and give me your thoughts, for now I will pray."

"I suppose we might as well too," muttered Hooker.

"I've done plenty of praying already," said Jimmy gloomily, "but a bit more won't do me any harm."

All the brethren, some of them already in a highly emotional state, were kneeling, and even the guards contrived a sort of compromise between prayer and sentry-duty, by dropping down on one knee and perhaps, as Malcolm could not help thinking, by keeping only one eye open. Malcolm had reached that queer exhausted condition in which a person wants either to cry or to giggle and is not certain which and swings idiotically between the two. But now he knelt, like the others, and tried to shut his ears and mind to what John was crying through the loud-speaker and to pray to another and less vengeful God than the one John invoked, not some jealous monster invented by fierce old Israelites who had spent their lives fighting for waterholes in the burning desert, a terrible patriarch of the tribe, but a patient and tolerant and infinitely wise Creator who had known ages ago that man was foolish and slow to learn and yet somehow gradually struggled upwards out of the slime. As he struggled to present before his mind some image of this Creator, he felt a sudden rush of somebody near him and then a warm sweet neighbouring presence. It was Andrea.

"I did telephone last night," she whispered, "but it was awfully difficult and the man seemed all confused—it was hard to make him understand but I think he did in the end. But what can he do? Oh—Malcolm—what can *we* do? And I know now how wrong it's all been." She was terribly contrite.

"Never mind," he whispered, very close to her ear, and putting an arm round her as she knelt beside him. "Are you frightened, Andrea?"

"Not much now, darling. It's no longer quite real. You're real—and being out here in the sun with you—that's real. But not the rest of it."

The high priest of the strange ceremony now temporarily concluded his prayer and left them to their meditations, which gave Malcolm a chance to tell Jimmy what had happened.

"He's probably spent the last twelve hours trying to persuade people he's not off his nut," Jimmy said mournfully. "And he's not the right sort of chap to do it. But who would be, with this packet to handle? Even me—and I've seen it coming and been damnably mixed up in it for days—even me—why, I feel half barmy. It just can't be true. He'll give the signal, and we'll all wake up somewhere else."

"If half of what he told me last night is true," said Hooker grimly, "and unless somebody manages to interfere, there'll be no waking up, unless it's in heaven."

There were strange cries, half mournful, half ecstatic, from the believers, for the most part simply-dressed middle-aged men and women, huddled together on the hill-side. They terrified Andrea, and rather frightened Malcolm, who began to talk to her quickly;

while Jimmy and Hooker, whom the cries simply seemed to anger, glared across at the emotional brethren.

"Blast 'em!" muttered Jimmy. "What a crowd to go popping off with! And why didn't I remember to send a message by Charlie to Rosalie Atwood?"

"Who's she, Mr. Edlin?" asked Andrea, who could still be curious even on this doomsday morning. "I think that man said something about her."

"She and I sort of started in this business together," said Jimmy, "and if everybody's going to go off—bang!—then I wish to God she was here with me, to see the finish of it together. There's one grand little woman."

"Were you going to marry her?"

"That I don't know," he replied gloomily, "and the less we talk about such things, it seems to me, the better. What's the use? And I thought Charlie might have tried something, but they've probably got him in a strait-jacket and a padded cell by now." But anxiously he searched the sky and listened for some sign of poor old Bendy.

"It's ten minutes of ten," said Hooker, with a fine appearance of being casual.

John MacMichael was now asking them to pray with him again, for the last time, and all his followers, with shouts and groans, threw themselves down and put up their clasped worn hands. And the sun still smiled out of a bright empty sky. Andrea gripped and squeezed Malcolm's hand until it hurt. Hooker kept glancing from the tower to his watch. Jimmy stared angrily into the western blue.

"Let us now depart in peace, O Lord, from this earth, which is altogether lost in evil, to a new earth," cried the voice from the tower, "an earth that is another Eden straight from Thy hand, where Thy word shall be fulfilled and we shall hunger no more, neither thirst any more—"

"Listen!" cried Jimmy. And as they listened, they heard, cutting through the voice from the tower, the sound of an approaching plane. They looked over the western hills, from which the sound came, and after a few moments the plane itself could be seen making straight towards them at a high speed. Before the prayer was ended, it had come roaring above the valley.

"It's Bendy," shouted Jimmy, dancing with impatience. "Charlie,

Charlie," he yelled ineffectually into the blue, waving like a mad-man, "for Pete's sake, do something, boy."

But what could he do? John MacMichael, having finished his prayer, gave a glance upwards, and then obviously decided to ignore the intruder, though they saw him descend for a moment from his rostrum, presumably to call down to his brothers below. But a moment later, he stood erect again, and now raising his voice because the plane was circling lower and making more noise, he asked them all to ignore it, for it could do nothing, and implored them to receive his blessing, for the hour had arrived. The old biplane went circling round in an unsteady bewildered fashion. Jimmy, joined now by Hooker, was waving and shouting to it, and the two armed men near them were uneasily dividing their time between their charges, whom they were telling to be quiet, and the approaching plane, which they threatened, as ineffectually as Jimmy had shouted to it, with their guns.

The white figure on the tower now raised its two arms high, and at the sight of this first solemn warning, the watching crowd of brethren, most of them still huddled together on their knees, gave a shout.

The plane turned and rose, as if its pilot had decided there was nothing he could do and was leaving them. Though Jimmy and Malcolm and Hooker could not have said what they had expected the plane to do, yet now their hearts sank, and Jimmy groaned. "Oh—Charlie—boy—for God's sake!"

Again, the white figure raised its arms, very high this time, and the responding cries of the crowd were louder still. And now Malcolm felt terribly afraid, and held Andrea, who had suddenly turned to bury her face in his shoulder, closely to him, praying hard that the vast coming terror would not find him a gibbering coward. But the plane was not leaving them. It had swung round sharply, with a sudden accelerated roar, then shot down like a great projectile. Poor Charlie Atwood, who had performed so many stunts for meagre pay, now did his last stunt for nothing, and perhaps saved the world. He sent old Bendy crashing into the nearest pylon, and as she splintered and flamed and he went to his death, the cables parted. No more electric current was flowing into the tower.

Nevertheless, high above the burning wreckage, the white figure still raised its arms, to give the final signal, ignoring the confusion and tumult below. As the arms fell, it seemed as if the earth gave a shiver and then split. All the watchers were struck down as if by a hammer; the air went screaming above their prone bodies; the ground shuddered and heaved; and only half-conscious now they heard dimly the earthquake thunder of toppling buildings. It was indeed like the end of the world.

Yet after some moments, which in their fear, darkness and utter confusion could not be reckoned by ordinary time, one after another they lifted their aching heads, and looked to see what had happened. The tower had vanished; the house itself was a ruin; and the steep slope behind was scarred and fissured, and still seemed to smoke like a battlefield. A vast cloud of dust was rising slowly above the head of the valley. The sky was thick and yellowed. The air was hard to breathe. From the ruins there came licking out a long thin tongue of flame, and now in the terrible silence, like that which accompanies a deeply ironic stare, they could hear the crackling of fire. Malcolm and Andrea, Jimmy and Hooker were shaken but not hurt, and those near them were also uninjured. But some of the brethren farther along the hill-side were still lying motionless. One of the guards who had been posted near the tower could be seen crawling out of the wreckage, bleeding as he came. Most of the others must have been killed. The three MacMichaels were buried in the ruins of their tower.

It was then as if the world, which had laughed at the warning messages of last night, was suddenly awakened by the final crash itself, or the air that had fled screaming from the valley had carried with it rumours of catastrophe; for within a few hours planes filled with reporters, cameramen, radio and news-film commentators, and the like, were roaring and circling over the ruins, and a host of cars were burning up the road through Barstow, which, distant though it was from the actual scene, now became the headquarters of the news campaign and found itself suddenly famous. All that night the world stared at its headlines and listened to its broadcast news in wonder and amazement that were clouded with a new apprehension. A shudder of fear went through the world as the commentators drew vivid and largely imaginary pictures of the narrow escape everybody had just had, as distinguished scientists, dragged out of their quiet sane laboratories into the shrieking arena of big news, talked of this possibility and that, as photographs of the ruined remote valley went jerkily across a myriad screens to the accompaniment of shouting voices explaining what had been attempted and what might have happened, those voices so hot with human interest and yet so strangely inhuman in their amplified mechanical excitement. Now that they were dead and gone, the three MacMichaels suddenly cast shadows that stretched menacingly across whole continents and oceans. Their sinister biographies blackened innumerable columns. Dubious dots to represent their faces were flashed from capital to capital. Thus as the arch-criminals of our time they towered while what remained of them on earth still lay beneath their own ruined tower. To end the world? Millions of men and women stared at each other, their minds busy with crashing images of destruction. For an hour or two, clouded by this vision of what might have been, the producers forgot to blame the distributors; the distributors forgave both producers and consumers; the industrialists and the bankers were at one; the farmers stopped disliking the city folks; men who worked in black coats made common cause with men who worked in overalls; associations of employers made light of trade unions; capitalist and proletarian remembered they shared the same earth; fascists and communists were haunted by the same vision; patriotic imperialists failed to salute the battle-torn flags waving above their dividends; foreign secretaries neglected the drafted agreements that nobody intended to keep; the Class Struggle, the Red Menace, the Fascist Will, the Jewish Problem, the German Destiny, the Failure of the New Deal, the Decadence of Britain, Japan Over Asia, Italy Over Africa, Stalin Over Russia, the Threat to Democracy, the Decay of Liberalism, the Collapse of Civilisation, all were temporarily forgotten, and for a few hours all the currents of prejudice and mistrust and fear and hate were dammed behind one gigantic barrier, and though men were haunted by this one dark vision of doomsday, somehow for that little time they breathed a larger and nobler air. It did not last long, of course, for we live in an eventful age and have a magnificent news service, and so, flinging a few last curses at the memory of those three insane brothers who had tried to destroy the world at one stroke, men returned to their ordinary tasks and thoughts, perhaps to destroy the world piece by piece.

Towards the end of that insane day, which remained just as much a nightmare after the world had discovered that it was not to be destroyed, Andrea and the three friends fled from the scene, now rapidly turning into a vast garbage heap, lit by photographers' flash-lights and raked through by newspapermen. Jimmy had had a bright idea, and packing them into Andrea's big car had driven them himself, as fast as he could go along those narrow roads, with much blinding traffic coming into the valley, and with many stops when he was not sure of the way, over the dark mountains and under the wide glitter of stars, to another remote valley and a little ranch there, where there was as yet no hostess to look after them. But they were all still dazed and completely exhausted, and throwing themselves down anywhere they slept and slept, and were hardly fully awake when Mrs. Atwood herself arrived in the middle of the following afternoon. And there they stayed, telling their stories over and over again, under the peaceful sky, for many days. Mrs. Atwood, brighter of eye than ever, for even when she remembered Charlie her eyes were bright with tears, tears of pride as well as of sorrow, fussed happily over them; and she made Andrea, who was very quiet, very mournful, these days, and even kept aloof from the bewildered and unhappy Malcolm, answer all her questions so that the girl could not imprison herself in her silent brooding. Malcolm wandered and wondered about the place, a pale, gloomy, handsome young man, asking himself what was to be done next. Jimmy and Hooker, sent off with smiles and nods by their hostess, mysteriously departed for Barstow and, after that, Los Angeles, to return with Jimmy's baggage and a host of things for the others at the ranch.

Now it was the morning after they had returned, a late October morning as clean as a new pin, with the little valley all smiling and the hills all sparkling and winking. Jimmy had gone off by himself in good time, taking his easel and paint-box to a little rocky knoll overlooking the ranch-house. Hooker was sprawling in a deck-chair under one of the cottonwoods, but not idling, for he never lifted his eyes from the notebook he held, a notebook that never seemed out of his hand now. Malcolm, becoming desperate, had implored Andrea to come into the sunshine with him and she had at last agreed, after being strongly urged to go by Mrs. Atwood, who pretended that she could do nothing round the place if they did not leave her to herself in the mornings, but seemed to be more full of smiles and nods and little secrets than ever. Indeed, when the lovers had gone, she appeared to be curiously expectant and kept looking down the road through the valley. She also took quite a number of peeps at Mr. Edlin, who could just be seen painting away on the hillside, but when she looked in that direction, the smiles and nods vanished, and it appeared then as if she were a bit anxious and a bit disappointed and in general rather puzzled by and dissatisfied with the distant Jimmy, so entirely absorbed up there.

Slowly leaving the ranch-house, Andrea and Malcolm came up to Hooker under his tree. "What are you doing, Hooker?" asked Malcolm, with that touch of irritation often felt by the idle for the deeply employed.

Before Hooker, coming out of his mathematical dream, could reply, Andrea looked hard at the notebook he was holding. "I'm nearly sure my uncle used to have that kind."

Hooker blinked a little. "This was one of your uncle's," he mumbled, looking rather shamefaced. "I don't know if you remember, but I managed to get into his room, before the fire had reached that end of the house, and though it was all smashed up, I salvaged three of these notebooks of his. I'm trying to follow his tracks, because he only dropped a hint or two, that last night, about what he'd discovered. I haven't got fairly on to them yet, but these notes of his look dandy to me. I never liked him, I guess, but—say, he was a great physicist."

"I've never asked before—though I suppose you're tired of talking about it," said Andrea, hesitantly, "but why was it such a failure then?"

"He was too rushed. That's the first thing. I don't know why," said Hooker thoughtfully, "though I might when I've been through these notebooks, but he felt compelled to hurry it on too quickly at the end. And then, of course, the current being cut off at the last moment, that upset all his calculations. What really happened, down there under the tower and way back under the hill itself, we don't know yet, but as soon as they've cleaned it up a bit on the surface, I'm going to have a look. I've been given permission, officially, to investigate. That's why I'm concentrating on these note-books. And—boy—are we going to have something to tell 'em! Here, sorry, Andrea—I oughtn't to be talking this way, I guess, to you," he concluded lamely.

Andrea shook her head and smiled rather wanly, then she and Malcolm walked slowly across the tiny pasture towards the hill away from the road and opposite to that on which Jimmy was sitting. They never noticed the little cloud of dust moving up the valley, and if they heard the distant sound of a car they were not sufficiently curious about it to turn round. But now they had begun to talk, after several despairing appeals from Malcolm, and as they talked they wandered towards a tiny clump of box-elder trees, which were almost as white and dusty above as the strange and ghostly desert holly scattered on the valley floor, but which seemed still to cast a friendly green shade. And here in this shade, they stopped.

"You see," said Andrea miserably, "I can't marry you. I couldn't marry anybody, but anyhow that's not the point because I don't want to. No, it's not because of all the horrible talk and fuss, which I suppose may go on for ages. That's bad enough, but it isn't that."

"Well, what is it then?" cried Malcolm. "Is it—something about me?"

"No, you idiot, how could it be?" she cried, smiling for once. "It's me. Don't you see, my—those three—as everybody says now—must have been mad. All three. And I believe my grandfather was queer too——"

"That doesn't matter," said Malcolm sturdily. "You're not off your head, except at this minute, and you're never going to be."

"You can't tell. And everybody knows that it runs in families. Even if I'm all right, suppose we—I—had some children—and they began to be queer?"

"You know," said Malcolm gently, following his own thought and not hers, perhaps deliberately, "those three—I suppose they were mad in a way—they'd got shut up inside themselves——"

"As you tell me I do," she put in, hastily.

"No, not like that. They had somehow got themselves all shut in, so that they could only see everything from one point of view—I mean, they were different among themselves, of course, but each just saw everything from his own point of view—but there was a kind of grandeur—a sort of nobility—about them, quite different from ordinary lunatic stuff."

"There you go, you see—even you—talking about lunatic stuff. And whatever you may say, I'm one of them. One of them was my father—that seems very strange now, but after all it's true—and the other two were my uncles."

She looked at him mournfully, and he tried to take it easily and smile but somehow he couldn't. And there they stood, dumb and frustrated, in the middle of the shining day. They were silent for some time, just staring at each other, with the same melancholy little troop of thoughts going round and round in their heads.

"No, Malcolm, it's hopeless. I seem to have been saying that about one thing or another ever since we first met. But there it is. Still hopeless. However much I may pretend, or you pretend for me, I'm a MacMichael."

"Hey, what's that you're saying?"

They swung round, and were surprised, rather annoyed. The intruder came up cheerfully.

"Hello, Mr. Mitchell," said Andrea, without enthusiasm, though trying to be friendly, "how do you come to be here?"

"Oh!—I just wandered along," said the bearded man, who still wore the same disreputable garments and the same surprising air of distinction in them. "Hallo, young man! You both seem to have recovered from your adventure pretty well. But now, young woman, I know I shouldn't ask and it's the height of bad manners and tactlessness, but would you mind repeating what you just said to this not very cheerful young man?"

"If you must know," said Andrea, not snubbing him unpleasantly, however, but rather as if she were showing poor Malcolm the strength of mind she had in the presence of this comparative stranger, "I was telling him I couldn't marry him because I'm a MacMichael."

"Is that the only reason?" asked Mr. Mitchell, who appeared to think it amusing.

"Golly—yes, of course," she replied in a sort of fine confused mixture of enthusiasm, tenderness and misery.

"Then go ahead, because, you see, you're not a MacMichael."

"What?" And they shouted it together.

"You're not a MacMichael. You were Henry MacMichael's step-daughter, not his own daughter. And your name's really Mitchell."

"But you're——"

"No, I'm not your father, if that's what you were going to say. I wish I was. I'm merely your uncle, your father's brother. He died two years ago, in Peru. His name was Scott Mitchell—like me, a mining engineer. You see, my dear, we both wanted to marry your mother, whom we'd known since we were boys, and he—well, he was the lucky one, though poor Scott was never lucky long. He was a bit wild, never kept a dollar, and not long after you were born, your mother left him. I took Scott away, had to do something with him. There was a divorce, and then, while you were still a baby, Henry MacMichael became your step-father and insisted upon giving you his name. If your mother had lived, well she'd probably have told you herself—but she didn't, and then there was nobody to tell you. My brother, who'd had dealings with the MacMichaels before and didn't like them or their methods, wouldn't come back here at all. But he knew I'd be coming back—and he asked me— it was about the last thing he ever said to me—to see what was happening to you, though I'd have done that without being asked. I've some things of his—old photographs and so on—that you'd probably like to have. And that," he turned suddenly to Malcolm, in order to leave Andrea to herself a moment, "explains a little urgent conversation you and I had last week, not far from Jubilee Pass."

"I tried to act on your advice then," said Malcolm happily, "and I'm still going to act on it."

"I'll leave you to get on with it," said Mr. Mitchell, twinkling away, and after giving Andrea a new avuncular smile, he showed them the very creased and stained back of his disreputable jacket, as he took it and himself back to the ranch-house, out of which a very impatient Mrs. Atwood, almost dancing with curiosity, suddenly appeared. But she did not remain long with Mr. Mitchell. After firmly introducing him to Hooker, and compelling that long lean young man to emerge from his notebook and be sociable, she tripped up the hill, ostensibly to tell Jimmy Edlin the news. On the way there she told herself not to be a silly woman, that she'd no right to feel disappointed with Jimmy, that they were all good friends and what more could she expect, and much more stuff of the same kind. And there he was, painting away like a real artist, his pipe stuck in his mouth but no smoke coming out of it, his broad face very red and moist, his eyes screwed up comically, an entirely unromantic figure to every possible person in the world except one. But she was remembering, though she didn't want to at this particular moment, and felt it was downright tiresome of her to do so, the terrible afternoon—and who could believe it was only a week ago?—when he had put her in that plane beside poor Charlie and remained behind himself. Unromantic figure indeed! Just the right age and size and shape of a man!

Jimmy had nearly finished his picture of the ranch, and it might as well be said at once that it was one of his more characteristic creations, a genuine horror in pigment, which firmly set the ranch and its valley in the very centre of some metallic hell, with acid greens and poisonous pinks and yellows that were like acute attacks of bilious headache. He glanced up from this monster to the approaching Rosalie Atwood, who was looking more of a bright-eyed peach than ever, and took his pipe out of his mouth to give her a grin; but it was, she noticed at once, an anxious grin, and she wondered unhappily if she was a nuisance.

Before she could speak, however, he got up and stepped back a few paces and beckoned her to his side, so that she would see the canvas from a proper distance.

"Well," he said hoarsely, "what do you think of it?"

But he had hardly time to ask before she was exclaiming, obviously without any need of prompting: "Why, Jimmy, it's lovely."

"Do you mean it?"

"Of course I do," she told him indignantly. "Why shouldn't I? It's really beautiful. I never imagined you could do anything like that." And she moved away a few steps, to look at it from another angle.

Great Christopher, what a woman! He moved across to her masterfully. "If you like that, what about this, Rosalie?"

"I like that too," she cried, as best she could, for there was not much room, so masterfully had she been enfolded. "And here's one for you. No, no, please, Jimmy. Let me go. No more now. Yes, of course I do, you silly. But let me go—somebody's coming." There wasn't, but now she was free, and stood at a reasonably safe distance, and tried to look reproachful. "A nice way to behave!" But she couldn't stop her eyes dancing at him. "What do you think you're doing, Jimmy?"

Jimmy put on one of his more aggressive looks. "Finishing this picture, and when it's done, you'll have it and you'll like it. And then, you'll marry me and you'll like it."

"Jimmy! And did I tell you about Andrea and Malcolm——?"

"No, but I can see them down there, thinking they're in the garden of Eden. And I can see Hooker getting all excited explaining something to that chap with the beard. And I know you're there, just bursting to ask me fifty thousand questions——"

"Well, who wouldn't be?"

"And," continued Jimmy firmly, "I'm not bothering my head about any of you for the next ten minutes. I've had my adventures. The world's not done with yet. We're still alive and kicking. So just be quiet while I finish this job."

But he gave her a wink, and she replied with a smile, and as he returned to his painting, she stared dreamily down at the other four below, at the quiet valley trembling in the heat of noon, at the peaks of enduring rock, shining in the sunlight.

THE END

ALSO AVAILABLE FROM VALANCOURT BOOKS

WHAT CRITICS ARE SAYING ABOUT VALANCOURT BOOKS

"Valancourt are doing a magnificent job in making these books not only available but—in many cases—known at all . . . these reprints are well chosen and well designed (often using the original dust jackets), and have excellent introductions."

Times Literary Supplement (London)

"Valancourt Books champions neglected but important works of fantastic, occult, decadent and gay literature. The press's Web site not only lists scores of titles but also explains why these often obscure books are still worth reading. . . . So if you're a real reader, one who looks beyond the bestseller list and the touted books of the moment, Valancourt's publications may be just what you're searching for."

MICHAEL DIRDA, *Washington Post*

"Valancourt Books are fast becoming my favourite publisher. They have made it their business, with considerable taste and integrity, to put back into print a considerable amount of work which has been in serious need of republication. If you ever felt there were gaps in your reading experience or are simply frustrated that you can't find enough good, substantial fiction in the shops or even online, then this is the publisher for you."

MICHAEL MOORCOCK

TO LEARN MORE AND TO SEE A COMPLETE LIST OF AVAILABLE TITLES, VISIT US AT VALANCOURTBOOKS.COM

CPSIA information can be obtained
at www.ICGtesting.com
Printed in the USA
FFOW02n1329221216
30373FF

9 781941 147146